W9-BLK-823

THE UNWANTEDS

Island of Fire

Also by Lisa McMann

» » « «

The Unwanteds

Island of Silence

» » « «

For Older Readers:

Wake

Fade

Gone

Cryer's Cross

Dead to You

Crash

Bang

» » « «

LISA McMANN

THE UNWANTEDS

Island of Fire

Aladdin

NEW YORK   LONDON   TORONTO   SYDNEY   NEW DELHI

For Chloe

» » « «

ALADDIN

An imprint of Simon & Schuster Children's Publishing Division

1230 Avenue of the Americas, New York, NY 10020

First Aladdin hardcover edition September 2013

For information about special discounts for bulk purchases, please contact Simon & Schuster Special Sales at 1-866-506-1949 or business@simonandschuster.com.

The Simon & Schuster Speakers Bureau can bring authors to your live event. For more information or to book an event contact the Simon & Schuster Speakers Bureau at 1-866-248-3049 or visit our website at www.simonspeakers.com.

Designed by Karin Paprocki

The text of this book was set in Truesdell Regular.

Manufactured in the United States of America   0713 FFG

2 4 6 8 10 9 7 5 3 1

Library of Congress Cataloging-in-Publication Data

McMann, Lisa.

Island of fire / by Lisa McMann. — First Aladdin hardcover edition.

pages cm. — (Unwanteds ; [book 3])

Summary: "The magical world of Artimé is gone and the Unwanteds are looking to Alex Stowe for answers, but while his twin brother Aaron continues to build his army in Quill, a very dangerous common enemy is revealed."—Provided by publisher.

[1. Fantasy. 2. Brothers—Fiction. 3. Twins—Fiction.] I. Title.

PZ7.M478757Iq 2013   [Fic]—dc23   2012031939

ISBN 978-1-4424-5845-1 (hardcover : alk. paper) — ISBN 978-1-4424-5847-5 (eBook)

Acknowledgements

I offer heartfelt thanks to all the amazing booksellers I've had the pleasure to meet along this journey, and no less thanks to the ones I haven't met yet. I hope our paths cross soon.

To teachers and librarians: I see what you did there with that kid and that book. Your tireless work is inspiring. Thank you.

To my team of superheroes at Simon & Schuster, in the field, and around the globe, you amaze me with your fresh ideas, your enthusiasm, your dedication, and your kindness. You have become dear friends to me over the years, and you give me reasons to be thankful for you every single day. Special thanks to my fabulous editor, Liesa Abrams, and my publicist, Nicole Russo, for making me look good when I don't deserve it.

To my astounding agent, Michael Bourret—lover of villains, master of plot twist ideas—my career and my life would be so boring without you.

To all my family and friends, your support is incredible and it means so much to me. Thank you.

Last but not least, sincere thanks to my amazing fans for reading my books. Thank you for going on this Unwanteds journey with me. I hope you'll see it through to the end.

Contents

The Death Farm » » 1

Broken Harmony » » 6

The High Priest Aaron » » 17

Gondoleery's Secret » » 21

Caves » » 24

From a Closet in Quill » » 28

Descent » » 34

Exodus » » 38

At the Palace Gate » » 42

Finding the Dots » » 48

A Little Help » » 54

Magnify, Focus, Every One » » 58

Patience » » 65

The Sun Also Rises » » 69

Together, Apart » » 74

In a Word » » 79

Where You First Saw Me » » 85

Repeat Times Three » » 90

Breaking the News » » 98

Behind the Wall » » 104

The Gray Shack » » 111

Ol' Tater » » 117

Touch and Go » » 124

Nasty Places » » 133

The First Rescue » » 138

The Second Rescue » » 142

Approaching Normal » » 147

Alone » » 152

Empty Chairs and Empty Tables » » 157

Life on Warbler Island » » 162

A Still, Small Voice » » 171

For a Brief Moment » » 180

On the Move » » 185

The Birds, the Birds! » » 191

Information Overload » » 197

Lessons in Warblish » » 204

A Ray of Light » » 212

Making Plans » » 215

More Plans » » 224

And Finally, They're Off » » 231

Across the Sea » » 240

A Small Problem » » 246

Destination: Unknown » » 250

Pirate Island » » 257

A Long Night » » 265

Still Stuck » » 272

A Face in the Pool » » 279

Waiting » » 285

The Death Enchantment » » 290

Gondoleery Rising » » 296

Warbler Calls » » 301

The Front Line » » 305

Hope at Last » » 313

Finally, the Beginning of the Third Rescue » » 319

The First Loss » » 327

Finding Lani » » 334

A Somber Ride » » 349

The Long Night » » 358

The Tale Is Told » » 370

One Last Tale » » 374

A Sleepless Night for the High Priest » » 380

Land Ho! » » 385

The Fourth Rescue » » 391

While Alex Slept » » 396

The Eighth Day » » 405

A Fight » » 414

A Promise » » 420

Back to Normal » » 425

Masquerade » » 430

A Visitor » » 436

Lights » » 441

Death Farm

It was as if Artimé had never existed.

In the weeks since the death of Marcus Today, Alexander Stowe was often seen sitting on a rickety stool, staring out the window of the gray shack, clouding the glass with his breath. Sometimes he leaned his head of dark tangled curls or pressed a dirty cheek against the pane to catch a few moments of sleep when he could stay awake no longer.

Today was no different. He stared even now, but he wasn't seeing anything at all.

In his hand he gripped a piece of paper with a colorful

LISA McMANN

border, which was beginning to smudge, and he never let it go even though he'd memorized the words on it. It was his last message from Mr. Today, a cryptic, poetic spell that would fix all Alex's problems if only he could decipher the clues. He went over the words for the millionth time in his mind.

> *Follow the dots as the traveling sun,*
> *Magnify, focus, every one.*
> *Stand enrobed where you first saw me,*
> *Utter in order; repeat times three.*

The only thing Alex truly understood about the clue was the "enrobed" part. Mr. Today had been famous for his colorful robes, and Alex imagined there was some hint of magic to the robes themselves—there must be if Alex had to wear one to make the world of Artimé come back. Alex had the good fortune of possessing the only robe in existence at this moment—the one Mr. Today had been wearing when Alex's Wanted twin brother, Aaron, killed him. The robe was Alex's only symbol of hope in a time that could not possibly be any darker.

"You should eat something," said a voice at Alex's shoulder. It was Henry Haluki, Lani's younger brother, and next to him stood the Silent boy, a ring of thorns threaded through the skin around his neck. When Alex turned and focused his bleary eyes on the boys, Henry held out a good-sized half shell he'd been using as a small bowl.

Alex smiled and took it. "Thanks," he said, breathing in the faint smell of a weak seafood broth. His empty stomach snarled, begging for it, but Alex hesitated. The Unwanteds were beginning to starve. He handed it back to Henry and shook his head. "Give it to Meg," he said. "No, wait . . . to Carina Fathom and her baby. They need it most." Alex swallowed hard and turned away so he wouldn't be tempted to grab it back again. It would be a sign of acceptance to Carina, who was so mortified that her mother, Eva, had turned against Artimé that she couldn't bear to look Alex in the eye.

Henry frowned, but he shuffled away obediently and left the shack carrying the soup. The Silent boy followed him, both of them careful not to disturb any sleeping bodies on the floor. After a minute Alex stood up, stretched his tired limbs, and left too. He walked around to the front of the shack, maneuvering over the still body of Jim, the winged tortoise, whose mosaic back sparkled in the sunshine, until he reached Florence, frozen in full stride. Nimbly he climbed, using Florence's legs and arms as a ladder, and he swung his body up to the roof as if he'd done it dozens of times.

He lifted a hand to shield his eyes and looked west, in the direction of the two islands that dotted the ocean. "Follow the dots as the traveling sun," he muttered. "The dots have got to mean the islands, but . . ." He didn't finish the sentence because there were so many unknowns. The phrase didn't even make sense. And then the next line—"magnify, focus, every one." How could Alex magnify and focus on the islands? He was stuck on *this* island. He couldn't get any closer. He had no binoculars. Sometimes, when conditions were less favorable, he couldn't even see the more distant one. And "every one"? There were only two visible, though Simber had told him once that there were actually three in that direction. Mr. Today certainly would've said "both" if he meant only the two he could see, but the clue said "every one." Could Mr. Today have meant to include the island of Quill, too? And what about the rest of the chain that they couldn't see, to the east? There were seven islands in all, with Quill in the center, Simber had said. . . .

Oh, Simber. A wave of grief flooded Alex. He closed his eyes for a moment. Nightmares had plagued him since Simber had plunged into the sea, deadweight. All the rest of the creatures Mr. Today had created in Artimé had ceased to be alive then too, from the moment of the mage's death. The mansion and every wonderful thing in it was gone. Worse, two of Alex's best friends remained missing on Warbler Island, where the Silents had come from, and Alex had no means by which to search for them.

Alex shook his head. "I don't know what to do," he whispered.

Just then he heard a shout from the gate that led to Quill. He stood up on the roof to see what was happening. The shout had come from Henry, who lay sprawled on the dusty ground. Two other Unwanteds ran off through the gate and disappeared into Quill, with the Silent boy giving chase. Henry didn't move.

Broken Harmony

Alex scrambled down to the ground and ran to see what had happened. By the time he got to Henry's side, Sean Ranger and the Silent girl had arrived on the scene, and Meghan Ranger ran from the water's edge. The girrinos sat near the gate, unmoving, in heaps like boulders.

"What happened?" Alex demanded. "Did you guys see anything?" He looked from the Silent girl to Meghan to Sean, who knelt next to the boy.

Henry rolled to his side, curled up, and sucked in a few sharp breaths, as if he'd fallen hard and had the wind knocked out of him. After a minute, he waved Sean away and rose to his feet, dusting off his pants. There was a trickle of blood coming from his nose. He wiped it gingerly on his sleeve and scowled. "They stole the broth," he said. His lip quivered for an instant, and then it stopped. "Crow ran after them."

Sean raised an eyebrow as Meghan took a closer look at Henry's injuries. "Crow?"

"The Silent boy," Alex said. "Henry named him."

"That *is* his name," Henry said. "He showed me. He drew a bird in the sand and I guessed it."

"I'm going after him," Alex said, finding it a little easier now to take charge than he had just a few short weeks ago. "Sean, you want to get the story?"

Sean nodded. Alex started off toward the gate and then stopped, turned, and called back, "We need to have a meeting. You, me, Meg, Henry, and the Silents. See if you guys can find out if Mr. Appleblossom and Carina are available too. They've had their hands full with the fish catchers the last few days."

"Got it," Sean said.

Alex's best friend, Meghan, whose skin was mostly healed

around the band of metal thorns on her neck, could only nod in response.

Alex didn't have to go far before he saw Crow walking back toward the gate. He caught up with the boy and turned around, walking with him. "You okay, little guy?" Alex asked.

Crow nodded and punched his fist into his other palm.

"I know," Alex said. "But I don't want you to fight. I shouldn't have sent you guys out in the open with food like that. People are mean when they get desperate." He pressed his hand into his own stomach, trying to batten down the hunger. He knew he didn't have much time before the little plot of land that had once been Artimé became a battleground of infighting. And if that happened, the Unwanteds were doomed.

Who was Alex trying to fool? If he didn't do something quick, they were already doomed.

Crow kicked the dusty road with his bare foot as they turned in at the gate.

"We're going to have a meeting. I'd like you to be there, okay?"

The Silent boy made a fist and tapped it to his chest. It was the new Artiméan symbol of loyalty, which meant "I am with you."

Alex smiled. "Good."

They made their way to the shack. Alex poked his head in and spied Henry sitting in the midst of dozens of other Unwanteds, most of whom were trying to get their six-hour shift of sleep. "Meet by Florence," Alex whispered, trying not to disturb the slumbering masses. The roof was the only private place around.

The small team of Unwanteds assembled one by one around Florence. It was a strange group, since three among them were unable to make a sound, and a fourth, Carina's baby boy, spoke only gibberish.

Henry scrambled up Florence's limbs to the roof and then reached down to take the baby. Alex, Meghan, Crow, the Silent girl, and Carina all climbed up too, and they sat in the shade— for the moment—of Quill's forty-foot-tall stone wall.

Alex looked at the Silents. "So, your name is really Crow?" he asked the boy.

The boy nodded.

Alex smiled. "Nice." He looked at the girl. "I wish I knew your name," he said.

She tilted her head and both she and Crow pointed upward.

Alex frowned and looked up. "Cloud?" he guessed. "Blue? Sunny? Star? Rain?"

The girl shook her head and pointed again.

Carina and Henry looked on, and then Henry piped up. "Is it Sky?"

The Silent girl nodded, her face breaking into a bright smile.

"Sky," Alex said, gazing at her. He liked the sound of that. And then he blushed and looked down to see if Sean was coming.

On the ground, Sean appeared, along with Mr. Appleblossom. "Um . . . ," Sean said, looking first at the man, who was one of the original Unwanteds Mr. Today had saved, then glancing up at the roof. "Is this going to be a problem, Sigfried?" he asked the theater instructor.

"Oh my," Mr. Appleblossom murmured, "what a predicament indeed." He gazed imploringly at Florence's ebony face. "It's not the height that bothers me, of course. I'm nimble quite enough, though lacking speed. But think of when she wakes! Severe remorse—without our gentle mage to intercede. I may as well attempt a pommel horse." Instead he drew back a few steps and gave Sean a measuring glance. "Or vault,"

LISA McMANN

he murmured, suddenly thoughtful. "At that I may perchance succeed." He brought a finger to his chin, calculating his odds of running and vaulting to the roof using Sean's back, rather than disrespecting the enormous warrior trainer.

"She'll never know. We won't tell her, I promise," said Sean, his eyes widening in alarm when he realized what Mr. Appleblossom was considering. "There's really no other way to get up there—I'm not nearly big enough to be used as a gymnastics apparatus. Besides, I'm sure Florence would be glad she helped us in her own way."

The theater instructor shuddered, then set his shoulders and carefully climbed up the statue to the roof, where he settled next to the others. Sean followed.

"Well then, everyone," Alex began, and then he cleared his throat a little. "It seems things are beginning to crumble."

Meghan's eyes shot open wide.

"To put it bluntly," Sean said.

"How much water is left?" Alex asked Sean.

"About a barrel and a half."

Alex turned to Carina. "And the fishing?"

"They're catching a dozen or so each day, and some

LISA McMANN

shellfish. Not enough to keep us all from starving, I'm afraid, no matter how thin we make the broth." Carina looked down at her hands. "People have been fighting over it the last few days. It's not good."

"I got attacked," Henry said. He still held baby Seth, who was content for the moment to sit and gnaw on Henry's shirt collar. "I was trying to bring you some broth, Carina. Two guys came up to me and Crow. They grabbed the food and shoved me." He shifted the baby to his other leg. "They took off and Crow chased them."

"I'm so sorry," Carina said. "How could anybody do that to you?" She looked at Crow. "Did you see what they looked like?"

Crow nodded.

"You'd be able to recognize them?"

The boy nodded again.

Mr. Appleblossom shook his head. "My guess is that these thugs will not be back. The high priest's guards are bribing Artimé. We've lost a score so far—I'm keeping track. What boy would starve when facing a soufflé? I blame them not for joining that wolf pack."

Alex winced. "Twenty gone? I guess it's not surprising."

"It won't be long before a true uprising," the theater teacher added in a quiet voice, completing Alex's couplet.

Alex turned to look at the instructor, his stomach feeling as pinched as Mr. Appleblossom's heat-flushed cheeks and sunburned forehead looked. "I know, Mr. A," he said with a hint of desperation. "I'm trying."

"Of course you are, my boy. I have no doubt." Mr. Appleblossom patted Alex's shoulder and gave him a sympathetic look. "I hope the rest of us can help you out."

"I'm open to any suggestions." Alex pulled Mr. Today's note from his pocket and unfolded it. "I know you've heard it before, but I'm going to read this to you all again," he said, looking around the group. "If you think of anything that might help me solve these clues, please say it, no matter how silly it sounds. We're desperate. Here goes:

> Follow the dots as the traveling sun,
> Magnify, focus, every one.
> Stand enrobed where you first saw me,
> Utter in order; repeat times three."

Alex looked around the group. "Anyone?"

Sky, the Silent girl, closed her eyes and frowned, a look of concentration on her face.

Carina looked out across the water to the west. "Do you still believe the dots are the islands?"

"I don't know what else they could be," Alex said. "Trees? We don't have any. Buildings? Ditto. The clue refers to the sun, and the sun sets over the islands we can see. It seems the most logical thing."

"But I don't get how you are supposed to magnify and focus on them when we can't see them all from here," Sean said. "And we're stranded. Maybe we shouldn't have used the raft for firewood."

Sky opened her eyes, sat straight up, and shook her head violently. She clutched her hands to her throat and fell back against the shingles, feigning death.

Alex gave his newest friend a small smile, impressed with her theatrics, though now wasn't the time to mention that. "She's right," he said. "The water is really too rough out there for a raft, as Sky and Crow know. Besides, I'm not sure what an excursion would do for us—I wouldn't have the first idea of what to magnify and focus on once we got to the other islands. Even with a powerboat it would take days and days to stop at all of them. And talk about dangerous—we have no idea what kinds of people we'd face. . . ." He trailed off and couldn't help but glance at Meghan's neck. She looked back at him, her sober gaze unwavering. How badly Alex wished he could fix her, but with no tools or magic or medical supplies, he didn't dare risk trying. He wondered if she'd ever be able to speak again. Or sing.

They discussed the clue at length, with the best suggestion coming from Mr. Appleblossom, who wondered aloud if one could see the other six islands in the chain from the top of the wall, and if so, perhaps there was a pattern to be found by viewing all of them at once.

"Okay," Alex said, "but how do we get up there?"

"I guess I'll get to work building a ladder," Sean said.

"Out of what?" Henry asked, incredulous. "We don't have any wood or metal, just a few barrels . . ."

Sean glanced down at Florence, his jaw set, and then turned his gaze to the multitude of frozen, once-magical creatures that lined this side of the wall: squirrelicorns, beavops, platyprots, and more lying stiff and helpless without Mr. Today's magic.

"With them," he said quietly. "Stack them up like a stair-case, I guess." And then he looked out over the sea, shaking his head. "Without a solution to Mr. Today's clue, they'll never come to life again to know the difference."

The High Priest Aaron

A s High Priest Gunnar Haluki was tied up at the moment, the new Associate High Priest Aaron Stowe wasted no time shortening his official title to High Priest Aaron. It was just easier for the people of Quill that way, he declared, and it took much less time to say and write.

Not that Aaron could write quite yet. But soon. He'd been practicing with one of the scholars, Crete Sepulcher, a middle-aged man with crinkly, paper-thin skin and the personality of a rock.

Aaron sat at his desk with a rare piece of paper, scratching on it with an ancient stick of a pencil. As a young boy, he'd always wondered how the markings got on the paper. He never imagined it was with a stick. It made him think of Alex, drawing with that stick in the mud in the midst of a downpour in the backyard. And how he'd tried it too. And how he'd been caught, but his father had mistaken him for Alex. With his eyes, Aaron had pleaded with Alex to go along with it, to take the blame so Aaron wouldn't get an infraction.

He looked at the pencil now, turning it in his hands, tracing the ridge with his finger, down to the dull, whittled point. Remembering. It all seemed a very long time ago. But the look of betrayal on Alex's face . . . Aaron closed his eyes and tried to forget it. Tried to stop the words that taunted him. *The only reason you're sitting here now is because of him.*

Standing abruptly, Aaron dropped the pencil on his desk and strode to the window. An ugly gargoyle statue wearing a pink bow around its horn rested on the ledge, very nearly staring up at the young high priest. "Haluki had the strangest sense of decor," Aaron muttered. He gazed through the glass down the long driveway, then turned his eyes back and traced his gaze along the ever-present, ever-boring wall.

"Secretary," Aaron said in a raised voice.

Eva Fathom appeared in the doorway, her name—and indeed her identity—discarded once again.

"Find me a dozen strong Necessaries and the most powerful tools we have. Giant hammers, sharp picks, shovels. My guards and I will meet them at the portcullis at sunrise tomorrow."

"Of course," murmured Eva, but she smirked to herself. The rusty, broken-down gate to the palace could hardly be called a portcullis, but the new high priest was fond of making his things sound important, especially when they weren't.

"Next," Aaron went on, "send two more guards to Artimé to infiltrate. Tell them not to fight—just create some more unrest and keep the grumbling going. It's been working. We've taken in nearly two dozen so far and have put them right to work for our Wanteds."

"Very good," Eva said. She folded her hands behind her back, waiting for more tasks.

Aaron turned, looking down his nose at the woman. "And get me an update on the whereabouts and activities of the Restorers. Is Haluki dead yet? Where's Gondoleery? She's all but disappeared."

LISA McMANN

Eva hadn't seen Gondoleery at all since the battle, but instinct nudged her not to admit that. Instead she said, "Many of the Restorers are taking a rest after all their hard work, but Liam Healy and Bethesda Dia Gloria are still stationed at High Priest Haluki's house."

Aaron narrowed his eyes at her. "*I'm* the high priest. Secretary."

Eva pursed her lips and turned them into a thin-lipped smile. "My apologies for the slip. I don't know what I'm to call him now."

"Call him . . . oh, who cares? Just don't call him *that*."

Eva nodded. "Anything else?"

Aaron turned back to the window and caught a glimpse of the gargoyle again. He frowned at it. "No. You may go."

Without a sound, the old woman turned and left the office.

Aaron picked up the gargoyle, held it away from himself as he walked, as if its hideousness might be contagious, and tossed it into a wooden box in the closet with the rest of Haluki's things. They'd melt the statue down to make weapons once Haluki was dead.

Gondoleery's Secret

In the weeks since Gondoleery Rattrapp had made the skies above her little gray house open up and pour down rain, she barely gave a thought to the Artiméans. She didn't think often about the new acting High Priest Aaron Stowe, either, though she'd been one of his prime supporters as he attempted to restore Quill to its former state of control.

No, Gondoleery had been awfully scarce around Quill lately. And for good reason. She was very busy sitting at her kitchen table, thinking about her childhood.

If she knew how to write, she'd be writing down everything

LISA McMANN

as she remembered it so she could free up her mind for more memories. But there were no pencils for ordinary people in Quill, and no knowledge of how to use them. So instead of writing, Gondoleery was thinking.

Sometimes she napped in her chair in the heat of the day, and she began to dream for the first time in decades. It was frightening at first, since dreams were not allowed in Quill, but she was wise enough to realize no one would ever know unless she told them. Her dreams were filled with ideas she could never have imagined when awake—dreams of fiery rivers of lava hurtling down a jagged mountainside. Dreams of swirling dust, of gusting winds, of frigid ice and quaking earth. Dreams of destruction that both frightened and thrilled her.

Yet when she awoke each day, she knew she had seen such things before, though none of the people of Quill ever had. None, that is, except for the three remaining droolers in the Ancients Sector.

And Eva Fathom.

Gondoleery needed time to think. She needed time to remember, and time to see just how powerful her own bit of magic really was. And so it was that she decided to disappear from Quill by staying right where she was, in her chair, and not emerging until she had thought every thought and dreamed every dream. And relearned every bit of magic she'd lost.

And then, when she was good and ready, when she was stronger and more powerful than any nonmagical high priest, when she required no team of Restorers to back her up . . . that's when she would make her move.

Caves

The breeze came, and the breeze went away.

Day after day, Samheed and Lani huddled together somewhere below ground on Warbler Island, telling time by the breezes that swept over them—the gentle wake of Silent people bringing them daily food and water. As on the first day, the two friends remained blind, deaf, and mute, and they still had metal bands of thorns threaded through the skin of their necks, which had finally begun to heal.

In the vastness of their dark days, they created a language with their fingers, tapping the other's palm or knee to spell out words. The letter *A* was one tap, *B* was two taps, and so on.

It was a long process to spell anything of length, but they had plenty of time in which to do it. After a few days, having memorized the number of taps that corresponded to each letter, they were able to go more quickly, using a full-palm slap to count for five. The twelfth letter of the alphabet, L, was two slaps, two taps. S, the nineteenth letter of the alphabet, was three slaps, four taps. A brush of the hand meant a space between words, and a closed fist meant the speaker was finished. Sometimes they skipped a letter to save time and effort if they thought the other would be able to figure the word out without it.

Through this method, Lani recounted what she had seen while Samheed was unconscious. She told Sam of her hope for Meghan's escape, which lifted his spirits, although only a little bit. If it weren't for each other and their new language, they might have gone insane by now.

Sometimes, when they were tired of tapping and there was nothing left to say, they linked arms or clasped their fingers together as they fell asleep, desperately afraid that if they didn't stay in constant physical contact, one of them could one day wake up alone and have no idea what had happened to the other.

A few times each day Lani pulled Alex's drawing from her

pocket, concentrated on his face in her mind, and tried to send him a seek spell. It was the only spell she could think of that could help them. The first few times she sent it, she had great hope that Alex would be coming soon.

But eventually she wondered what was taking him so long. Alex knew about the spell. She knew he'd be able to recognize that it came from her, because when it reached him, it would explode into a fiery picture of the drawing he gave her, and he only had to go in the direction from which the glowing ball had come. If Meghan hadn't made it back to safety in Artimé— Lani shuddered at the thought of what might have happened to her friend—then Alex wouldn't have the boat, but he could still ride Simber to get here. And she was certain Mr. Today could make another boat if he'd made the first one. She didn't understand why no one was coming for them.

Several thoughts kept plaguing her, joining together and chiseling away at her. What if Alex and Mr. Today had come already but couldn't find Lani and Samheed? What if they had come and been killed? What if Meghan had made it to the boat but couldn't find her way back to Artimé and had become lost at sea? What if . . . what if Alex just didn't care enough to come looking for them?

"Maybe magic doesn't work from here," Samheed spelled out. "There's no sound so could be burier?" He meant to spell "barrier" but didn't realize his mistake until he got to the end of the word, and he was too tired to redo it.

But Lani nodded her fist in Sam's hand. "Maybe." She gave a deep, silent sigh and closed her eyes as a wave of hopelessness washed over her. She couldn't stand this much longer. She wasn't used to being so helpless. "We've got to find a way out," she said daily. But each time they tried together to crawl around the perimeter of the cave looking for an exit, they couldn't find anything. They ended most days in total frustration, with no voice to express it.

After they'd been still and lost in thought for some time, sitting in the middle of the floor trying to waste away the endless darkness, Lani spelled, "I'd give anything to see my family agai—" And then she clapped her palm to her mouth. She'd forgotten about how Samheed's family had treated him. She felt Samheed fizzle and slump to his back. He turned away from her, but he didn't let go of her hand. Not even when the shuddering began.

From a Closet in Quill

Claire Morning leaned her head against a shelf in her closet prison. Every joint in her body ached, for she'd been sitting there in the dark, tied up, for all but one hour of every day for the past several weeks. Liam and Bethesda allowed her thirty minutes in the morning and thirty minutes in the evening to move around. She was growing thin and weak, and her early hopes for escape had faded.

The thing that kept her strong was the Unwanteds. She knew, of course, that her beloved father, Mr. Today, had been killed. And she knew that Artimé was gone. It was the thought of all the Unwanteds struggling to make sense of what had happened, struggling to survive without their magical world, that kept Claire motivated to survive so that she could get back there and help them.

She often heard the shuffling of footsteps and the low rumble of conversation between her two captors outside the closet. Now and then she was able to discern a word or two, but not enough to make sense of anything. And as much as she wanted to ask about the state of Quill and Artimé, she refused to speak to Liam or Bethesda.

She closed her eyes and thought about her father, determined to remember all he had done for the Unwanteds so she could write everything down someday. *Someday.* The day dragged onward.

She startled when she heard a commotion followed by the bang of the front door. Then there was silence once again. Very soon she heard soft footfalls coming toward her, but she knew it wasn't yet evening by the line of sunlight coming from the crack under the door. So whomever it was certainly wasn't coming to let her out. When, to her surprise, the door opened, she squinted as the light poured in and hurt her eyes.

"Claire," Liam said.

She didn't look at him.

He reached down and untied her wrists, then loosened the gag from her mouth and let it fall so that it hung around her neck like a scarf. He handed her a cup of water. She took it and drank, frowning at her hands, which insisted on shaking around the cup. When she finished, he helped her to her feet and didn't let go of her arm until he was sure she was stable.

Her legs pricked and burned as the blood rushed through them, and a wave of black crossed in front of her eyes. She reached for the door frame, willing herself not to black out. A moment later her vision cleared, and she hazarded a glance at her childhood friend. He looked disheveled and hadn't shaved in several days. His eyes were the same as they'd always been—surprisingly blue and intense.

"Bethesda stepped out," Liam said. He worked his jaw as if he might say more. Instead he looked away.

A wave of adrenaline pulsed through Claire, but she trained her eyes on the floor now, her face frozen. Could she escape? Why was he telling her this?

"I can't let you escape," he said in the softest voice. "I'd be sent to . . . well, you know where." He stepped away, shuffling his feet awkwardly, and then he hastened to the stove and plated a thick slice of toasted bread and a hunk of cheese. "Here." He set it on the table, and then refilled her cup and set it next to the plate.

Claire stared at the food and walked to the table. She didn't think it was a trick. She looked up at Liam, her brows knitting together, wondering.

He looked back at her with softer eyes now, giving away the slightest hint of emotion. Perhaps there was a soul inside, somewhere.

"Why?" Claire asked, her voice clotting on the word, leaving it stuck in her throat.

Liam opened his lips as if to speak, and then closed them and turned away. He went to the window and peered out, keeping an eye on her as well. "Just hurry," he said.

Claire, gripping the back of the chair to hold herself steady, bit her lip and glanced at the door.

"Don't," Liam said. He shook his head slightly, a warning. "You won't make it."

She swallowed hard, the food wavering in front of her. She

knew Liam was right. She wasn't strong enough. But maybe she could build up her strength again.

She tugged on the chair, straining to slide it back, and then sat down. "Thank you," she whispered. She ate.

Liam watched her out of the corner of his eye.

When she finished, she asked, "Is it all right if I stand?"

"Sure," he said. "Stay over there, though."

She nodded, and stretched her muscles carefully.

From the back part of the house came a thump. Liam tensed immediately, and then relaxed.

"Bethesda?" Claire whispered, ready to hide.

"No."

Claire's eyes widened. She had suspected something for days, whenever she'd heard people moving about. "Is someone else . . . here?"

Liam looked at her.

"Liam," Claire said, "is it Gunnar?"

After a moment, Liam nodded so slightly that Claire almost didn't see it.

A sigh escaped her. She closed her eyes and brought her hands to her face, shaking her head, wondering what would become of them all. The situation was beyond hope. And then she turned, dejected, went back to her pantry cell, and sat on the floor, placing the gag back into her mouth, and waited for Liam to tie her up again.

Descent

The next day Alex was no closer to a solution. While Sean, Meghan, Henry, and the Silents began stacking frozen creatures to make a stairway to the top of the wall, Alex made the rounds of the Unwanteds, trying to boost morale and offer help in any way he could.

"We need more water," grumbled a woman on the beach. "The ration you're giving us is worse than in Quill."

"I'm starving," a man said. "I haven't eaten a thing in two days."

"This place is a disaster," voiced a group of Unwanted boys from Alex's year. A few of them jeered. Cole Wickett took

Alex aside. "Come on, Alex," he said earnestly. "You've got to do something. People are going to leave, you know?"

Alex pressed his lips together. So far today he had taken a number of verbal beatings from the people of Artimé, and he was beginning to feel defensive and desperate. "I know," he said. "We're doing everything we can. I don't know what else to say."

Cole shook his head. "I'm sorry, Al, but . . ." He looked around at all the Unwanteds, some weak and ill, sprawled on the ground, others grumbling in small groups, and still others lining the shore trying desperately to catch fish, with little success. "This place is starting to remind me of the Ancients Sector. *Somebody's* got to step it up here. Fast."

And it's obviously not you. Cole didn't say it, but it was implied. Alex felt the hopelessness of it all pulling him down, and at the same time a wave of reckless anger rushed up from his collarbone and he threw his hands up in the air. "Well, maybe you should be in charge, then. I never wanted this job, you know." His mouth twisted against his will. "What do you want me to do, anyway? What exactly does everybody expect me to do?"

Cole's eyes widened in alarm. "Alex . . . ," he began.

"It's not my fault this happened." Alex said. "It's Mr. Today's fault. How"—his voice quavered with pent-up anger—"how could he have done this to us? To all of us? How could he have left Artimé so . . . so *unstable* that it would disappear if he died?"

"Calm down, Alex—"

But Alex wouldn't stop, even though he couldn't believe his horrible thoughts, his sharp words against their beloved mage. "Don't tell me to calm down. This is not a calm situation! Answer me—I'm serious. What kind of leader would do that? Did he think he was invincible?" Alex was horrified at himself for asking the questions that had been plaguing him, but he felt helpless to stop them. "And now I'm the one who's supposed to fix it? I'm, like, practically still a *kid*. It's *so* not okay that he left me with this. It's a disaster!" he cried. "It's not fair!" He grasped Cole's arm and shook it. "Can you see what I'm saying? I'm saying I can't just fix this. I can't. I tried—I'm trying, and I'll keep trying. But as of right now, I can't figure it out, okay?"

Cole just stood there, color rising to his cheeks. Then he deliberately removed Alex's hand from his arm, stepped back, and wiped his sleeve. "Oo-kay," he said, his voice cold. He turned to his friends, who had stopped complaining long enough to listen. Cole nodded in the direction of the entrance to Quill and started walking away. To his friends he said, "Come on, guys. I know where we can get some food."

Alex's mouth dropped open. "Whoa," he said. "Wait. Seriously? You're going to be slaves to them again? You're disgusting!" He kicked the cracked earth and spun around. "Cowards. I can't believe this."

"Whatever, Alex," Cole called over his shoulder. He went through the gate, the others following him into Quill.

Alex raked his fingers through his hair and cursed under his breath. Now he was driving people away.

LISA McMANN

Exodus

Not far away in the yard, next to Jim the winged tortoise, stood Sky, on a break from stacking stiff, lifeless beavops, watching her new friend Alex fall apart. When she escaped from Warbler, she never once imagined that she would find a place where things were actually worse than what she'd endured.

She took a few steps through the crowd toward Alex, thinking she might be able to offer some form of comfort, when she saw Carina Fathom walk up to him. Sky admired Carina's pixie haircut and spunky style. But she slowed and then stopped when she saw Carina's face, which looked very serious.

"Alex," Carina said, looking up at him. She held young Seth on one hip and a knapsack over the opposite shoulder.

Alex turned, an almost bewildered look on his face. "Oh, hi," he said. "What's up?"

She took a deep breath. "Alex, I'm sorry."

He frowned. "Why?"

"Because I . . . we . . . need to go. I'm sorry." She pinched her lips together and didn't look away. "We're going. Leaving."

The color drained from Alex's face. He looked away quickly and took in a sharp breath, letting it out slowly through pursed lips. He squeezed his eyes shut, and then opened them again and looked back at the young woman. "You're leaving." He nodded, a little too swiftly, looking at the baby. "Of course you are. You have to." He absently reached out and smoothed the listless baby's hair. It was damp with sweat. Alex dropped his arm, like lead, to his side. "To your mother's, I suppose," he mused, almost to himself.

"No. She's, you know. Back in the palace, and I—"

"Of course," Alex murmured. "I— How could I forget?"

"I've changed my name, you know," Carina blurted out.

"Oh?"

"To Holiday. Carina Holiday, that is. I mean, I can't—I won't have *her* name anymore."

"I see." His words were feeble, like unstable puffs of air. "A bit ironic, that name," he said, looking past Carina now, to the sea. "Holiday. Day of the Purge and all that."

"It's—yes, it is. Intentionally so." She shifted the baby higher on her hip.

Alex looked at her again as if he was finally seeing her. "Can I help you? Carry something, I mean? I'm sorry, I should have—"

"No," she said quickly, shaking her head. "I'm used to it. I just . . . I should go."

Alex nodded. "Well." He opened his lanky arms awkwardly and hugged her.

Carina patted his back. "I'm sorry," she said again.

He shook his head and gave her a sad smile. "Don't—it's okay. Thank you for everything. I mean it."

"I'll be back."

"I know."

They stood face-to-face a moment longer, and then Carina nodded once. "Okay, then." She hesitated a second more, and then set off. "You'll figure it out, you know. The clue," she called over her shoulder. "You will. I'm sure of it. Good-bye for now, brave Alex Stowe." She grinned.

Alex nodded. He lifted his hand. "Good-bye, Carina Holiday."

He watched her go.

As she reached the gate, she paused, turned once again, and tilted her head. "I don't think it's the islands," she called. And then she shrugged and smiled. "For whatever that's worth."

With that, she disappeared around the wall.

When Alex's shoulders slumped and he turned away, dead-eyed, Sky was there.

At the Palace Gate

The High Priest Aaron donned his inherited black robe and made his way down the long driveway to the portcullis. He was flanked by four guards who carried rusty spearlike weapons in case the Necessaries acted up.

The workers stood waiting with shovels, picks, and some makeshift equipment.

"Release the lock," Aaron said to his guards. Without so much as a glance at the Necessaries outside the gate, Aaron motioned to them and said, "Follow me." One of Aaron's guards unlocked the gate and the Necessaries streamed in.

Aaron led them up the drive, to the forty-foot wall outside his palace office window.

"I want you to make a hole through the wall here, like a large doorway," he said. "As tall and wide as the door to the palace." He turned and looked at the dim-witted Necessaries to see if they understood. When he got to the last of them, his jaw slacked and he paled a shade, or perhaps two, but only someone who knew him well would have noticed. He held the unblinking man's gaze for a moment, and then nodded slightly and turned back to the first one. "Are you in charge here?" he barked.

"Y-yes, Associate High Priest," the man said.

"High Priest Aaron," corrected one of the guards.

The Necessary nodded, saying nothing.

"Well," Aaron said, impatient, "do you understand? Do you have any questions?"

The man was so flustered he didn't say a word.

"No?" Aaron continued. "Fine, then. You'll work until it's dark." He didn't wait for the man to respond. Instead Aaron gathered his cloak, whipping it around with a flourish, and stomped away to the palace.

"Secretary!" he yelled, even before he'd fully made it inside. "Secretary!"

There was a scuffle of shoes on echoing steps. A moment later, Eva Fathom rounded the corner and nearly bumped into Aaron.

"Yes?" she said, a bit breathless.

"Where did you find these workers?"

"Well, logically, I went to the Ancients Sector. The workers there have shovels and other tools, and they're accustomed to that sort of hard work. Is there a problem?"

Aaron narrowed his eyes at the woman, never quite sure if he could trust her. "And did you not ask them their names?"

"I spoke only to the one in charge. He rounded up the others." She held her chin steady and didn't look away.

Aaron studied her face for a long moment. Then he nodded his acceptance of her story. "That's all for now," he said. He pushed past her and went to his office, closing the door firmly, leaving Eva Fathom tapping her lips.

Aaron hung up his cloak and went to the window once more, looking out over the driveway at the men, who stood measuring and marking off a doorway on the wall using spit and dust, and then taking their tools and whacking them against the wall.

The one man in particular seemed to be pounding especially hard. He reached down to the pile of tools and found a thin piece of metal. Shoving it into the crack between two blocks of cement, he picked up a mallet, pulled back, and pounded the piece of metal with all his might, over and over until the block began to move.

The others, including the leader of the party, watched for a moment and then followed his example. Aaron frowned, and hollered once again, "Secretary!"

But this time there was no answer. Instead he saw Eva Fathom climb into the backseat of a Quillitary vehicle, which choked and slowly chugged its way down the hill, belching black smoke at the men, who had managed to remove a few blocks.

Aaron's attention turned to the beautiful view of the water through the hole in the wall, and he wondered once again how in the world Justine could have wanted to hide Quill from that. A prick of fear gnawed at him. There had to be a reason.

. . .

Eva Fathom, in the backseat of the rusty old vehicle, bounced along with a hint of a smile on her wrinkled lips, having quite possibly heard the high priest's last bellow but dodging it all the same. She had better jobs to do than run around chasing after things for a teenage boy.

The driver soon pulled up to the Haluki house, and the smile left Eva's face. She got out of the vehicle, went to the door, and opened it without knocking. She went inside.

"Good morning, Bethesda. Liam." She spoke more loudly than she needed to. "How are the prisoners today? Not trying anything tricky, I hope." She rounded the corner to Haluki's old office. "Is Claire Morning giving you any trouble in the pantry?" she called out.

Bethesda frowned in Liam's direction.

"I'll go quiet her down," Liam said, standing up. "She's old. Must be getting deaf," he whispered. He caught up to Eva in the short hallway. "No," he said to Eva. "She's fine."

"Too weak by now to try anything," Eva said, almost as a question.

"I suppose so."

"Tsk." Eva shook her head and leaned toward Liam, lowering her voice. "I can't say I understand why we're keeping them trapped like this. We should either kill them or let them go." She looked at the man. "Don't you agree?"

"I—" He shrugged, noncommittal.

"Do you think we should kill them, then?" Eva looked at him for a long moment, trying to gauge his loyalties. If anyone were going to cave in, it would be him.

He shifted his weight uncomfortably and looked away, and Eva had her answer.

Finding the Dots

T he clue from Mr. Today became a song in Alex's head, and even though music was still new and wonderful to Alex, this clue became the kind of annoying song that sometimes got stuck in his brain and left him wishing he could forget it. Trying to get some sleep on the hard ground, Alex couldn't get the words out of his head, so at last he got up, picked his way to Florence, and climbed up to the roof.

Sean Ranger was there already.

"Hey," Alex said.

Sean offered a bleak smile. "You okay?" He'd heard about Carina Holiday leaving them.

Alex was quiet for a moment, and then he said, "Sometimes I don't know if we're going to make it."

"Yeah, I know," Sean said. "Carina will be back, though."

Deep down, Alex thought that Carina would probably not be back at all. "Does she have any other . . . family? Out there?" he asked, meaning Quill.

"No." Sean pulled a thin, whittled stick from his pocket and began to clean his teeth. "You knew her husband, Seth, was killed in the first battle, didn't you? Before the baby was born. He's named for his father."

Alex looked at Sean. "I—I didn't know her then." He'd wondered about it, but Carina never spoke of the past or about the baby's father, so Alex assumed she didn't want to talk about it. Now Alex felt even more terrible.

"She's a really strong person," Sean said. "I admire her. I remember her from Quill—she's just a few years ahead of me, you know. When she was Purged, she had this look on her face like she was going to get revenge on everybody one day."

Alex laughed softly. "I believe that."

"She'll do it, too."

Alex nodded.

"I remembered that when my name was announced. I wanted to be like her."

"You are. In a lot of ways."

Sean shrugged. "Thanks."

The song played in Alex's head during the silence that followed, and he recalled Carina's parting words. "She said she didn't think the dots were the islands."

Sean was quiet for a long moment. "Well, she has really good instincts. She might be right." He glanced at the wall, where two days' worth of effort stacking the creatures had gotten them nearly to the top of it. "I reckon I'll continue the project, though."

"Yes, definitely. We don't have anything else to go on."

Just then a face peeked up over the edge of the roof. Alex smiled. "Come on up," he said. "We're just talking."

Sky climbed up and sat next to Alex. All three lay on their backs or rested on their elbows, staring at the night sky.

Sean frowned. "Do you think the dots . . ."

Alex looked at him. "What?"

Sean sat up, peering intently at the sky. "Do you think the dots are the stars?"

Sky sat up too.

Alex shook his head. "I thought about that. But the sky is always changing. The stars don't stay in the same place all the time. So if we're supposed to follow a line of stars, how would we know what time of night to do it, or what time of the year they would all line up in the right part of the sky?"

"Oh. Good point." Sean sighed.

The Silent girl slumped.

"What if the dots weren't actually, you know, outside?" Sean asked.

"What do you mean?"

"Are there any dots in the shack, like on the walls or anything?" Sean leaned back on his elbows.

"Not that I noticed. Believe me, I looked everywhere. I see dots swimming in front of my eyes constantly."

Sky sat up again and stared out across the sea.

"Something in Artimé, maybe?"

Alex was quiet, considering that. He'd dismissed the idea once before, but now he couldn't remember why. "I don't know," he mused. "Maybe. Like what?" He pictured the lounge, the theater, the mansion, the library. "Books could be dots, maybe." But then he shook his head. "No, Mr. Today would be more clever with his clue if he meant books. Maybe there was something in his office." Alex felt a sharp pang of sadness. "If Samheed were here," he said, "he might remember." But no one else remaining had ever set foot in Mr. Today's office as far as Alex knew. Not even Mr. Appleblossom. It was depressing.

"What about the black-and-white tiles in the entrance to the mansion? Or statues in the hallways? Or—"

Alex slapped his forehead. "No. Now I remember why I don't think the dots are inside Artimé. It's because we can't magnify or focus on anything that doesn't exist. Which seems to be our biggest dead end."

"Right," Sean muttered. "Sorry. I'm not thinking straight." They lapsed into their thoughts.

Sky closed her eyes, thinking hard. And then her lids popped open and she turned toward Alex and gripped his leg.

He looked at her, alarmed. "What is it?"

Her hands flew through the air, speaking a language Alex didn't know.

"Whoa," he said. "Slow down."

But Sky wasn't slowing. Her face was wildly animated, her golden-orange eyes bright, her actions exaggerated—all indicating that something very important was happening, but Alex couldn't figure it out.

"I'm sorry," he said. "I'm sorry, I can't understand—" He bit his lip, frustrated, then glanced at Sean. "Any idea?"

"No," Sean said quietly, his eyes intent on the girl. "But now she's getting frustrated with us."

Sky rolled her eyes and gripped her hair, pulling her head down to her bent knees, shaking her head from side to side. Finally she sat up again and faced the two. She took a deep breath, and then calmly held up a hand, first to Alex, then to Sean.

"Stay here?" Alex guessed.

The Silent girl nodded wildly.

"Okay," Alex said, relieved to have gotten something right. "We'll stay here."

Sky pointed to herself, then pointed away, then pointed to herself again, then at the roof.

"She's going to leave and come back," Alex interpreted. "Right?"

The Silent girl rewarded Alex with a beautiful smile that made his stomach flip. She touched her nose and pointed at him, nodding. And then, after one more reminder to the boys to stay put, she scrambled down Florence to the ground.

A Little Help

Sky returned a few minutes later, just as the eastern edge of the morning sky turned orange. She was carrying something on her shoulder, gripping it tightly with one hand as she maneuvered her way up the statue. Alex reached down to help her up.

She held the miniature mansion that she'd found the first day, a replica of the true mansion, and she handed it to him with pride.

"Oh!" Alex grinned and took it, careful not to tip it. "Did I ever show you this?" he asked Sean. "Sky found it our first day here inside a cupboard in the shack. I think it's a model that

Mr. Today made as he was planning what Artimé would look like. Can't you just picture him sculpting this little miniature mansion and dreaming about creating it?"

Sean squinted in the dark. "Sweet," he said under his breath. He looked into the windows, opened and closed the doors. "There's a mini Florence and a mini Simber," he said with a hint of glee in his voice. "And look! A platyprot wandering the hallway. This is the best toy ever."

The Silent girl waved her hand in front of their faces. They looked up. She stared at them as if they were stupid, then pointed to the mini mansion. She tapped the air several times and shrugged.

"Dots? Oh! Now we can see if there are any dots. I get it." Alex smiled at Sky. "Good idea." He said it almost like it was a silly thought. Like the girl had made a big deal out of nothing.

She glared as Sean and Alex explored the miniature, pointing out the tubes and the giant kitchen, their mouths watering at the thought of all the food they could eat if only they had Artimé back. They stared at the black-and-white squares on the floor, but decided they weren't really dotlike.

A steadily growing light filled the skies, and the sleep-

LISA McMANN

ing Unwanteds began to stir. After a few minutes, Sean yawned and stretched, saying it was his turn to sleep inside the shack on the sofa, and he wasn't about to give up that luxury.

After Sean was gone, Alex looked at Sky, his eyelids heavy from lack of sleep. "Thanks for finding this," he said. "I didn't really see any dots, though. But it was a good idea." He set the model mansion on a flat part of the roof and lay down next to it. "I'm going to try to grab an hour of sleep here before it gets hot," he mumbled, and he closed his eyes.

The Silent girl frowned. She watched the sunrise, the words of Mr. Today's clue running through her head. She crawled over to the little mansion and looked inside. She didn't see any dots either.

Alex groaned in his sleep. The girl watched him for a moment. His clothes were ragged and dusty, his face smudged with dirt, his hair a tangled nest of dark brown curls. His chest rose and fell, rose and fell; he was finally getting some rest. Maybe it would help him think more clearly. The girl reached out a tentative hand and pushed aside a lock of his hair that had fallen in his face. And then she closed her eyes and made a wish for him to receive every good thing he needed to save his people . . . and himself.

When she opened her eyes, she was struck by another thought. A thought so simple she was surprised that no one had come up with it yet. She bit her lip as she mentally reviewed the clue, and she came to the same conclusion as before. And so it was that Sky climbed down Florence with an idea and went in search of the two people who would be the most helpful to her.

Magnify, Focus, Every One

Alex had tried not to spend much time thinking about Samheed and Lani. Everything in front of him was desperate enough to keep him barely able to function. Thinking about them, knowing he could do nothing to save them, would only put him over the edge. He had lots to do here before he could go there, so he chose to concentrate on one thing at a time.

But his dreams didn't care for that logic. He fell hard into crazy dreams of them—dreams of Lani and how nice his skin felt when she touched his arm, but then she turned around and cast a nasty spell on him, forcing him to fall face-first into his

LISA McMANN

soup while the walls of Quill crumbled around him. Dreams of Samheed and him working together to take down the Quill leaders with magic spells, followed by an angry Samheed shoving Alex into the glass partition in Mr. Today's mostly secret hallway, the glass shattering and giving Alex a thousand cuts, the noise ringing out.

He startled awake, breathing hard, and sat up, trying to get his bearings. Sweat dripped down his cheek from where it had been planted against his forearm. He took in a deep breath and let it out slowly, his stomach cramping from hunger and his heart aching from missing his friends. He longed for the safety of Mr. Today's office, hidden from most of the world. Unlike here, where he was surrounded by people every second of every day.

The song in his head started again. *Follow the dots, follow the dots, follow the dots.* It was more frustrating than he ever could have imagined. "Mr. Today, please," he muttered, "please help me out here. Where are your ridiculous dots?"

And just as he said it in such a fashion, thinking of them as Mr. Today's dots rather than the world's dots, it struck him like a magical glass wall to the face. "His office," he muttered, his eyes darting left and right as he pictured it. "Dots.

Mr. Today's dots." He scrambled to look at the miniature mansion, and lifted the roof clean off so he could stare into Mr. Today's office unhindered.

And there on the walls they were. Only they were the tiniest replicas of already tiny dots grouped together, so tiny they could hardly be seen, and instead the masses of dots looked like blobs. "That hideous artwork," he whispered, remembering how he'd noticed the odd series of paintings while waiting for Mr. Today. The words rang true and sounded right and solid in his head, so he said it again, louder. "That hideous artwork. It's the artwork! Great protuberating conch shells!"

With a shaky hand, Alex reached into the office and tried carefully to pluck one of the dot paintings from the wall, but it was stuck fast. He pulled his hand back and looked around the room. There were five paintings with unattractive dot designs, all hanging on one wall. "Clever beast," Alex said. "But what am I supposed to do with them?"

As he lay on his stomach, peering into Mr. Today's office, he heard a noise at the edge of the roof. Sky, Crow, and Henry Haluki clambered up. Sky had a wide grin on her face and pointed to Henry.

"Hi, guys," Alex said. "I don't have time for games now—I think I—" He stopped speaking when he saw the Silent girl's fiery glare. "I mean . . ."

"Alex," Henry said, "Sky figured out part of your clue! And I'm the only one who can help you." He grinned slyly. "Magnify. Because remember I have this?" From his trouser pocket he pulled his magnifying glass, one of the few items that had transported unharmed from Artimé when the world disappeared, because it had been in Henry's pocket during that time. It had been handy for starting fires. And now it was going to be even more useful.

Alex's jaw slacked. But Henry kept talking.

"I didn't think about it when we thought the dots were islands, because obviously," he said with a bit of a swagger, "this glass can't work from so far away. But Sky thought there was more to this little mansion. So do you want me to start magnifying things?"

Alex stared at the magnifying glass, and then he looked at the Silent girl. He felt the corners of his lips tug into a wispy smile as he processed the news. "Just before you got here, I figured out where the dots are," he said. He shook his head.

"I can't believe I didn't think of it earlier. The clue is totally literal. The dots aren't islands or stars or trees. They're dots! They're actual pictures of dots!" He pointed at the office wall. "And you guys just figured out the next part." He grinned like a maniac.

Henry reluctantly handed over the magnifying glass. "I guess you know what you're looking for."

Alex took it and gripped the boy's shoulder. "This is all thanks to you, Henry." He looked up at Sky and winked. She blushed. Alex held the magnifying glass up and leaned toward the first painting, his hands still quivering. He moved the glass until he could see the dots just as he remembered them. And then he blinked. "Okay," he said. "I magnified. I focused. And . . . I see dots." He looked over at the others. "Now what?"

The two Silents and Henry looked at one another and back at Alex. All three shrugged. "Aren't there any clues?" Henry asked.

"I don't see any. I just see dots."

"Well, try the next one."

Alex looked at the next painting the same way. Again he

saw dots and nothing more. He moved on to the next, and the next, until he had magnified and focused on all of them. "They're all just dots," he said. "They aren't in the shape of anything. They're just random."

"Let me see," Henry said. "Maybe you're doing it wrong." He grabbed the glass and peered into it.

"Yeah," Alex said sarcastically, "you're probably right. You have to really know how to use one of those things."

Sky laughed, her shoulders shaking. Alex made a face at her, then reluctantly laughed too.

Henry went through the same procedure as Alex, growing more and more perturbed. "There's nothing there," he declared after a while.

"Thanks a lot, Aristotle," Alex said.

Henry proceeded to magnify everything else in Mr. Today's office and in all the other rooms and hallways—the floors, walls, ceilings, staircases, and even statues. It took him well over a quarter of an hour to declare that there were no clues whatsoever hidden in the miniature mansion.

Crow poked Henry in the ribs. He looked bored. He pointed to the shack and raised an eyebrow.

Henry shrugged and nodded.

"Can I hold on to your magnifying glass for a bit?" Alex asked.

Henry considered the request, looking doubtful, but then Sky clasped her hands around Henry's and offered up a pleading smile. "Oh, all right," he said. He gave it to Alex. "Don't break it."

"Yes, boss," Alex said, rumpling the younger boy's hair, and then he pretended to drop it.

Henry glared, but then Crow tugged at his shirt, and off they went, Crow signing rapidly to his sister, to which she nodded her approval. And Alex and Sky were alone once more.

Alex sighed heavily. "We're back to having nothing." He wiped sweat off his forehead with his sleeve, and then he looked over his shoulder at Warbler Island. His recent dreams had him thinking of his friends more urgently than ever. After a minute, he turned back to the girl and squeezed his eyes shut to stop them from burning, pressing his fingers into the corners as if that would hide the defeat in them. He shook his head and whispered into his hands, "I honestly don't know how much more of this I can take."

Patience

After the wave of emotion passed, Alex looked up at Sky. "Sorry about that," he said with a crooked smile. "Apparently you're the one who always gets to see the real me." After a moment he hung his head. "Sorry I didn't take you seriously at first. That was not very cool of me."

The Silent girl's lips twitched. She moved closer and took Alex's hand, and for a moment he forgot to breathe. Without thinking, he brushed a finger across her cheek, wiping away a smudge of dust. "You're pretty . . . awesome," he said. Saying it made him feel like a dolt, but she didn't laugh. She blinked and looked down as the blush rose to her cheeks. He didn't

LISA McMANN

know why she made him feel so weird. Maybe because she seemed to understand so well all the anxiety he was feeling, all the responsibility. And all the pain, too. Whatever it was about her, it was starting to make him act like a total dork. Maybe it was because he liked her both as a friend and as a girl. Kind of like Lani, only this girl was . . .

His eyes sprang open, and he pulled his hand from hers. What was he doing? What would Meghan think if she saw him holding hands with Sky? How could he do that when Lani was out there somewhere, probably suffering? A couple days ago he didn't even know this girl's name!

He scrambled to pick up the magnifying glass. "Uhhh . . . here," Alex said, shoving it at her. "You want to try?"

She looked startled for a moment, and perhaps a bit annoyed, but then nodded and took it. Kneeling, she magnified one of the pictures. Then another, and another, concentrating harder on each one, but nothing came of it. Finally, on the fourth picture, she really looked at the dots. Was there something they weren't seeing? She gazed at the picture for several moments, looking at the pattern of the colors, the various sizes of the dots. Some were open circles, and some were solid, filled in.

She let her mind wander and kept her gaze unwavering. And then she reeled back and almost dropped the glass.

"What? What is it? Did you see something?" Alex gripped her shoulder, nothing but business now.

She nodded. She tried to trace what she had seen on the palm of her hand, but gave up and instead waved Alex to slide in next to her, which he did. She held up a finger, squeezed his shoulders, and wiped a hand across his furrowed brow, trying to tell him to relax. She breathed in and out, then tapped his chest so he would do it too.

"Okay, okay. I get it. I need to be calm. I was watching you, you know."

Sky nodded and held up the glass to the fourth painting. She pointed two fingers to her eyes, then to the painting, encircling it to indicate he should focus on the big picture, not just the center of it.

"Got it," he said. He took a deep breath, let it out, and gazed calmly at the picture. He let his eyes blur just slightly as he looked at the dots. He noticed they were all different sizes, and some were a solid color while others were just rings. He stared and stared, and when the girl next to him shifted and her

LISA McMANN

shoulder brushed against his, he stopped thinking about how important it was to get this clue and started thinking about what it would feel like to kiss a girl on the lips, not that he ever would, but maybe someday, and then he wondered if she thought he was cute, even though he was really a mess after weeks of cleaning up in seawater, and then without even realizing it, before his very eyes, the dots began to shimmer and move.

Alex was so startled that he gasped and stopped relaxing, and the dots went back the way they were. "Bricks and mortar!" he cried. "Something almost happened." He focused again.

The girl gripped his knee, excited, and that was enough to distract poor Alex in such a way that the dots began to shimmer and move again very soon. He stayed very still, and within seconds all the purple dots had moved to form letters, and the letters solidified and popped out from the painting one at a time, kind of like a 3-D door when you finally get it right. It was almost as if Alex could reach out and grab the letter blocks. But the most hopeful and exciting thing happened when the letters stopped popping, because they twirled around like they were dancing, and they rearranged themselves until the letters spelled a word.

And that word was "BREATHE."

The Sun Also Rises

On the cool stone floor of their prison, Samheed and Lani huddled together to try to sleep.

"When it's cold like this, I bet it's nighttime," Samheed tapped into Lani's hand, but she didn't answer. She was already asleep. Samheed uttered a silent sigh. He was uncomfortable with Lani's head resting on his upper arm, treating it as a pillow, and he debated whether he could slide his arm out without disturbing her or letting go of her hand. They were tethered by a promise. Their hands weren't tied together by anything but fear of the other being snatched away. They didn't know who could see them or if someone—

LISA McMANN

or a whole roomful of people—might even be standing a few feet away. It was a creepy feeling. Samheed shivered and tried to stop thinking about it.

Soon enough Sam knew he had to either pull his arm out from under Lani's head or lose a limb due to lack of circulation, so he nudged Lani and yanked his arm away, stopping in time to catch her head in his hand. He set her head gently on the stone floor and freed his fingers from her hair, then instinctively smoothed it away from her face, knowing how much it tickled his own nose when she flung it about. He found the most comfortable position under the circumstances and took a fresh grasp of Lani's fingers while he waited for the numbness in his arm to subside. Eventually his lids drooped, and he slept too.

When Lani awoke, she didn't bother to open her eyes—what was the point? Instead she readjusted her grip on Samheed's hand and rolled to her side, pushing her back against his to try to warm it. Under different circumstances, she might delight in holding a boy's hand for an extended period of time, even if it wasn't Alex, because it was a new feeling, and Lani was nothing if not an explorer of new things. But there came a time when enough was enough, and after what must have been many days, even weeks, she was so tired of holding Samheed's hand that she sometimes squeezed it very hard to try and get some of her frustrations out.

The crazy thing was that Sam, who was such a hothead when she first met him, didn't seem to mind. He let it happen, knowing there was no other way to express emotions in their mute world. He'd squeeze back, but not like one might expect Samheed to squeeze when angry, so it never hurt Lani. Something had changed in him since his early days in Artimé. He'd grown mellower. Lani liked that. She liked it a lot.

She sniffed deeply, trying to determine if anyone had brought food recently. Smelling nothing, she scooted over, rolled to her back, and slowly let her eyelids open.

She frowned. And then she sat up. She craned her neck, squinting, turning her head all around, and frowned again. And then she pounded Samheed's arm.

Her heart raced, and she pounded him again, and then began to tap into his hand, "Wake up! I think . . ."

He didn't move, so she pounded him harder until he moved and sat up.

LISA McMANN

She began again. "Something's different. Can you"—she paused, not quite sure—"see? A little bit?"

Samheed turned his head about, and Lani almost thought she saw a shadow, or a silhouette of his face. "I can see you!" she tapped. "Sam!"

"No," he tapped. "I can't." He turned toward her, but she couldn't make out his features at all. He was just an outline, black on dark gray. A moment passed. "Nothing," he tapped slowly. "Are you sure?"

Lani strained her eyes, and the usual blackness was definitely gray now. She could see Samheed's profile, and a blob not far away—the bucket of water. "It's very faint," she tapped. "Gray instead of black. Outlines. The bucket." She turned toward him. "I'll touch your nose," she said, and reached out toward the line where gray became black along his profile and the tip of his nose was apparent. Her finger landed on it, and she could feel him breathe in surprise.

"I . . . ," he began to tap, and shook his head. His heart twisted as he yearned to see anything, but all was still black. "Still nothing," he finally tapped.

In wonder, just barely able to see the outline of him, Lani

guided her finger down his nose, across his cheek, and then she squeezed his shoulder. Tears jumped to her eyes as the world lightened before her at the slowest possible pace. "I can see you," her lips mouthed, but she didn't tap it. Instead she tapped, "I'm sorry."

Samheed was still for a moment, and Lani watched him bring his free hand to his bowed head. She could almost feel his longing. Then he dropped his hand to his lap, deadweight, and tapped, "Tell me everything you see. And—" He stopped.

Lani waited. "And?"

Samheed turned his blind eyes toward her. She could see the outline of his body, feel his breath on her bare arm, his hand on her knee. Slowly, softly, he tapped, "Please don't leave me."

Together, Apart

Lani squeezed Samheed's arm. "Of course I won't leave you!" she tapped. She flung her arms around his neck, surprising him, catching him off balance. He righted himself and, after a second, hugged her tightly, squeezing his eyes shut and biting the inside of his cheek, wishing he weren't so helpless. He hated this feeling—had always hated it. Before today he could be thankful that Lani couldn't see the fear on his face, but now . . . He didn't want to have to count on anybody at any time, not after all that had happened to him.

But when he was truthful with himself, and when he

remembered that Lani hadn't left him the last time she'd had a chance, while he lay helpless and knocked out on a table, and when he thought about the past weeks in this stupid, horrible cave of darkness and silence, no one coming to their rescue, only Lani there, and the two in turn acting both vulnerable and strong, he knew that Lani was probably the one and only person in the whole world with whom he could truly let down his guard.

He clutched at her, devastated that she could see shadows and he couldn't, yet trying not to lose hope. If she could see, she could try to escape. But if she had to drag him with her, he was only a liability. And despite her response, despite knowing deep down that she wouldn't leave him willingly, he was still scared beyond anything he'd ever been through—beyond the Purge, beyond the battle, beyond the excruciating implanta-tion of the necklace of thorns. Samheed was frightened that something would separate them, and that he would be left blind, deaf, mute, and alone in this stark cave once again, this time forever.

Lani's lips parted in surprise when Samheed didn't let go of her. And even though she'd been concentrating, straining her

LISA McMANN

eyes to see more and more as the light slowly increased, something in her stomach flitted about just then, and she became
highly aware of Sam's warm cheek against hers. She swallowed
hard and her breathing grew shallower, almost as if she was
afraid her intake of air would disturb the moment or cause
Sam to come to his senses and let go. But he didn't. Lani's eyes
fluttered closed, and she turned her attention from things she
could barely see to things intangible and invisible inside of her,
and for the briefest of moments, the two breathed together in
time.

When they drew apart at last, it was with a somber realization that they were alone in this strange and horrible world,
and that hope for rescue was waning. That despite the trauma
and horror of their predicament, all they had was the person
sitting next to them. And all they could do was wait for Alex.

But Alex hadn't come.

Neither needed to say it. They sat side by side, backs against
the wall, fingers intertwined, with no pressing need for sight or
sound in this moment, as long as they had each other.

It was perhaps an hour later that a towering shadow dark-
ened the brightening space in front of Lani. She startled with

force and scrambled closer to Samheed, gripping his hand tightly as she tried to explain what was happening with taps from her other hand on his knee. But it became apparent that the figure, in the process of setting down a tray of food, noticed her commotion. In the grainy light, Lani saw the black holes that were his eye sockets, two dull orange spots coming from the depths of them, and a slow, evil smile spreading across his face.

He lunged at her, snatching her by her free arm, and pulled her toward him. Lani's mouth opened wide in a silent scream, her body being pulled upward by the figure and down again by Samheed, who hung on to her hand and arm with all his might, knowing only that his worst fears must be coming true.

Pain tore through Lani's body as the figure grasped her around the waist and yanked her up and away from Samheed. He stomped on Sam's foot and kneed the boy in the stomach, but even breathless and racked with pain, Samheed hung on to Lani's arm. "I'm not letting go!" he screamed, but the words could be heard only in his head. He kicked out wildly, trying to connect with whatever it was that was taking Lani away, but he missed over and over. Sweat slickened his grasp, and with one lurch into the air and a kick from the enemy, Samheed lost his hold and hit the ground hard.

Lani nearly went flying in the other direction, but the figure tightened his grip around her waist as she kicked and pounded at him, and he carried her away, leaving Sam motionless on the stone floor of the cave.

In a Word

B reathe,'" Alex murmured. He looked up at Sky. "It says 'breathe'!"

Sky looked back at him, her eyes shiny. She nodded. Then she pointed at another picture inside the miniature mansion.

Alex turned back to Mr. Today's tiny office and aimed the magnifying glass on another picture. Sweat poured down his face as he concentrated, then tried not to concentrate too hard. This picture was similar to the first, but the colors of the dots were different, as was the pattern. Alex wiped away the sweat that dripped into his eyes, which made him have to start over. "Crud," he muttered.

LISA McMANN

The girl rested her hand on Alex's arm and gave him a stern look. He took a deep breath and relaxed. "I know," he said. "I know." He closed his eyes and focused his thoughts on being calm. Then he started again.

After a few minutes, something wavered before his eyes, and then it turned cloudy. Without warning, Sky pulled the magnifying glass from Alex's hand and started blowing into the mansion with all her might.

Alex, startled, was mad. "What? I almost had it!"

She spoke with her hands furiously fast, even though Alex couldn't understand what she was saying. Then she jabbed her finger at a black spot on the wall of Mr. Today's office just below the picture Alex had been focusing on. It was a scorch mark. Alex sniffed and smelled smoke.

"Oh," he said. "Wow. I almost burned the place down."

Sky rolled her eyes and pointed down to the roof of the shack.

"Go inside the shack?" Alex guessed.

Sky answered by leading the way down the statue.

Inside, on the floor of the little kitchen, they found an unoccupied niche in which to sit. Once their eyes adjusted to the difference in lighting, Alex tried again. This time it took only a few moments for the dots to start swimming around. Alex strained to hold the connection, and soon enough, letters popped out into space, danced, and then formed another word. This time, the word was "BELIEVE."

"'Believe!'" Alex whispered to the girl. She nodded excitedly and prodded him to go to the next one. He did, and a few minutes later, he had deciphered the third: "COMMENCE."

Alex said the words in his head several times so that he wouldn't forget, and he said them to Sky as well so that she could memorize them. He chose a new picture and soon he had his fourth word: "IMAGINE." When he had that one, he glanced at the Silent girl. "Which one haven't I done?" he asked, his voice pitching high with nerves. He didn't want to waste any time by doing any of them more than once, but he'd been too shocked and excited at the beginning to keep track of where he'd started.

She pointed to the one in the middle.

Alex grinned. Sky was amazing, he thought. No wonder she'd been to able escape from Warbler. "You are the best," he said.

She nodded.

Alex laughed softly. He loved that she knew she was smart and clever. He turned back to the miniature and trained the

LISA McMANN

glass on the middle picture. He was getting quite good at it now, and within moments the last one jumped to life. "'WHISPER,'" he whispered.

Alex scanned the other walls of the office to see if there were any more dot pictures. When he was quite certain there weren't, he said all the words aloud. "Breathe, believe, commence, imagine, whisper." He pulled Mr. Today's spell from his pocket once more and read it through silently.

> Follow the dots as the traveling sun,
>
> Magnify, focus, every one.
>
> Stand enrobed where you first saw me,
>
> Utter in order; repeat times three.

With every line, Alex's heart pounded faster. He'd found the dots, magnified, focused on all the pictures, he had the robe . . . Now all he had to do was figure out what the sun had to do with the dots, and remember where he first saw Mr. Today, then say the words in order three times, and Artimé would be back.

He looked at Sky. "We're so close," he whispered, and he could feel the intensity about to burst through his veins. He stared at the first line. "The traveling sun . . ." He pressed his fingers to his temples. "How does the sun travel?" he asked himself. "Actually, it doesn't travel," he mused, having read about it in the library once. "It only appears to." He shook his head. "No, too technical. This is simpler than that. How does the sun appear to travel? In a line. In the sky." He mumbled a bit more, thinking aloud. "Wait." His eyes sprang open. He grabbed the mini mansion and turned it. "This is the way it sat on the property," he muttered, placing it just so and looking over his shoulder out the window to make sure he had his bearings. "The sun travels from east to west. So that means . . . if Mr. Today's office stands like this, which it does, or it would if the mansion were here, the first picture if we follow the sun is the one on the east end of the wall. So, that one. 'Imagine,' wasn't it?"

Sky nodded with enthusiasm. She pointed her forefinger to her temple, then fluttered her fingers like a bird, stretching her arm away, teaching him her silent word for it.

"Cool," Alex said, delighted. "Okay, so 'imagine' is the first word, and then we go in order to the west. Does that sound right to you?" Alex asked.

Sky agreed, and pointed at the pictures in that order. Then

she went back and pointed to the second one. She looked up at Alex, as if willing him to say the right one. She made fists and brought them together, knuckles to knuckles in front of her, then pulled them to her chest.

Alex took a deep breath, thinking back. "'Believe,'" he said. He imitated the word in her language, bringing his fists together.

Sky smiled and pointed to the one in the middle, then held a finger to her lips. "'Whisper,'" Alex said with confidence.

She moved her finger to the fourth one.

Alex looked at it. His mind drew a blank. "Um . . . crud."

Sky shook her head in mock disgust, a wide grin on her face. She put her hand on Alex's chest, pressed gently, then released.

"Oh! That one is 'breathe.'" He flashed her a sheepish smile. He had such trouble remembering that word sometimes. "And that means the last one is 'commence.' Right?"

Sky rolled her hand in the air, doing the sign for it, then clapped her hands.

"Okay. Help me remember the order." He glanced back at the clue and frowned. "Stand enrobed where . . . ," he said, trailing off. "Hmm." He scrambled to his feet and looked around. "Where's Meghan?"

Where You First Saw Me

Alex didn't see Meghan anywhere near Henry and Crow or among the fifty or so other sleeping Unwanteds inside the shack. He weaved through the people on the floor and slipped outside, Sky following him. Together they ran, zigzagging through the crowded property.

"Alex!" someone shouted. "We're out of water!"

Alex felt his stomach churn at the words he'd been dreading, but this time a wave of hope followed it. "Okay!" he shouted back. "I'm working on it. Don't panic!"

Three others tried to stop him with the same complaint,

LISA McMANN

but Alex hurriedly thanked them for the information and explained that he was working on it. Finally Alex and Sky found Meghan on the sand at the water's edge, sorting through the collection of shells, seaweed, branches, and tiny fish in a net.

"Meg!" Alex said, breathless. "I think we almost have it!" He and Sky slid to a stop at Meghan's feet, chests heaving, throats parched.

Meghan's eyes widened. "Well?" she mouthed. She gripped Alex's arm.

"We've got the dots, the rising sun part, everything! Except I don't know where we first saw Mr. Today. That day was so crazy. I remember the bus, and walking in and seeing the Eliminators," he said, shuddering. "But the sight of them about put me into a coma. Everything after that is a little fuzzy, with Jim and the world swirling around. Was Mr. Today at the gate with Jim? Do you remember? Please say you do." Alex pressed his lips together.

Meghan's face grew thoughtful. She looked at the sky for a long moment as Alex tried not to rush her. Her brows knitted together, and she ran her finger over the thorns around her neck, as if that helped her concentrate. She closed her eyes and let out a breath of impatience. Not only was it difficult for Meghan to think back to that frightening moment, but also it was so incredibly frustrating not being able to speak, especially when speaking was crucial to helping Alex get Artimé back.

She pictured the moment they'd shuffled into the Death Farm all shackled together. She saw the Eliminators coming toward the Unwanteds, their beady red eyes glowing, their black cloaks dragging on the ground as they walked. She remembered her heart pounding, her breath stopped in her lungs as she awaited the end. She remembered her surprise when the Eliminators stopped and turned to look at the sky, and then Jim landed. She remembered how agonizingly slowly he spoke when he called out for Mr. Today.

Meghan's eyes flew open. She grabbed Alex's and Sky's arms and tugged at them to follow as she ran toward the gray shack, straight to the door that faced the gate, where Mr. Today had first appeared, his shock of brilliant white hair standing on end, his bright-colored robe, his gentle words.

When she reached the spot just outside the door, she stopped and pointed to the ground below her feet, and nodded.

"Here?" Alex asked. He scratched his head. "I thought he

LISA McMANN

came from the seaside door and walked the along the path around the shack."

Meghan shook her head, her eyes flaring, her lips moving at great speed, scolding him without making a sound.

"Okay, okay," Alex said. "I'm sorry. You're right." It was horrible to watch Meghan trying to ream him out and being unable to. It was worse than being reamed out the old way. But he didn't have time to think about it now. He took a deep breath, attempting to remember the words and their order. "Ready, guys?"

Sky grabbed her head in frustration. She waved her arms, calling it off. Then she feigned putting on a . . . a coat?

Alex frowned, and then his face cleared. "Oh. Geez! The robe. I'm an idiot. Hold on a minute." But Meghan held out her hands, telling him to stay put. She flung the door open and ran inside the shack. A moment later she was back with the robe. From the doorway, she made Alex twirl around so she could help him put the robe on. It was a bit too long, a bit too wide, but it draped nicely.

Alex took another deep breath as he looked first at Meghan to his right in the doorway, then at Sky on the other side of him. He nodded. "Ready."

Sky nodded back, touched her finger to her temple and fluttered her fingers away from her head to remind him.

Alex felt faint. But he began nevertheless. "Imagine." The word wavered a bit in his throat but it seemed clear enough, so he continued. "Believe."

And then he paused. "No, wait. I need to start over."

Repeat Times Three

Meghan rolled her eyes. Sky raised a brow.

"I think I need to do more than say the words," Alex explained. "I need to act them out in my head, like when I made the hospital wing. I bet that's what Mr. Today did when he first created Artimé."

So he closed his eyes and imagined Artimé, the way it had been, the way he wanted it to be again. His hands reached out to include the entire plot of land. "Imagine," he said in a soft voice, picturing it all, room by room, the lawn with the fountains, the trees, the creatures. When he was certain he'd imagined it all, he went on.

"Believe." He believed with all his heart that Artimé could exist again. Believed that when he was finished with the spell and he opened his eyes, it would be there.

"Whisper." Alex imagined Mr. Today whispering these words over the desolate plot of land so many years ago, calling it to live a new, vibrant life, and he realized that he'd been whispering the words all along.

"Breathe." Alex took in a deep, satisfying breath and let it out slowly. He didn't forget it this time. He pictured himself breathing life into the world, giving it the air it needed to flourish once again.

And then: "Commence." The command to make it all happen. The beginning of everything.

Alex waited a moment, and very nearly opened his eyes before he remembered the clue. *Utter in order, repeat times three.* Hoping he hadn't messed anything up, he began the second round and went through the five words in order, all the while imagining, believing, whispering, breathing, and commencing with all his might.

When he finished the second round, he started one last time, his voice remaining soft. "Imagine. Believe. Whisper.

LISA McMANN

Breathe." He hesitated, swallowing hard, before the last one. And finally: "Commence."

Nothing happened. All was deathly silent.

Alex remained very still, eyes closed, arms outstretched, feeling a sort of calmness inside him that he hadn't felt ever before. It almost seemed like he was beginning to float, peacefully alone in the world.

And then something *did* happen. The light through his closed lids grew pinkish-white, bright, and soon lights swirled around him, faster and faster, with colors joining in and growing stronger. He opened his eyes just as the land in front of him turned a luscious green and, with a great rumble, the enormous fountain broke through the ground, spewing up from the earth, the growing expanse of lawn rippling and resettling around it. The land spread farther, making Unwanteds along the shore lose their footing and tumble to the ground. Trees popped up to dot the lawn and form the jungle on the opposite side of Artimé. The gray shack spun and grew into the enormous mansion once again. The heat dissipated in an instant, and a cool breeze rushed in from the sea.

Alex gaped. "I did it," he whispered. And then he yelled

at the top of his voice, "I did it!" He began to run toward the center of the lawn so he could see if all was in order as people along the shore sprang to their feet, annoyed at first, then their faces awash in joy. "I did it!" he screamed once more, his voice growing ragged. He gripped his head and stared all around.

The Artiméans jumped and danced, laughing and shouting the news to their friends, as if their friends weren't seeing it just as they were. Dozens of them raced for the fountain and threw themselves in to celebrate, cool off, and quench their thirst. A number of Artiméans saw Alex standing in the center of Artimé, turning slowly, taking it all in. They surrounded him, hugging him and patting him on the back and lifting him in the air, praising and thanking him, all the frustration of the past weeks forgotten. Alex felt all the anxieties of the world wash away as a surge of joy rushed through him. "I did it," he repeated softly as the crowd set him down and went on cele-brating. "I actually did it." He rubbed his eyes and slapped his own cheek to make sure he wasn't dreaming, and indeed, he had done it. Artimé was back, and everything was good.

Well, not quite everything. All around, reminders of things gone wrong pelted him again, and Alex knew he had other

LISA McMANN

extremely important things to tend to. He broke free from the crowd and ran smack into the biggest, hardest, movingest statue he'd ever run into. He reeled back, not quite catching himself before he fell to the grass. "Florence!" he cried out. He scrambled to his feet.

She looked about, bewildered at the commotion. "What on earth is happening? Are we under attack?"

"No—" Alex opened his mouth to tell her, having nearly forgotten that she and all the creatures and statues had no idea that Mr. Today was . . . gone. "Oh," he said. A fresh wave of grief flooded through him alongside the rush of relief at Artimé's grand return, and with so much emotion of so many kinds, the overwhelmingness of it all threatened to overflow from his body into a soggy mess at Alex's feet. Tears formed and dripped from his eyes. "Find Sean or Mr. Appleblossom. Hurry." It was all he could squeak out.

Florence, alarmed, nearly took a step toward Alex to comfort him, but the look on his face told her to do as he'd asked. "I will," she said. "Whatever it is, it's going to be okay." She turned around just as the enormous pile of owlbats, beavops, rabbitkeys, squirrelicorns, and platyprots, all still propped

LISA McMANN

against the wall in the design of the spectacular towering ladder Sean had been building, began to wriggle and squeal. Alex turned to look too, just as the gigantic heap combusted into a hurricane of feathers, beaks, horns, and tails. The ones who could fly wriggled free and did so, while the ones who couldn't fell like plump, squishy sacks, splatting to the ground, screeching and squealing and yipping, but unhurt. All the platyprots began imitating the noises of the others, so it sounded like three times as many creatures in an instant cacophony strong enough to make the Unwanteds nearby hit the dirt in fear.

Alex put his hands over his ears and watched in horror. "Oh dear," he said. He hadn't thought *that* one through, that was for sure. He whipped his head around as creatures flew and stormed past him, some joyous, others furious, all of them still not understanding what had happened. "Rufus!" Alex called out when he saw his squirrelicorn teammate from the battle, but it was no use. Everyone else was shouting too, and no one could be understood.

Alex's eyes landed on Jim, who stood up rather gingerly, testing his legs and wings, but he seemed well enough. The ground shook as the girrinos got to their feet. And then Alex's

LISA McMANN

heart caught in his throat. Abruptly he turned and shouldered his way desperately through the masses, trying not to get trampled, trying to head toward the shore against the flow of traffic as everyone else went to find friends and make their way into the mansion to find shelter, food, and the comfort of their rooms. Nearby Alex saw the beloved octogator, Ms. Octavia, rise to her tentacles, and he watched as someone unwittingly knocked her glasses off her alligator snout. Alex reached for them and handed them to her, thrilled to see his instructor alive again. "Find Sean or Mr. Appleblossom!" Alex called out to her before she was picked up by some students and swept to safety.

Each second that passed was excruciating as Alex forced his way through the bodies toward the shore, but finally the crowd thinned. Before long Alex was left alone on the beach, a most bizarre feeling after weeks of no room to breathe, much less stand alone and contemplate. But Alex wasn't thinking about that. He held his trembling hand up to shield his eyes from the sun and stared at the water.

"Come on," he whispered, the breeze tumbling around him, and he ripped his fingers through his hair to move it out

Island of Fire » 96

of his eyes. "Come on," Alex said again, pleading this time. He sank to his knees, not trusting himself to stand any longer, the waves lapping up around his legs. He strained forward, blinking away the burn in his eyes. "Come on!" he shouted at the water, his voice ragged and catching on the words. "Come on, Simber! You should be here by now! Everyone else is alive!"

Another moment of silence and nothingness. Then two. Alex lowered his head, picturing the cat reduced to a pile of sand at the bottom of the sea. His chest caved in to sobs. "You said you wouldn't leave me," he whispered. He covered his face, overwhelmed with sorrow.

And so it was that in the midst of chaos and color and light, in the glorious rebirth of a magical world, there remained two small vessels dark and drained. And those vessels were the heart and the soul of a brokenhearted young mage, sobbing alone in the sand.

It was only then that the sea before him exploded.

Breaking the News

I t was as if the sea had wings, its destination the sky. The water shot up like a geyser to an enormous height, and once it reached its zenith, it fell back to the sur-face in sheets, slapping and booming like thunder, until only the creature responsible for the watery show remained airborne.

At the first sound Alex had looked up, and now, with his chest stuck in a gasp and his heart throbbing in his throat, he scrambled to his feet and began waving like mad to the giant stone cheetah half a mile out.

It took Simber a good deal less time to cover the distance

than it had taken Alex, who'd been dragging the unconscious Meghan through the water, and before Alex could fully comprehend that his beloved Simber was truly not melted into silt on the sea's floor, the cheetah descended and came to an elegant stop next to Alex. He arched his back and shook himself wildly, his stone skin rippling as water fell around him.

"Simber," Alex breathed, and when the beast had finished shaking, Alex flung himself around the cat's neck and held on for dear life.

After a long moment, Alex found his voice again. "I don't even know where to start," he said, his face pressed against the cold stone of Simber's neck. He smeared his tears across his dirty cheek, trying to wipe them away.

"I can only guess what went wrrrong," Simber gargled. He cleared his throat.

"We lost . . . a lot," Alex said, then closed his lips and pressed them together.

"The last I rrrememberrr, we werrre on ourrr way home. Then I woke, of all places, underrrwaterrr." He shuddered at the thought. "It took a bit of time to get my bearrrrings and swim towarrrd the surrrface."

Alex nodded and let go of the cheetah but was unable to look the statue in the eye.

Simber regarded the boy's ragged, dirty appearance carefully, and wrinkled up his nose. "How long has it been since I . . . frrrroze?" He began to lick the remaining droplets of water off his back and legs.

Alex took a breath, hoping to steady his voice. "Weeks," Alex said.

Simber stopped licking and stared hard at the boy. His expression didn't falter, but his eyes gave away everything. "Couldn't Marrrcus . . . ?" He stood alert and sampled the air, his ears moving wildly. "Wherrre is he? Why arrre you wearrring his rrrobe?"

Alex couldn't speak. His lip trembled.

"Alex!" Simber roared. "Answerrr me!"

"He's dead!" Alex shouted, more from fear than anything. When the cat reared back in shock, Alex said it again, softer this time. "He's dead. Most likely from the moment you fell to the bottom of the sea."

Simber stared at Alex for a long moment, searching the boy's face. And then he closed his eyes. His head fell. "Tell me," he whispered.

Alex swallowed hard, his throat still sore and dry as toast. "Meghan and I were thrown from the boat. She almost drowned. We barely made it to shore. When we did, Artimé was gone."

"Oh, Marrrcus." Simber, eyes still closed, winced as he imagined it. His beloved creator, his closest friend. The cat held very still for an excruciatingly long moment, as if pulling his thoughts together to make sense, accepting the realization of it, bracing himself for what was to come. And then he opened his eyes. "And you brrrought Arrrtimé back," he said, not a question.

Alex swallowed hard. "Yeah. Finally. I'm sorry it took me so long. I'm just . . . I'm so glad to see you."

Simber lowered his head so that his eyes were even with the young mage's. "I'm verrry prrroud of you," he said.

"Some people left," Alex whispered. He dropped his gaze, the lump in his throat too big to allow his voice to come through.

It may have been an accident, but Simber's muzzle brushed against the side of Alex's head, which nearly looked like an act of kindness, but no one was around to point it out. In a gentle voice, Simber asked, "Wherrre do things stand now?"

When Alex could speak, he said, "It's pretty crazy right now. Everyone headed for the mansion because we've been, sort of, well, starving to death, I guess. I sent Florence and Ms. Octavia to find Sean and Mr. Appleblossom for answers. I hope they're settling everyone down. I had to come here. I had to . . . wait for you."

"Of courrrse," Simber murmured, but his stony brow furrowed. "Sean and Sigfrrried? Not Clairrre?"

"She's . . . ," Alex said, and shook his head. "She's gone too."

"No," Simber said, the word turning into a ferocious growl that hurt Alex's ears. "Who is rrresponsible forrr this?"

Alex's face paled. He gazed in the direction of the gate. "The new high priest of Quill. Aaron Stowe."

"The new . . . ?" Simber's jaw opened, but for once he was incapable of finishing. Just as he attempted to repeat Alex's words a second time, Sky came running up at full speed. She seemed surprised at the size of Simber and planted her feet into the sand to stop her momentum just short of her goal, not wanting to get too close to the beast, as she'd never seen him before. She reached out carefully to grab Alex's arm, tugging at him and gesturing for him to follow.

Her expression worried Alex. "Something's wrong," Alex said to Simber. "I'll tell you everything when I get a chance. Come on." He followed Sky, who had taken off at a run.

"Indeed," Simber said, and he loped alongside the two. Several yards before they reached the mansion, Simber stopped. "Something's shaking," he said.

Alex held up. "What? I don't feel anything."

Sky urged Alex onward.

"Something is shaking," Simber said again. "The mansion. It's shaking." He looked hard at the mansion and then bounded toward it. "Something is terrribly wrrrong inside."

Behind the Wall

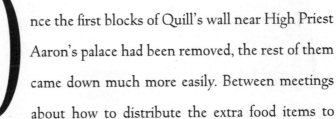

Once the first blocks of Quill's wall near High Priest Aaron's palace had been removed, the rest of them came down much more easily. Between meetings about how to distribute the extra food items to those who had earned it, and planning sessions where Aaron gave Eva lists upon lists of fairly useless chores to keep her busy and test her loyalty, the new high priest made his way to his office window to watch the progress. All day, the same something niggled at him: Why would Justine have built the wall in the first place if there was nothing to worry about on the other side? Was it simply her way of controlling the people of Quill through fear? If so, it didn't sit quite right with Aaron.

Toward the end of the day, all the workers but one had begun to slow down, much to Aaron's distaste. It was distracting to have to keep checking on them only to see most of them taking short breaks to drink water or rest their tired backs. Even more frustrating was the one who worked solidly, for Aaron would have liked to find fault with him especially.

After one such trip to the window, Aaron had had enough of their slacking. Frowning, he strode out of his office and down to the palace entry, flying out the door with his cloak billowing behind him. There was a strong breeze coming through the opening, which was both delightful and unsettling, for Quill rarely had much more than a tiny hint of wind coming over the walls. Aaron felt so exposed. Putting a hole in the wall alongside the palace—perhaps that was not one of Aaron's smarter ideas. *But look at Artimé,* he argued. *They're even more exposed, and nothing ill ever befell them from the outside.*

He approached the men, who began working much harder at the sight of him. "You're slacking off," he said to them. "If you continue at that pace, I'll make you stay past dark."

The one who'd been working hard all along put his shovel

LISA McMANN

down and looked at Aaron. The others who'd noticed did double takes and backed away.

"I haven't slowed my pace," the man said, wiping the sweat from his brow.

The other workers gaped.

Aaron's nostrils flared. "You'll address me properly, or . . . ," He couldn't think of anything, and his face flushed.

The man nodded solidly, but his voice quavered. "All right. I haven't slowed my pace, *Son*, and you know it. I've always worked my hardest and taught my children to do that too." He hesitated, then blindly barreled onward, his voice cracking. "I don't care who you are now. You'll show your father some respect." He stood stone still, but his eyes flitted about, as if he knew he'd gone too far.

Aaron flinched and heat rose from his collar. His mind whirled. He couldn't allow a Necessary to speak to him like that—not even his father. Not in front of other Necessaries. If he didn't do something, word would spread that he was weak. If he didn't do something immediately . . .

"Guards!" Aaron shouted. Two of them came running to Aaron's side. "Take this man to the Ancients Sector," he said, his voice wavering the slightest bit. "His time of service in Quill is done."

Mr. Stowe stared at Aaron. Aaron stared back, a feeling of horror growing inside his chest when he realized what he'd just done. But he didn't take it back.

The guards grabbed Mr. Stowe by the arms and shoved him toward a Quillitary vehicle. The man's lips parted and a shocked look came over his face, then one of pain. "Aaron, no," he said. "Your mother . . ."

Aaron's face was stone. His mother—she was pregnant, he remembered from when he'd seen them in the crowd at his speech several weeks prior. Would she care that her husband was dead? She hadn't seemed to care about Alex when she thought he was dead.

Mr. Stowe's shoes slipped in the gravel as he struggled to look back at Aaron, his eyes pleading. Aaron's gaze narrowed, and as the guards pushed his father into the vehicle, Aaron turned to the other workers. "You may want to work harder," he said in a sinister voice.

Stricken with fear, the workers began at a frantic pace to disassemble the remaining blocks. Behind Aaron, the guards

LISA McMANN

drove off with Mr. Stowe, the man's bowed head visible through the back window. As soon as the noise of the jalopy had quieted, Aaron turned back to the palace and stomped inside to his office.

"Secretary!" he screamed. "Come at once!"

Eva was there in a flash. "What is it?" she asked, alarmed.

"I've sent my father to the Ancients Sector." He looked at her, and now he couldn't stop the fear that bled into his eyes. "He was disrespectful."

"Your father?"

"He was one of the workers."

Eva had to work very hard not to react. What she really wanted to do was punish the spoiled boy herself, right that minute. But all she said was, "I see."

Aaron turned and began to pace. "He didn't address me properly! He made me look like a fool!" He swiped his hand across his desk, sending papers flying. "What else could I have done?"

Eva didn't think he wanted an answer. "If you want me to tell you that you did the right thing . . ." She didn't finish, for fear it would get her sent to join Mr. Stowe.

Aaron rounded his desk and gripped the back of his chair,

muttering to himself. "He deserved it. He knew very well what he should have done."

Eva closed her eyes briefly and sighed, not loud enough to be heard.

"Even if he was right, he shouldn't have said it like he said it." He began pacing again.

Eva waited until Aaron had finished muttering, and then she said, "Shall I send a vehicle to retrieve him, High Priest?"

Aaron's face twisted in indecision. He pounded his hands on his desk in anger. And then he pressed his fingers to his temples. "Yes," he said finally. "Send him home, on the condition that he remains silent on the matter."

Eva Fathom nodded and set off to stop an untimely death.

"Wait," Aaron called after her, and she stopped and turned to look at him.

"There is one more condition. Tell him that he and my mother and any future . . . children . . . of theirs must be loyal to Quill. They will make an oath never to pledge loyalty of any sort to my brother, or to Artimé, as long as they live."

Eva waited to make sure he was finished, and then she said, "I will see to it myself."

LISA McMANN

Eva left the palace and Aaron went again to the window, watching her go, watching the other men working and struggling below to finish their job before they collapsed.

He was so deep in thought, he didn't notice that a little gargoyle statue named Matilda had climbed up and out of a box in the closet and now stood very still, ear pointed at the opening in the door.

The Gray Shack

Sean met Alex, Simber, and Sky at the door to the mansion. Hundreds of Unwanteds celebrated beyond the entryway, spilling out of the dining room and kitchen. "Simber!" Sean exclaimed. "Man, I'm glad to see you." But he looked more distracted than glad. He turned to Alex. "We're missing people," he said, getting back to business. "Meghan, Henry, Crow, Mr. Appleblossom, and dozens of others."

Alex's eyes widened. "Meghan? She was with me when I changed the world back."

"Well, she's not here now. She's nowhere."

"She was standing right inside the doorway of the shack," Alex said, alarm growing in his voice. "Henry and Crow were sleeping on the floor inside. They can't have gone far. Did you check their rooms?"

Sean reached out and shook Alex's shoulders. "I'm obviously not explaining this right. Yes, we checked everywhere. They're gone now. Everyone in the gray shack—all of them are gone. Disappeared. Wiped out."

Alex gaped. "What?"

"Gone."

"B-b-but," Alex sputtered, "why wouldn't the people inside the gray shack just turn up inside the mansion once Artimé is back? It's basically the same house, isn't it?" The Silent girl grabbed his hand and tugged at him.

Sean raised his voice. "They're not here, Alex! That's all I know. My sister is not here. I've been all through the place."

"Okay, okay," Alex said. "I'm worried too, I'm just trying to figure it out, is all. Did you call out for her or the others?"

"Of course I did," Sean said, annoyed.

"What's shaking the mansion?" Simber growled.

Sean turned to Simber. "I don't feel anything shaking."

Sky stomped her foot and jumped up and down, waving to get their attention. She pointed up the staircase.

"I think you ought to be paying morrre attention to the young woman," Simber remarked.

The girl started up the stairs, looking over her shoulder to see if anyone was coming. Simber bounded up the stairs after her, with Sean and Alex right behind. As they neared the top of the staircase, they too could feel a bit of a tremble in the floor.

Sean and Sky stopped on the landing, the girl feeling along the wall where the mostly secret hallway was. Sean pressed his ear up against what was an open space to Alex. "It's behind this wall," Sean said.

Alex gave Simber a questioning look. Simber's eyes narrowed. He nodded at Alex, urging him to take the lead.

"There's a secret hallway here," Alex said quietly to Sean and Sky. "Simber and I can see it. You guys stay here. If anything weird happens, or if we don't come back, find Octavia and Florence. They can get in too."

Sean raised an eyebrow. "Well. I guess I never knew about that." He seemed a bit put out.

LISA McMANN

Alex smiled grimly. "Not many people can see it." He turned to Simber. "Let's go."

They entered the mostly secret hallway, leaving Sean and a very startled Silent girl watching them disappear through the wall.

Simber and Alex both glanced to the left at the door to Mr. Today's private chambers. They caught each other's eye but didn't speak. They would have to pay a visit to that room eventually, when things settled down. But now Simber stopped in front of the door across the hallway from it. "Have you everrr been in herrre?"

Alex nodded. "Once. It's the Museum of Large." His memory of that visit was foggy after all he'd encountered in the past weeks.

"Can you get in?"

Alex thought hard. "I can . . . if I remember the spell." He pressed his ear against the door but heard nothing, only feeling the shaking against his cheek. He racked his brains for the spell to get in. It had been so long since he'd been able to do magic, and such a long time since he'd had even a second to think about any spells other than the one to restore the world, that it took

LISA McMANN

him a while to engage that part of his brain. He turned to Simber. "Can you tell what's going on in there? What if it . . . what if it's dangerous?"

"That hasn't stopped you beforrre," Simber said. He sniffed under the door. "Something's familiar . . . ," he said, and then he shook his head. "But the doorrr is magically sealed. I can't rrreally tell."

Alex closed his eyes and let his forehead rest against the door, trying to picture his visit to this room with Mr. Today. What was that dratted spell? He mentally ran through all the museum's items that he could remember in case they offered a clue. The library, the pirate ship, the whale, the gray shack . . .

"The shack," Alex murmured. He opened his eyes and stared, unseeing, at the door. "Oh, say! The gray shack is in *there*," he said, getting excited. "Whoa, wait. Let me think this through. When I was in here before, I remember seeing the gray shack, only it was behind this really awesome whale skeleton, and I didn't go over to look at it. Do you think . . . ," he said, and then he paused and started again. "Do you think that when Artimé disappears, all that remains on the plot of land is

LISA McMANN

the gray shack, and that when Artimé exists, the shack automatically stores itself in this room?"

"What *I* think is that you should open the doorrr," Simber said dryly, but he looked relieved at Alex's revelation. "The shaking is prrrobably a few dozen angrrry Unwanteds jumping up and down in therrre, trrrying to get ourrr attention."

"Probably. Phew," Alex said. And now that the pressure was off him, the spell filtered into his brain. "Ah, that's right. I've got it." He reached for the handle and muttered, "Door number one."

When the door popped open, the sounds of fifty or more screaming Unwanteds pierced Alex's ears, but none of them were jumping. Instead they ran about hysterically, being chased by an enormous mastodon statue, whose thunderous steps were doing all the shaking.

Alex and Simber stared at the scene, and then Alex gasped and pointed. The Silent boy, Crow, hung precariously thirty feet above the floor from one of the mastodon's gleaming tusks.

Ol' Tater

Alex and Simber charged into the room and assessed the situation at top speed. "Buckets of crud! When I brought the world back to life, I think it woke up this guy," Alex yelled over the din.

"You *think*? Hey! Ol' Taterrr!" Simber roared to get the statue's attention, and then he turned back to Alex. "I thought Marrrcus got rrrid of him yearrrs ago."

"He couldn't stand to get rid of him!"

"Why am I not surrrprrrised?"

Alex nearly grinned despite the situation. "Okay, let's get the people out of here. Then you distract him and I'll see if I

LISA McMANN

can locate a spell in one of these books to . . . put him back to sleep." He gulped.

The two bounded over to a huddled group of Unwanteds, Alex waving and pointing to the open door, and Simber racing around the perimeter of the museum, shouting instructions and nudging Unwanteds in the proper direction. Within a few minutes, the majority of the people had made it out into the hallway safely. There were a few injured, and after Simber had flown up high enough to wrap his jaws around Crow and pull him from the mastodon's tusk, he deftly picked up the injured ones who couldn't make it out on their own. Just as the last Unwanted exited the museum, Alex lunged and slammed the door shut—not that the creature could get through it, at his size, of course. But Alex wasn't taking any chances on a stray tusk or a beefy leg reaching through the opening.

Simber raced around the museum like a kitten at play, letting the giant beast nearly catch him but getting away just in time, while Alex scrambled for the books, searching for spells that would be powerful enough to soothe this beast and turn him back into a nonliving statue.

"It would've been nice if Mr. Today had kept this place a little more organized!" Alex shouted.

"Orrrganized wasn't exactly his modus operrrandi, if you know what I mean," Simber said as he circled close to Alex.

Alex wasn't sure what that term meant, but he liked how it sounded and vowed to look it up just as soon as everything calmed down.

The mastodon took a swipe at Simber and missed, tripping and falling into the whale skeleton and sending hundreds of bones flying in all directions.

Alex ducked as a rib flew past his ear, and he yelled, "Aw, man, that's a pity right there!"

"You'rrre telling me!"

"Maybe you could keep him away from the breakables, eh?"

"Maybe I could let him crrrush you into tiny bits," Simber replied, charging to the darkest corners of the museum where Alex hadn't even begun to explore. The mastodon followed.

"Well, there's always that," Alex muttered, flipping pages.

Ten more minutes of tireless chasing had gone by before Alex happened upon a thin book called *Tater*. He whipped through the pages outlining diet, likes and dislikes, and disposition issues, all the way to the end, where his eyes alighted on the one spell that might actually do him some good. It was a song spell called "Nighty-Night, Tater," so he knew it was probably the right one. He studied it carefully, still not totally comfortable using spells without components to go with them—he never knew what to do with his hands.

Once he'd memorized it, he tossed the book over his shoulder and snuck between the enormous museum items to try to give himself a good angle. "Lead him back to this empty spot!" he shouted to Simber.

Simber did it, and when the mastodon was in the general area where Alex wanted him, Alex began to sing a little lullaby. It was undoubtedly the dumbest, most embarrassing song Alex had ever sung, but what choice did he have? He was glad almost no one was there to hear it. He took a deep breath and sang:

> "Tater boy, Tater boy,
> Too much sadness, no repeats.
> I am sorry, more than sorry,
> But it's time for you to sleep."

When Alex finished, the giant mastodon statue froze in place, and everything was quiet again.

Simber harrumphed a few times, trying not to laugh.

"Knock it off," Alex muttered, and then hoped Simber hadn't heard him. "This place is trashed," he said as he met up with the cat at the door. "We'll have to come back here and clean it later." He reached for the handle. "Door number one." The door opened to the hallway, and approximately fifty pairs of eyes met their gaze.

"Oh," Alex said, surprised. "Hello. I thought you'd have headed down by now." He saw that the injured among them were feeling better now that the danger had passed, and everyone was sitting up. Henry snuck through a space between two adults. "We're still trapped," he announced. "Walled in over here, glass wall here." He tapped it to prove the predicament. "How'd you find us, anyway? And where are we?" The crowd murmured its concerns.

Alex's lips parted, but he didn't quite know what to say. They couldn't see out to where Sean stood on the other side of the wall. How was he going to get them all out of here if they couldn't go through the opening to the balcony? He caught

LISA McMANN

sight of Meghan just then, and he was relieved to see her acting completely fine. She had her arm around Crow, who looked more scared of Simber than he'd been of the mastodon. After all, he'd seen neither before today, and had been inside the mouth of only one of them.

"Well," Alex said, scrambling to sound calm, "I can at least give you a little more room to stretch out. He pointed to the clear wall and muttered, "Glass." The wall shimmered to the ground and disappeared. "Okay," he said, turning back to the Unwanteds. "You can move to the end now, but please stay in the hallway. Don't go into any of the side rooms, okay? I'll get you some water from the kitchenette and move you out of here just as soon as I can figure out how to open up that wall."

Alex had no idea how to do that, or if it was even possible. He didn't know if there actually *was* a specific spell on this hallway at all—he'd always thought it just took a certain kind of magical ability to see it. Mr. Today had never made it visible or invisible to anyone as far as Alex knew. Eva Fathom had been able to get in on her own. And when Lani and Meg couldn't get in for the magical weapons meeting, Mr. Today had moved

LISA McMANN

Island of Fire » 122

the meeting to the lawn—he hadn't tried to rig it so they could get in. But what about Simber? He didn't do magic, but maybe Mr. Today had created him with the ability to see the secret hallway.

"I'm not sure I can fix this," Alex murmured to Simber as the people spread out down the entire length of the hallway and sat leaning against the wall.

"You don't have a choice," Simber muttered back.

Alex, facing yet another obstacle and feeling extremely hungry and thirsty himself, gripped his head and let out a frustrated groan. He headed down the hall toward the kitchenette across from Mr. Today's office, Unwanteds lining the hallway all the way to the end, where the big picture window was. And just when Alex was trying to figure out how to tell the Unwanteds that he didn't know how to get them out of there without putting them all back into the gray shack and somehow shutting down the world all over again, a small voice in the doorway of the kitchenette uttered a single word. The voice belonged to Henry, and the word he said was "Dad?"

Touch and Go

Henry ran into the kitchenette, Alex right behind him. Gunnar Haluki's limp body spilled out of the corner tube onto the floor. His hands were tied behind his back, and his ankles were tied together too. His eyes were nearly closed, his face thin and drawn, his lips parched, and his gray hair ragged and unkempt. His clothes were ripped and ruined, and they hung loosely on him. It wasn't clear how long he'd been lying there or where he'd come from.

The boys kneeled down beside the former high priest. "Simber, we need healers!" Alex called out. Simber loped down the center of the hall and, to the Unwanteds, seemed to disappear through the solid wall at the end.

"Dad?" Henry said again, pulling his father's sleeve. "Dad. Can you hear me?" Like a natural, Henry checked his father's vitals while Alex untied the man and rolled him onto his back. Murmurs wafted through the group of Unwanteds as people expressed cautious joy that the good man was alive and here with them. Henry glanced at them when he heard the kind words, and he smiled gratefully as he worked. He got up and poured some water into a cup as Simber returned.

"None of the nurrrses can get in," he said, "but I know Gunnarrr can get out. Shall I take him thrrrough to them on my back?"

"Great idea. Good thinking, Simber," Alex said. He and a few of the others helped hoist Gunnar onto the giant stone cheetah's back.

"But what about me?" Henry said. "I need to stay with him."

His lip quivered enough to make Alex hesitate, but in the end, Alex knew what was best.

"I'm sorry, little guy," Alex said. He kneeled next to the boy. "Now that Artimé is back, the nurses can help him way better than we can. And we need him to get help right away."

He glanced at Simber. "Did you happen to notice if the hospital wing is still in place?"

"I did, and it is, just as it was beforrre."

Finally one thing is working out right, Alex thought. "Good. Okay, Henry, give your dad some encouragement, and then off he goes."

Henry leaned down and spoke softly in his father's ear. Then he patted his father's shoulder and stepped out of the way, his face a facade of bravery. Simber carried Gunnar carefully down the hallway so he wouldn't slip off. They disappeared through the wall, and all was quiet.

The Unwanteds' faces were troubled. High Priest Haluki had been good to them. And they certainly didn't want to see young Henry lose the last remaining member of his family.

A few of the people went over to Henry to offer him comfort and distraction, while Alex assigned others to pass out water and some of Mr. Today's favorite cookies, which he found in the cupboard. When everyone was busy, Alex returned to the kitchenette and approached the tube to see if he could send something up from the main kitchen.

Don't ever use that tube, Mr. Today had once told Alex. *It goes to Haluki's house and other nasty places.*

"Like where?" Alex muttered to himself. He hesitated, and then stepped toward it. Without setting foot inside, he poked his head in so he could see the mini blackboard and the controls. But instead of the destination descriptions he was used to seeing in all the other tubes—lounge, library, dining, and room service—this one had only numbers with no explanations to go with them.

Alex pressed his fingers to his throbbing temples. Everything was happening all at once. He couldn't seem to catch a break. He had to focus now on getting the people out of this hallway. But how?

A cool hand touched his arm, and he turned to see that it was Meghan. She smiled at him, but there was a question in her eyes. He knew the look well enough.

"I'm okay," he said, and then the words flooded out. "There are just so many crazy things happening. I don't even know how to get everybody out of here. And Haluki . . . he obviously escaped, but how? And I feel so bad about not trying to rescue him before, you know? But how could we?"

Meghan nodded.

"I mean, I had no idea he'd been treated like this. And wow," he said, shaking his head, "we just barely had enough energy to keep ourselves alive. How could we possibly go rescue him, too? It's all so much . . . it's too much. But did you look at him? I feel terrible."

Meghan reached her arms around her friend and hugged him.

Just then Simber bounded down the hallway and stopped at the open door to the kitchenette. "Alex," he said, "Gunnarrr spoke."

"Oh, good," Alex breathed. Maybe the man had looked worse off than he really was.

"He said Clairrre's alive. She's in his house, locked in the pantrrry."

Meghan's hand went to her mouth and Alex's jaw dropped. "She is? Is he sure?"

"He hearrrd Eva Fathom talk about herrr just yesterrrday. Therrre are two guarrrds, sometimes thrrree, in the house at all times." Simber's stone face was earnest. "If you use the tube and yourrr spells, you may be able to surrrprrrise them."

Alex pressed his lips together. "If we . . . but the tube—it's all numbers. I don't know which button to press, and I don't know—"

"It's numberrr one to Haluki's office," Simber said in a low voice. "I know that much from Marrrcus. Two of you could go togetherrr in the tube if you can fit. That would . . . that would be the best way, I think."

Alex looked hard at Simber. "You're serious."

"Yes."

"Okay." Alex sighed a heavy sigh and squeezed his eyes shut. "Sorry," he said. "Of course we need to go. We need to go now. Let me just, ah, get some components, and then Meg . . . are you up for it?"

Meghan's eyebrows shot up. She shook her head, pointing to her neck.

"She can't use verrrbal components," Simber translated, though Alex didn't really need him too—he'd just forgotten for a moment.

"Okay, well . . . who from this group?" Alex muttered, peeking around the corner of the doorway and scanning the crowd. He didn't really know very many of the adults well, and he didn't trust the ones he knew to be great at magic since

LISA McMANN

they'd never had to use it for defense until recently. He turned back to Simber and whispered, "Or is there anybody else who can get into this stupid hallway?"

"Perrrhaps Octavia," Simber began. "But she's . . ."

Meghan frowned, shaking her head, and then she turned Alex around by the shoulders and pointed to someone.

"Who?" Alex asked.

She pointed especially hard, and Alex followed her finger. "Henry? Are you kidding?"

Meghan rolled her eyes and looked at Simber.

Simber spoke. "It's a good choice."

"He's a little kid! Hasn't he been through enough?"

"It's his house. Think, Alex."

Alex thought. And then he said, "Oooh. He'll know his way around. Places to hide. And how to find the pantry."

"And he's small enough to fit in the tube with you, so you can attack togetherrr rrratherrr than one at a time."

Alex thought about that, too. He thought about how well Henry picked up the spells even though he'd only been in Artimé for a short time. The kid was levelheaded and smart, sure. And he was quick. But . . . Alex cringed. "What if some-

LISA McMANN

thing happens to him? I mean . . ." He thought of Lani and nearly lost his composure.

Simber looked at the floor. "I know. But he's the best choice. And we need her." He glanced at Meghan. "We need Clairrre. She's morrre than a frrriend. She's . . . like family. To me, that is, now that . . ." Simber growled sharply to clear his throat, causing many of the Unwanteds in the hall to cast a nervous glance in the direction of the kitchenette.

Meghan gave Alex an imploring look.

Alex gazed from one face to the other and closed his eyes wearily. "Okay."

While Simber spoke with Henry, Alex ran out of the secret hallway and into the boys' hallway to his room to collect as many components as his now-tattered vest could hold. It was strange to be back in his comfy quarters again. He yearned for a nap in his bed.

"What happened to you?" Alex's blackboard, Clive, sneered as if he'd just seen him this morning.

"Nothing," Alex said. "Just . . . I'll tell you everything someday." He grabbed handfuls of origami dragons, scatter-clips, balls of clay for shackles, and blinding highlighters, and stuffed them into his pockets. He paused, looking at the little pile of heart attack components, so simple and innocent. He grabbed them, his face twisting into a grimace. He hesitated, and then he tossed them into a drawer and slammed it shut. "Never again," he muttered.

As he rushed out the door, he heard the old familiar words ring out from Clive: "Don't die!"

Nasty Places

Alex met Henry at the tube in the kitchenette. Henry's lashes were still wet from crying when he couldn't go with his father, but the tears had stopped and his eyes held an eager look now.

"Here," Alex said, handing him some components. "Do you know how to use all these?"

Henry looked them over carefully. "Yes," he said. He sounded more sure of himself than Alex felt.

"Do you know what room of your house the tube is in?"

"It's in my father's office," Henry said. "End of the hall."

Alex nodded, and the two strategized. When they had their

LISA McMANN

plan together, they stepped into the tube. Alex gave Meghan a reassuring smile that didn't come from any sort of confidence within himself, but she looked relieved to see it.

Alex regarded the tube's strange numbers-only blackboard and hesitated. He glanced at Simber. "How will we know which button to press to get back here?" he asked.

"I don't know forrr surrre," Simber said. "Marrrcus never spoke of that one. But I think that tube in Haluki's office only comes herrre to Arrrtimé, so therrre should only be one option."

"Let's hope so," Alex muttered. He looked down at Henry. "Ready?"

Henry nodded. They each gripped components in their hands.

"Here we go," Alex said. He pushed the button with his elbow and the two boys disappeared.

In a blink, they were cast into darkness that didn't lighten again.

"Where are we?" Alex whispered after a time.

"Inside a closet. The door's closed."

"Oh." Alex reached outside the tube and felt the door, moving his hand across it to get his bearings, trying to find a handle, but there was none. A line of light ran across the bottom and up the center of the closet, indicating there was a double door. "Which direction is the hallway?" he whispered.

"Straight ahead about ten or twelve feet."

"Okay." Alex took a deep breath. "Components ready?"

"Yeah."

Alex pushed on the door. It didn't budge. He pushed again with both hands this time, and then with his shoulder, hard. Still nothing. He frowned in the dark. "It's stuck." He ran his hand up and pricked his finger on a nail, but he didn't make a sound. He found several more nail points along the top edge. He almost told Henry that it was nailed shut, but then he thought about it and decided Henry didn't need to know that right now. "We're going to have to make noise. No voices, though, okay? Just pounding. We want them to think it's your dad. On the count of four."

"Okay."

Alex counted off, and they both began pounding on the door, though not too hard, since Haluki was weak. Nothing happened.

135 « Island of Fire

LISA McMANN

Alex hoped the captors hadn't discovered that Haluki was gone already. Maybe that was why the door was nailed shut.

"Again," Alex whispered, and they pounded once more.

This time they were rewarded with footsteps.

"Knock it off!" said a woman. She sounded grumpy.

Alex started knocking again, too afraid to cue Henry this time.

"All right," the woman muttered. "Liam, bring the crowbar. We'll do Haluki's break now. He's . . . noisy." Her words trailed off, her voice weary.

A few minutes later, Alex and Henry could hear the crack and squeak of nails being pulled through wood. Alex squeezed Henry's shoulder and bent down to whisper in his ear when the noise continued. "You take the right side, I've got the left. Spells ready?"

Henry nodded.

When the door swung open, the two boys jumped out, yelling, "Attack left!" and "Attack right!" to their origami dragons, and while they squinted to get their pupils used to the bright light, the fire-breathing dragons nearly scared the two guards to death. It was long enough to keep them distracted while Alex and Henry focused and aimed highlighters at the two. Both found their mark, blinding the shrieking guards.

Before the Quillans understood what was happening, Alex and Henry grabbed scatterclips and fired them, sticking the guards to the walls by their clothing, and pelted the two with the clay bits, shackling them. Finally Alex uttered a silence soliloquy, and their work was done. Alex inspected their handiwork as the two struggled. Then Alex nodded at Henry. "Lead the way," he said. "Be ready to attack."

Henry set off, trying very hard not to chatter on about the house or stop to show Alex the bedroom that had been his when he lived there, though he was tempted. He peered around the corner into the kitchen. Seeing no one, he continued to the pantry, Alex at his heels.

"Guard me," Alex said. Henry stood ready with his components, turning this way and that at the slightest imagined noise. Alex reached out for the pantry door and turned the knob.

The First Rescue

Whenever Claire Morning heard the voices of Liam and Bethesda in conversation, it reminded her that she was still alive, and that maybe someday, if she could just get her strength back, she'd be able to break out of here. She didn't blame anyone for not coming to find her—how could they possibly know where she was? And she could only imagine what the Artiméans were dealing with . . . if any of them were still alive. For all she knew, Aaron could have killed them all.

The voices Claire was hearing now seemed different. There was some sort of ruckus going on, she could tell, and she hoped something horrible hadn't happened to Gunnar. But she could barely lift her head to rouse herself completely. Whatever was happening, it would happen without her.

Or so she thought until the pantry door swung open, blinding her with light. She turned her face toward the towering shadow, but she couldn't focus. And with the gag in her mouth, she couldn't speak.

The figure gasped. "Ms. Morning," he said, which puzzled her. Liam had always called her Claire.

Soon her gag was off her numb wrists and ankles untied, and the figure lifted her to her feet. "Can you stand?" he whispered.

Claire nodded, but her legs buckled.

"It's okay. I've got you," the figure said, and he hoisted her off the ground, over his shoulder.

Claire opened her eyes a slit, letting the painful light in.

"It's Alex," the figure said. "And Henry Haluki. We came to take you home."

Relief flooded through Claire's weak body, and she closed her eyes again as Alex directed Henry to lead the way.

"Give the guards another dose from the highlighters and silence spells. All three of us can't fit inside the tube at once, so you go first to let Simber know we're coming," Alex said to Henry, who did exactly as he was told.

When Henry was gone, Alex turned to the shackled, blind Liam and Bethesda, and said in a measured voice, "I'm sure someone will come along eventually for you. But even if they don't, you won't suffer any worse than what you've put these people through." He maneuvered his way into the tube, careful not to bump Claire's head against the glass as he squeezed into the space with her, and gave the guards one last hard look. In the voice of a man, he spoke with a measured tone. "If you ever dare show your faces in Artimé, I will not be so kind as to allow you to leave it alive."

With that, he pressed the only button on the blackboard, and in the blink of an eye, Alex, still carrying Ms. Morning, stepped out of the tube into Mr. Today's kitchenette. He moved swiftly to the hallway, where scores of Artiméans parted to allow them to pass.

"They'rrre expecting you," Simber said. "You take herrr. I'll stay herrre until we've got time to sorrrt out this mess."

Alex looked at him in surprise, but then nodded. He hurried down the hall, stopping at the Museum of Large. "Meghan?" he called out, and she came to his side. He adjusted the limp body of Ms. Morning and whispered the words that reopened the door. Then he turned back to Meghan. "See if you can find a spell in the museum library that will open this hallway for everyone."

Meghan nodded, going inside as Alex and Ms. Morning disappeared through the wall that for now held the rest of them prisoner.

Alex glided down the stairs, surprised that his strength hadn't given out yet, but Ms. Morning was not very heavy, and truth be told, Alex had probably bulked up just a bit in the past several weeks from the constant hard labor. Or maybe it was simply adrenaline.

So many thoughts swirled through his mind as he rushed into the hospital wing and set Ms. Morning down on the bed that was prepared and awaiting her. The nurses swarmed around the beloved instructor, pushing Alex back. He moved willingly to the doorway to stay out of their way as they worked, and with a chance to breathe, Alex finally let his mind go. He leaned his head against the wall and watched, unseeing, the actions before him as his brain sorted out every option he could think of to free the Unwanteds from the secret hallway.

The Second Rescue

As he stood watching the hospital workers and thinking about the trapped people, Alex realized that the very last thing he wanted to do was shut Artimé down again, even if he could figure out how to do it. It would most assuredly free them, but no one wanted to go back to that desolate world, not even for a second, now that they had Artimé back. What if the restore spell didn't work next time?

Alex could take the trapped people through the tube to Haluki's house one at a time and then walk back to Artimé from there. But that would be dangerous, most certainly

LISA McMANN

arousing suspicion and attracting unwanted attention in Quill.

There was always a chance that Meghan would find a spell. But Alex wasn't feeling it—he was doubtful a spell existed, as access to the secret hallway seemed as random as the color patterns of Mr. Today's robes.

Alex could allow them to try to break through the wall, but their strongest Artiméans, Simber and Florence, couldn't help with that—they'd go right through it without disturbing so much as a piece of dust. This was an option, but not a nice one. He couldn't really imagine what that would mean for the wall, or for the secret hallway's secrets in the future.

He closed his eyes and wished for the millionth time that Lani and Samheed were there to help him. Alex was so anxious to find them now that he had better means to do so, but he had to get everything under control here first before he could do anything else. He thought about Sky and smiled a little, knowing she'd be reminding him to breathe right now. He took a deep breath and let it out, listening to the soothing voices of the men and women who were caring for Gunnar Haluki and Ms. Morning. He wondered if there was any other way to get

LISA McMANN

the trapped Artiméans out of there. If only he'd had more time with Mr. Today. His face burned when he thought of the years of learning he should have had. But he'd been robbed of that, and Aaron was the thief.

Alex opened his eyes when a young man he didn't know touched his arm and handed him a cup of cider.

"Thank you," Alex said. He drank it down. Nothing had tasted better in all his life.

"We're all grateful, Alex," the man said in a low voice. "Things were rough, but Mr. Today clearly made the right choice with you. I'm sorry some folks lost hope." He turned and went on with his duties, leaving Alex to return to his problem solving.

After a while, Alex slipped through the mansion, checking on things, making sure nothing else was falling apart, and remarkably everything was under control. Florence patrolled the dining hall, where many of the Artiméans sat and ate. It was good to hear their happy voices again. He caught Florence's eye and they exchanged the steady, solemn gaze of comrades. It would take time for the creatures and statues to come to terms with the news. Alex nodded and lifted his hand to her. They would talk later.

He walked around to the other side of the mansion to the classrooms, peeking into Ms. Morning's flawlessly clean music studio, where he'd seen Meghan so many times, singing. . . . A lump grew in his throat, and he vowed to do everything he could to get Meghan's beautiful voice back.

And then he stopped in the most familiar classroom of all, the one where he spent so much time working on his art. Chalks, paints, pencils, brushes, and all the wonderful spells that went with them. It was too bad he couldn't draw a way out of the secret hallway, he thought.

And then he froze. His eyes opened wide and he groaned as he slapped his forehead. "That's it!" he cried. He whirled around and ran through the mansion, looking in every room, in every hall, in every corner. And then he sped outside and turned this way and that, until finally he spied his beloved instructor at the shore. He sprinted to her.

"Ms. Octavia," he said, breathless as he reached her, and then he stopped short. Her glasses were askew, eyes red. She'd been crying into the water as gentle waves licked her tentacles, and Alex remembered how Mr. Today had created her—she came from the sea, he'd said. Alex's heart surged, knowing what loss she was feeling. "It's very hard, isn't it?" he said.

"Indeed it is," the octogator said, drawing a dry tentacle across her snout to catch the tears. "It feels a bit like my soul has been torn away. Like perhaps I shouldn't exist without him."

Alex remained quiet. Nothing he could say was important enough to stand next to her words, for she, like all creatures and statues, had something from Mr. Today that he did not, and that was life itself. Instead of trying to pretend that he knew how she felt, he peered out over the waves and waited.

After a time, Ms. Octavia cleared her throat and inhaled a large, reverberating sniff. She turned to Alex. "Now then," she said, not quite in her regular, stern voice, but almost. "How can I help you, my dear boy?"

Alex regarded her with a solemn look, wondering if she were up to the task but knowing it would take him days, even weeks, and they couldn't afford that kind of time. He had no choice but to ask. "Ms. Octavia, for reasons I don't have time to explain right now, there are upward of fifty Unwanteds trapped in Mr. Today's secret hallway, and they can't get out. How quickly can you make a 3-D door?"

Approaching
Normal

A s it turned out, Ms. Octavia had a stash of 3-D doors in her classroom that she employed for various purposes throughout the years. She grabbed the theater door drawing, which she used fairly often to get Simber and Florence in and out of the theater for assemblies. She and Alex brought it upstairs to the secret hallway, where people were beginning to get anxious.

Alex cleared a space. Ms. Octavia unrolled the large drawing and pasted it to the wall between the museum and the kitchenette.

The door wavered and then pushed out from the wall: wooden slats, hinges, and all.

"Now then," Ms. Octavia said as she reached for the protruding handle and pulled open the enormous, creaking door that led to Mr. Appleblossom's sanctuary, "head through the theater to the tubes and be on your way."

The Artiméans cheered and pressed forward through the door. In no time, the hallway was clear once again, except for Simber, Ms. Octavia, and Alex.

Ms. Octavia swished over to peek into Mr. Today's office and the kitchenette. "Is that everyone?"

"Seems to be." Alex frowned. "Wait—not quite. I almost forgot! I'll be right back." He rushed over to the Museum of Large, where the door was still open a crack. He went in and looked around, spying Meghan sitting near the enormous restored pirate ship, surrounded by stacks of books. Alex walked over to her and looked at them. The book closest to him looked quite new, though some of its pages were wavy, as if they'd gotten wet. It was the strangest title he'd seen yet: *Yodeling Groceries: 100 Awesome Slang Words for Vomit*.

"Any luck?" Alex leaned against the bow of the ship. It whispered unintelligibly as it had done in the past.

Meghan looked up and smiled sadly. Then shook her head.

"Well," Alex said with a grin, "the good news is that we've found another way out. Come on."

Meghan's eyes lit up.

Alex pulled her to her feet. Meghan grabbed the vomit book, grinned, and showed Alex a page, making him laugh out loud for the first time in a long time. "What are groceries, anyway?" he asked.

Meghan shrugged. Her shoulders shook with silent laughter. She tucked the book inside her vest to read later.

As they walked out of the museum, Alex grew serious again. "So, um, do you want us to try to get that thing off your neck? I mean, if the medical people think it's safe to do?"

Meghan looked at him. She nodded and her mouth opened to say a silent yes. Her face was desperate.

"Even if there's a chance your voice never comes back?"

Meghan hesitated, closing her eyes for a second and taking a deep breath. When she opened her eyes, she nodded again.

"You go it," Alex said. "I promise we'll do everything we can to hear you sing again."

Meghan teared up and grabbed Alex's arm. Together they

left the museum, Alex sealing it magically once again. They moved down the hallway.

"I'll walk with Meg through the door," Alex said to his instructor, who waited patiently to take the door down and store it away safely once again.

Ms. Octavia, who hadn't seen Meghan since before Artimé disappeared, startled at the sight of the girl's necklace of thorns. "Oh dear," she said, reaching out to give Meghan a hug, while looking vastly puzzled all the same. "I can't begin to imagine the depths of heartache I missed."

Alex gave her and Simber a grim smile. *I can't begin to tell you,* he thought, but he didn't say it. Instead he said, "Now that everything seems to have settled, I'd like to meet with you two and Florence as soon as possible." He looked down at his clothes, still partially covered by Mr. Today's oversized robe. "But I have a feeling I should probably clean up first," he said, realizing he must smell pretty bad by now. He looked from Ms. Octavia to Simber. "Mr. Today's office in an hour, then?"

The cat regarded the dirty, disheveled new leader of Artimé, who had grown considerably more confident and decisive in the time Simber had been at the bottom of the ocean. He tipped his head in solemn agreement. "An hourrr," he agree[d]

"But it's *yourrr* office now."

At those words, Alex felt his lungs turn to ice. He closed his eyes and pinched the bridge of his nose, trying to comprehend it. When he looked up once more, he gave Simber and Ms. Octavia a grim nod. He turned to Meghan, who gave him a reassuring smile as they stepped through the door to the theater.

After Ms. Octavia had closed the door and pulled the 3-D drawing from the wall, she rolled it up and tucked it under an appendage. She and Simber left to check on tasks below, while Charlie the gargoyle wandered into the secret hallway unnoticed. He tottered to the end and peered into the office, then turned, crossed the hallway, and peeked into the kitchenette. A moment later he retreated from there as well and went back down the hallway the way he'd come, a puzzled look on his face. He stopped at the door of Mr. Today's private living quarters and pressed his ear against it. And then he knocked.

When no one answered, Charlie turned around and sat down in front of the door, drew his knees close to his chest, tilted his head to lean it against the molding, and waited for his master to return.

Alone

Lani kicked and wriggled until she was exhausted, but the large man carrying her only squeezed the breath out of her. She stopped fighting and started trying to focus her limited sight on where they were going, but she was soon totally turned around in the maze of tunnels, all lit by candle sconces attached to the walls. Every now and then, when the man walked close enough to the wall, Lani kicked out, hoping she was making a mark of some sort. Her sight wasn't quite good enough to tell at this point, but the low lighting certainly helped her see a little bit better.

After a ten-minute walk through a warren of underground

LISA McMANN

passageways, the man finally ducked into a room with elaborate decorations. At the far end was a low, round platform upon which a jeweled gold throne stood. Sitting on the throne was a stately woman with long silver hair and thin, wrinkled lips. She wore a cloth band around her head, from which strings of tiny, bright sparkling stones fell all around her shoulders. She had a stern look on her face.

The man carrying Lani flipped the girl around, setting her on her feet. He pulled a chain from his pocket and clipped one end to her thorny necklace and locked it in place. The other end had a clasp, which he snapped onto to a thin wire above their heads, well out of Lani's reach. He locked that end as well.

Lani squinted at the woman sitting on the throne. Her clothes were simple enough—light-colored linen, like the clothes worn by the other people Lani had seen before they put the painful acid in her eyes. But the one thing that was different about this woman was that she didn't wear a necklace of thorns like nearly everyone else.

"Still causing trouble, I see."

Lani almost fell over—there was no other sound anywhere

on this strange, creepy island, and she hadn't heard a single thing in weeks. It was almost with relief that she discovered she wasn't deaf. So it took her a few moments to recover enough to realize that the woman's voice seemed eerily familiar.

Squinting even more as her eyes adjusted to the light, Lani took in the woman's features. Her erect stature, her long silver hair, her pale, wrinkled skin . . . and that voice. It gave Lani chills, and not the good kind.

"I wonder where you came from." The queen, or whoever she was, tapped her lips with her forefinger. Her fingernails were several inches long, and they curled around in various fascinating ways.

Lani's eyes widened.

"*Tch*. Shame you can't speak. You'll learn the sign language soon enough, and then we'll have a chat about your friend who got away. Guards!" she called.

Lani sucked in a gasp, but it made no sound. *Meghan got away!* As two more hulking men came out of nowhere to grab her by the elbows, she realized this queen bore a striking resemblance to the woman Lani had destroyed—the High Priest Justine.

Back in the cave, Samheed lay still for a long time. When he awoke, he was alone and his hands were empty. He blinked a few times before he remembered what had happened. His head pounded and ached, and when he reached back to the source of the pain, his fingers came away sticky with blood.

But he didn't care. He didn't care about the blood, or about his aching head, or about his sore body from being slammed to the ground. All he cared about was Lani, and Lani was gone.

He covered his face. His hand felt so empty without hers. And for the first time in Samheed's life, he felt like giving up. He'd faced death before, twice. But this abandonment felt worse somehow. Maybe it was because at the Purge he wasn't alone, and when his father had tried to kill him during the battle, he wasn't alone then, either, and he was able to use his anger to stand up against fear. As long as he had people on his side, he gathered strength and courage from them.

But the people of this island had apparently found Samheed's ultimate weakness. He rolled to his side and curled up, hoping to become small enough to disappear. As he lay there, a very subtle change began to take place. It was so slight that he didn't notice it at first, but after a time, he blinked. And then he sat up. He craned his neck and squinted. And then he crawled on his hands and knees in a straight line and reached out.

His fingers grasped the water bucket on the first try.

Samheed could see.

Empty Chairs and
Empty Tables

Alex took the theater tube directly to his room, avoiding the excited Artiméans who roamed the hallways and staircase. He put his hand up to shush Clive and went straight into his private quarters, drew a steamy, soapy bath, and scrubbed and soaked in it. He even had to drain it once and refill it because he was so dirty after weeks of not showering at all.

"You should burn those clothes. They're practically rancid," he heard Clive point out from the other room.

"Shove a sock in it, Clive!" Alex called back, before sinking deep into the fresh water such that only his nose and mouth remained above it. His body ached terribly, and he was exhausted. Now that he had a few moments alone, he never wanted to go back out there again. But he had so much more to do before things got back to normal. As he soaked, he made a mental list.

1. *Get the thorn necklace off Meghan.*
2. *See if Sky and Crow want theirs off too.*
3. *Figure out how to find Lani and Samheed.*
4. *Find them.*
5. *Rescue them.*
6. *Sleep.*
7. *Do something about the . . .*

He drifted off. Half an hour later, he jerked awake. The water was cold. "You'd think there'd be a spell to keep bath-water warm," he grumbled.

After another ten minutes his hair was combed, his body was clean, his clothes were fresh, and he felt like a new mage. He smiled at Clive as he headed for the door, and then he stopped and turned. "Do you know, uh, what happened?" he asked the blackboard.

Clive's eyes darted around the room. "When? Where? What?"

Alex sighed and added a note to his mental list. "Never mind."

"Come on, tell me. I won't tell anybody. I don't even know anybody."

Alex flashed a grim smile. "Not yet. I don't have time. Soon." He opened the door and slipped out.

He made his way out of the boys' hallway and into the not-very-secret-anymore-but-still-mostly-hidden hallway. It was quiet there. Alex walked toward Mr. Today's office, his footsteps echoing, and then he stopped in front of Mr. Today's private quarters.

"Charlie!" he exclaimed.

The gargoyle approached and began speaking with hand signals.

"I don't understand," Alex said. "I— There's a book somewhere, I'm sure . . ."

Charlie pointed to Mr. Today's door and then lifted his shoulders in question.

LISA McMANN

"Oh no," Alex muttered, his heart sinking. *Is it ever going to end?* "Come on," he said. "Let's go in here. I'm going to explain everything."

Charlie loped alongside Alex, snapping his finger and thumbs.

Alex had avoided the office so far, but now he took a few tentative steps inside. It was painful going in and seeing all of Mr. Today's things. He glanced at the wall behind him, and there, as always, were the crazy, stupid dot pictures that were the answer to the riddle that had driven him nuts for the past month. If only he'd been more observant, he might have fig-ured out the clue much faster.

Alex took off Mr. Today's robe and hung it next to a spare one on the rack in the corner. He ran his fingers along the fabric and let the sleeve drop, and then he turned away. The blackboards were in order as usual. Alex had no idea how they worked. Or how anything worked, really. He had a lot of books to read, for sure. And hopefully, once Ms. Morning was feeling better, she'd be able to help.

Alex looked at Mr. Today's chair. He'd sat in it before once or twice, during his nightly visits alone or with Sam. But now

LISA McMANN

Island of Fire » 160

it seemed too big to fill. Instead he sat in the armchair on the other side of the desk, which was his usual spot. It felt more comfortable for now.

One by one the others trickled in—Florence, Octavia, and Simber—and they sat down in their usual spots as well. Claire Morning's chair remained empty, and so did Mr. Today's.

For a few moments, no one said a word. And during those minutes, Alex finally accepted the truth—that from this point forward, he would lead the meetings. He would be the caretaker of Artimé. He would have to protect, provide for, and serve the people here. He would be in charge of everything, and he would be responsible. He would make decisions that could save lives, or cost lives. It was he who would take the wheel and keep Artimé going in the same direction, or change it. He, young Alexander Stowe, Unwanted, was the new mage of Artimé. Like it or not.

There was no time to look back. Only to move forward, to the dots on the horizon, and steer for them.

Life on Warbler Island

When the next breeze came, Samheed opened his eyes and sat up, hoping it was Lani. He peered around the dimly lit cave, and his newly seeing eyes alighted on a hulk of a man. Samheed stared at him and swallowed hard, trying not to react. But the man was staring at Samheed as well, as if he expected the boy could see.

The man's orange eyes glowed faintly, and he took three or four rapid steps toward the boy.

Samheed couldn't help it. He cowered and drew back.

The man gave a sinister smile, reached out as Samheed

scrambled to get away, and scooped up the boy with little effort.

Samheed fought, but not as hard as he could—there was really nothing to fight for. He didn't want to stay in the cave alone. He'd rather die than be stuck there forever. So after a time, he stopped struggling and just watched as the man opened the secret door and took him through a maze of tunnels.

Thorn-necked, orange-eyed people walked about, a few of them chained to the wire above Samheed's head, but most roamed independently. Some of them carried things like buckets of gold coins, baskets of bread, or armloads of clothing or firewood. Others walked with purpose as if they were in a hurry to get somewhere. He saw one woman with scars around her neck, but no thorns.

Samheed took in everything he could, trying to understand why anyone who had gone through the process of the thorns and the eye colorization would not try to run away. He didn't understand it.

Then again, he'd been a big supporter of Quill even after he'd been Purged—for a short time, anyway. He wondered what kinds of lies *this* island's ruler was telling these people to make them want to stay here.

After a few minutes, the man turned into a cave where a woman sat on a throne watching them. The man set Samheed down and hooked a wire around the boy's thorny necklace. He locked it with a tiny key, and then connected the other end to the wire above their heads and did the same.

"Well, well, well." The woman's voice boomed like a cannon in the silence, startling Samheed. "Your healing period has ended. Time to put a strong young person like you to work."

Samheed stared. He tried to respond, thinking maybe if the woman could speak, then he might be able to as well, but no sound came out. He wanted to know where Lani was, and if she was okay.

The stately woman narrowed her eyes. "There's a reason we don't allow you to speak, you know. I trust you're smart enough to figure out why eventually." She rose from the throne to her full height. "Follow your orders and you'll be treated fairly. If you don't? It's back to the dark cave. Simple enough." She descended from the throne's platform with languid strides and walked in a slow circle around Samheed.

He stared straight ahead, some of the old anger beginning to stir inside him once again. But he'd follow the rules. For now.

"Oh, your friend," the woman said, drawing a ridiculously long, curled fingernail across her lips so that it almost disguised a cold smile. "I nearly forgot. She's fitting in just fine in the women's compound. Very obedient now, that one. I'm sure you, dear boy, will do just as well in the men's compound." She stopped circling when she reached the throne platform once again, and held Samheed's gaze. "If you wish to see her again, that is."

Samheed's face betrayed him. He turned away, glaring at the floor as his stomach clenched for Lani. Did this mean he wouldn't see her? How long would they be separated? In the absence of Lani's cool fingers entwined in his, he folded his hands together in front of him and sucked in a deep breath, letting it out slowly. He knew what this woman was saying. Obey or else. It was exactly like Quill here, only there were no walls— instead the "safety" came from living underground.

Is every island in the world like this? he wondered.

The brute led Samheed to the men's compound. He pointed to the wire along the ceiling that Sam was connected to. It was purple. There was another wire next to it that was green. Both

LISA McMANN

wires had elaborate roundabout intersections every twenty feet or so, which would allow two people on the same wire to pass each other.

After walking for a few minutes, they came to a circular cavern with hallways branching off in multiple directions. The purple and green lines split up.

Samheed peered down the green hallways to see if there was any sign of Lani, but there was no long black hair to be seen anywhere. The man pointed to the hallway that he wanted Samheed to take, and they walked down it to a large room filled with cots in neat rows. The man brought him to an empty cot that had a book lying on top of it, titled *Handbook for Vaga-bonds*. Samheed sat down on the bed. He picked up the book and looked at the man.

The man nodded, and then he turned and left.

Samheed opened the book and read the first page.

Welcome, wanderer, and congratulations. By setting foot on our shores, you have become the sole property of Warbler Island and Queen Eagala. As you have likely discovered in your travels, there is no way to leave the sea that surrounds

Warbler and the other six islands contained within.

We wish to inform you that Warbler has a growing fleet of ships. Escapees will be hunted and killed. Your orange eyes will forevermore be proof that you are the branded property of Warbler.

Your golden thorns are for your protection and the protection of Warbler. As travelers land on our shores, they are removed of the burden of speech in favor of a simple, quiet life of quality without distraction. Indeed, a spell of silence has been cast over the entire island, quieting all incidental sounds except for human voices, allowing Warblerians to work in the most optimal conditions. As a possibly unwilling newcomer, you will learn to appreciate that we've removed the temptation to speak ill of Warbler or its leader to anyone passing by our shores. It was a necessary move to keep Warbler strong and loyal after the recent revolt.

Samheed's mouth hung open. *This place is nuts,* he thought. He looked back at the opening paragraph, which contained a line that was news to him. *"As you have likely discovered in your* travels, there is no way to leave the sea that surrounds Warbler and the other six islands contained within."

Sam had never thought about traveling beyond the seven islands. Until recently he'd never even thought that there could be more than one island, and that was Quill. But now, thanks to Artimé and Mr. Today, he knew how to think, how to use his imagination. Obviously, based on this book, someone must have tried going beyond the other islands. But what did it mean, *"there's no way to leave"*? How would anyone know there was another place to go to? And if there was no way to leave, did that also mean there was no way to enter? And if so . . . how did everyone get here in the first place? It was extremely puzzling.

Plus, there was magic here—a spell of silence, which explained why nothing made a sound except Queen Eagala's voice. Samheed had thought he'd lost his hearing. But he'd always equated magic with good places. This was no good place, that was for sure.

He turned the page.

Warbler uses a simple system of sign language created by Queen Eagala. You will be taught a small vocabulary of signs that pertain to your personal needs and the work to which you are assigned. You will find a loose piece of paper inside this booklet instructing you about your job, hours, requirements, and behavior expectations.

Samheed turned the page and a slip of paper fluttered to the floor. He picked it up and read:

SHIPBUILDER

Report immediately to shipbuilding. Hours are sunup to sundown with one break at midday. You are not allowed to touch any tools until you have been assessed.

Sunup to sundown? How was anybody to know when the sun was up or down, here in this warren of caves? Samheed sighed. He looked at the bottom of the note, where there was a makeshift map guiding him to the shipbuilding area.

After a cursory glance around his new living quarters, Samheed stood up. He tugged at the thin chain that con-nected his thorn necklace to the wire above. It was locked, stuck fast. Finally he started walking, carrying the note with

LISA McMANN

the map, weaving his way through tunnels. Straining his eyes for a glimpse of Lani and hoping she was okay.

When he neared the end of the directions, he squinted. Afternoon sunlight poured in through a hole above his head. He hadn't seen sunlight in weeks. As he stood there at the base of the stone-carved ladder, basking in the warmth of the sun, taking a moment to enjoy it before starting his new job, a bright ball of fire whizzed past his ear and flew up through the hole, leaving a faint trail of light skating down the passageway behind it.

A Still, Small Voice

hen Alex woke up late the next morning, he almost couldn't remember where he was. He lay in the soft bed surrounded by pillows and blankets feeling refreshed for the first time in a long time.

"Alex," Clive called from the other room. "Aaaalex!"

Alex cringed. "What?" he shouted back.

"Nothing."

Alex rolled his eyes and reluctantly climbed out of bed. He cleaned up and got ready for what would surely be another busy day, and then he went into his living area and

LISA McMANN

stood in front of the blackboard. "What?" he said again.

Clive looked away. A tear pressed out from the surface of the blackboard and rolled down his cheek.

Alex's eyes widened. "Oh no," he said. "You heard the news?"

Clive gave a curt nod. "Yes. And may I say that when Mr. Today was alive, the blackboards were the first to know everything," he said, his voice containing a hint of accusation.

"Clive . . . ," Alex began. Clive wrenched his head in the other direction for dramatic effect. Alex kind of wanted to punch him, but he gathered up as much patience as he could muster. "Look, I'm really sorry. I had a lot of stuff to do yesterday, and I wanted to tell you the whole story so you could deliver it to the others. But it's a really long story, and there was so much happening—rescuing Ms. Morning, getting the people out of the secret hallway—"

"There's a secret hallway?" Clive cried out.

Alex sighed, but he couldn't help saying, "I guess Mr. Today never told you that."

"Stop! The pain! It's still so fresh. . . ."

Alex gritted his teeth and started loading up his spell components for the day. "Oh, come off it. I've really had enough drama for now. I know you're sad, I know everybody's sad, and I am too, but I've got to go help take the THORNS out of MEGHAN'S NECK now," he said, punching the words out and slamming components into his pockets as anger built inside him, "because SHE CAN'T SPEAK. I bet nobody mentioned that to you, either. And then I have to figure out how to rescue Samheed and Lani, because they are PRISONERS at a NEARBY ISLAND. What's that? You didn't know about that, either? That's because I'm so busy saving everything and everybody that I didn't have TWO SECONDS to tell you before the next crisis happened. Okay?" Alex hadn't felt so unforgiving in a long time.

Clive's forehead wrinkled in alarm. "Gosh," he muttered. And then he sank back into the blackboard and disappeared.

Alex's mouth opened briefly, and then he closed it again and shook his head. "Whatever." He refilled the pockets of his newly cleaned component vest, ordered a breakfast sandwich sent up from the kitchen, and set off with it. As he closed the door behind him, he paused, listening for Clive's usual parting words, but this time there was nothing to hear. He bit his lip

LISA McMANN

and looked down at the floor, and then shrugged and walked to the balcony, inhaling his sandwich in three bites.

Meghan stood waiting. People buzzed about as usual. It was almost freaky how normal things seemed again.

"Ready?" Alex asked. He licked his fingers and wiped them dry on his pants.

Meghan's face was verging on light gray. She rolled her shoulders a few times and nodded. Together they descended and walked into the hospital ward. Florence and Octavia were already there, and so were Sean and a team of nurses.

Meghan grabbed her brother's hand and sat down on the cot as Florence explained the procedure. Octavia and the nurses performed as much medicine magic as they could think of to help her through the pain to come. And then . . .

And then.

Florence picked up an enormous sterilized wire cutter with long handles, and very carefully she clamped it down on a stretch of thorny necklace, not touching Meghan's skin. She pressed the cutter handles together and there was a loud, swift click as the metal broke.

Everyone breathed. Florence pulled the cutter back and

inspected her work. "Doing okay, Meghan?" she asked.

Meghan nodded.

Florence went to a second section and cut through that piece as well. She did a third and a fourth and a fifth, all the way around Meghan's neck. And then she stepped back. Her part was done.

Meghan offered up a strained grin. Everyone knew that the hard part was still to come. The nurses surrounded Meghan to the point that Alex couldn't see what they were doing, but perhaps, he thought, it was better that way. His stomach was feeling a bit queasy, and maybe it hadn't been such a good idea after all to gulp down a big breakfast sandwich ten seconds before coming here.

The nurses murmured to Meghan and to each other, little bits of encouragement that gave Alex hints at what was happening as they applied a magical ointment and tried working the metal bits loose so they could tug them out of her skin. But the incisions had healed well, fusing together with the metal, and the thorns were stuck fast.

After several minutes of struggling with nothing giving way, the nurses stepped back. Meghan searched Alex's face wildly, begging him with teary eyes to do something.

Alex swallowed hard. He felt so helpless. He had no idea what to do.

Sean tugged at his hair. "Isn't there a spell or something? Anything?"

The loss of Mr. Today hit hard at that moment. There would be many times like this in the future, they all felt it.

But then, from across the room, came a weak whisper. "Alex."

Alex rushed over to Ms. Morning's side. "She's awake!" he cried. His hands shook.

Claire closed her eyes again, and with great effort, she nodded. When he leaned down, she whispered in his ear, "Dissipate. Using the robe may help." She drew a pained breath. "Careful. Dangerous. Be very . . . ," she rasped, and paused to take another breath. "Precise. And concentrate on the thorns."

Alex's eyes widened. "Okay," he whispered. He glanced up at the others, who were all looking on anxiously. "I'll be right back."

He ran out of the hospital ward and took the steps three at a time—he'd never been able to do that before, he noted, but there was no time to marvel at his own awesomeness. Across the balcony and down the secret hallway he went, turning sharply into Mr. Today's office and grabbing one of the robes from the rack. He tore back through the hallway, shoving his arms into the robe, and clipped down the stairs into the hospital ward, coming to an abrupt stop in front of Meghan.

He caught his breath and fastened the robe properly, then flexed his fingers and looked his best friend in the eye. "Ms. Morning said this is a dangerous spell." His eyes roamed the room, stopping at Ms. Octavia. "I suppose I should just be here alone with Meghan so no one hears me say it. . . ."

Ms. Octavia held up three tentacles. "Say no more. Let's go, everyone. Out."

Florence, Octavia, and the nurses filed out. Sean looked concerned. He turned to Meghan. "Are you okay with him trying it?"

Meghan gazed into his eyes. After a moment she nodded.

Sean looked at Alex. "Don't mess it up," he warned.

Alex's stomach twisted. "Right. Of course not. No pressure."

As Sean reluctantly left the room, Alex grabbed Meghan's hand. "Are you absolutely sure? I don't know what could happen, but I promise I'll be extremely careful."

Meghan nodded firmly. She'd made up her mind.

"Okay, then. Hold very still." Alex let go of her and made a fist with his left hand, trying to stop it from shaking, but Ms. Morning's warning to be precise had seemed to set his body off in the opposite direction. He stretched his fingers out, blew on them, and took a deep breath. And then he carefully placed the tip of his thumb and forefinger on the end of a section of metal, making sure his fingers didn't touch Meghan's hair, neck, or any other part of her body. And then he closed his eyes and concentrated on the thorns, thought about what he wanted to do. He made one last check to be sure he wasn't touching any part of Meghan, only the metal, and then whispered, "Dissipate."

The section of metal faded away, and the skin deflated and puckered around the holes.

Alex stepped back and breathed. "Whoa," he said, "it worked. A piece totally just disappeared. Unbelievable."

Meghan bit her lip. She poked Alex in the arm and nodded impatiently, pointing to her neck.

"Okay, okay. Let's do the next section." Now that he knew what would happen, the thought of accidentally touching Meghan while saying the spell gave him a slight stroke. What if he accidentally made Meghan's neck—or worse, Meghan's whole self—disappear? No wonder nobody seemed to know about this spell.

"Hold still," he said. He placed his fingers on the next section, focused, and repeated the spell. The section disappeared just like the other had, leaving a strange, intriguing pattern of scars around her neck. "It's working," he muttered. "Next one." He did the third section, and then the fourth, and the fifth, all the way around, until he came to the last one, the piece right in front. It was the piece that kept her from being able to speak at all.

"Here we go," he said. Nervous sweat dripped from his temples. He touched the metal piece, whispered the verbal component, and watched it slowly disappear. With an enormous sigh of relief, he stepped back and wiped his face with his sleeve. "I'm done," he said softly.

Meghan lifted her hand to her neck and touched it gingerly, all around, feeling the tiny holes and scar lines.

"Does it hurt?"

Meghan bit her lip, and then she parted them as if to speak. Alex leaned forward, straining, as Meghan took a breath and whispered in a cluttered, choked sort of way, "Only a little."

For a Brief Moment

An enormous grin spread across Meghan's face. "I can talk!" she half whispered, half croaked. "It feels so weird. . . ." She trailed off. "I hope the squeaks go away," she said, squeaking.

"Woo-hoo!" Alex shouted. He embraced her, and then they flung open the doors to the hall outside the hospital ward, where Sean and the others had been standing around anxiously.

"Hi-iii!" Meghan said, her voice continuing to screech and creak. She did a little impromptu dance in the foyer. "I can talk!"

The group rushed over to her, chattering excitedly, surrounding her, and Alex stepped aside to give them room. He went back into the hospital ward to thank Ms. Morning, but both she and Gunnar were sleeping.

He tiptoed out and began to search the mansion for Sky and Crow—they needed to see this. But he couldn't find them anywhere. He hadn't seen much of them since Artimé had returned, actually, though he'd heard that Crow and Henry did everything together.

Alex headed outside and was reminded of how lucky they were not to be sleeping on concrete in desertlike heat. Now that he had a second to breathe, he took in the sights and sounds of the brightly colored world. The peaceful lull of the bubbling fountain, creatures walking down pathways or sitting together in trees, talking or resting or entertaining one another, and the gentle scents of flowers and the musk of the jungle at the edge of the lawn. It almost felt like the first day he'd been here.

A moment later he spied Sky sitting on the edge of the fountain. Her face brightened at the sight of Alex, and he felt his stomach flip as he ran over to her. He sat down at her side.

LISA McMANN

"Hey! I feel like I haven't seen you in days," he said, laughing, and then his laugh softened into a crooked smile. "Isn't it fun being clean again? Ha-ha. Um . . ." He blushed. "I missed you. And I never got to thank you for . . . wow, for everything. Helping with the clue, and figuring out there was something wrong upstairs . . ." He trailed off, realizing all the things she'd done for him the past few weeks.

Sky smiled and waved him off.

"No, I mean it," he said in earnest. "You've been, like, the one person I could count on through this whole mess. You're just really, really cool, and amazing, and smart, and level-headed—"

Sky covered her face with her hands, embarrassed.

Alex stopped talking and waited for her to look at him again.

She spread her fingers and peeked between them.

"And clever," Alex said.

She pinched the space closed again.

Alex grinned. "Okay," he said. He punched her softly in the arm. "I'll stop. I promise."

She pulled her fingers away and raised an eyebrow.

"Promise," Alex said again. He liked her orange eyes.

They smiled at one another as if they shared a secret, but when the girl blinked her long lashes and let her hand rest on the fountain between her knee and his, Alex was sure he didn't know what that secret might be. His brain turned to scrambled eggs. He knew he had a goofy grin on his face, but he couldn't help it. There was something almost magical about the girl. Her plump lips, her light brown skin, and those deep, golden sunset-colored eyes. Alex swallowed hard as he felt his body lean ever so slowly toward her, as if his shoulder was magnetized to hers. Sky, her eyes on his, didn't lean away.

Just then a flaming ball of light streaked between their faces and stopped a few feet in front of Alex. As he reared back and turned to see what had happened, it exploded, leaving only a glowing pencil-drawn picture of Lani and a thin trail of light stretching across the sea, pointing out the direction from which it had come.

Alex stared at it, his face growing pale just as the picture faded away. He swung around to look at the trail of light streaking toward Warbler Island. And then he turned back to Sky. His lips parted as if to speak, but he didn't have a clue what to say. Sky held his gaze solemnly for a moment, reached

LISA McMANN

up and squeezed his arm, and then smiled, bringing her hands together in her lap.

"I'm sorry," Alex whispered, though he wasn't sure why he was saying that. His gut twisted with guilt—here he was relaxing and smiling when Sam and Lani were still captured. He looked at the ground. "I'm such a dolt." He lifted his eyes up to hers again. "I came to tell you that we took Meghan's thorn necklace off, and she can speak again. And if you want, we can do yours and Crow's, too."

Sky's eyes grew wide, fearful. Her fingers fluttered to her neck, and now it was her turn to look away.

Alex got to his feet, knowing he had no time to waste, knowing he had to do something fast to get the rescue effort started, but desperately wanting to be with Sky. "I'm sorry," he said once more. "I have to go." Impulsively he reached out and squeezed her hand. And then he turned and ran to the mansion to find Simber, every step he took reinforcing the confusion of feelings he had in his head and in his heart.

On the Move

hen Alex had gathered up his group of trusted friends and advisors, he, Sean, Meghan, Florence, Simber, and Ms. Octavia picked a spot on the lawn to talk strategy. But first he invited Meghan to tell them all about her experiences on Warbler.

As she told her story, the others looked on in shocked silence. Sean sat silent and still, staring at the grass, fists balled up and jaw set.

She remembered making it to Claire's boat and not having the strength to climb inside, instead hanging on to the ladder for dear life. And that was the last thing she could recall before she woke up inside the gray shack. She didn't remember the rescue or flying out of the boat or nearly drowning.

"I can't imagine what they've done to Lani and Samheed," she said. "But you have to understand—we have one shot at getting them out of there. And almost everything is underground. There are spies in the trees with sleep darts—they got us on the way in, but I don't think they were expecting me to escape. They must only be looking out to sea. So by the time they saw me running for the boat, I was too far away and they missed." She thought for a moment. "We're going to need a lot of help."

"Simber," Alex said, "I'd like to do a flyover of Warbler as soon as possible. We need to get an idea of what we're dealing with and figure out where the cave entrances are." He looked at the afternoon sun. "Tomorrow, first thing?"

"I'll be rrready," Simber said.

Meghan frowned. "I should go."

Alex looked at her. "I didn't think you'd want to."

"I don't. But I should," she said. Her voice was growing clearer as the day wore on, and it was easier to understand her now. "I'll be able to show you where I escaped from."

"No," Sean said. "You're not going."

Meghan flared. "Yes, I think I am."

"Then so am I," he said. His face was stone.

Ms. Octavia cleared her throat.

Everyone looked at her.

She smiled, her sharp teeth gleaming, and then looked at Alex. "Alex, I think Artimé needs you to stay on the grounds for now as we plan things."

Alex flashed a confused look, which cleared a moment later. "Oh. To keep things stable around here," he murmured. "Rally the troops, as they say."

"At least until Claire is feeling better," Ms. Octavia said.

"I agrrree," Simber said, and Florence nodded.

Alex pressed his lips together. He wasn't sure he liked counting on someone else to get things right. But then he thought about it. Who better than Sean and Meghan to take on this task? They were certainly invested enough—Meghan had the scars to prove it—and Sean had been a great leader. "Okay," he said. "Both of you go with Simber tomorrow."

The brother and sister team wore nearly identical grim smiles.

"And I'll work on Sky and Crow," Alex said. He rubbed his temples. "If we could only convince them to let me take those chokers off, we could communicate. They could tell us everything."

"What do you mean?" Florence asked. "Are they hesitant?"

"Sky seems to be really worried that something bad will happen. I wonder what kind of nonsense they were told would happen if they removed them."

Meghan gulped. "You mean something could have happened to me?"

"The point is, nothing did happen," Alex said. "See? You're fine." He tapped his lips. "Maybe you could go talk to Sky this afternoon, Meg. Show her that you're okay."

"Sure," Meghan said.

"As for Sam and Lani," Alex said, "well, Lani, at least, is still alive. She sent a seek spell about an hour ago." He pointed to the fading trail of light that streaked across the water to the west. "I hope they can hang on a bit longer. They must think we've abandoned them."

"They won't give up waiting for us," Meghan said. "They must have figured out by now that things aren't normal."

Alex raised an eyebrow. "Could *you* have imagined what happened here?"

Meghan paused. "No, I guess not. But if Lani has been doing the seek spell, she had to have seen that it wasn't working for a while."

"I suppose that's true."

They sat in contemplative silence. "Anything else?" Alex asked. He looked around. "I'll send out a message to everyone's blackboards just to make sure everybody's doing okay, like Mr. Today would do. I don't see a need for a big meeting—everyone seems to have gone back to their routines quite easily."

The others agreed.

"What about the gate?" Simber asked. "I don't think Quill has discoverrred that we'rrre back in business yet, but they will soon."

Alex nodded. "I've thought about it. We need to keep it open in case some of our Unwanteds return. Let's get another line of guards in place, and maybe Rufus can act as lookout from above."

"I'll handle that," Florence said. "Shall I start up the Magical Warrior Training again?"

"Yes," Alex said. He looked at Ms. Octavia. "And let's get regular classes going again too."

The octogator nodded. "That will be good. Poor Siggy doesn't know what to do with himself. He's still so distraught over Samheed." She wrung two or three tentacles in her lap.

After they had sorted out all the most urgent tasks, Alex looked around the group. "Well, I guess that's enough for today. Thanks, everybody." He smiled. "It's good to have you back."

The Birds, the Birds!

When the advisors dispersed to take care of their tasks, Alex made his way inside the mansion. He peeked into the hospital ward, seeing Gunnar and Henry Haluki, along with Crow and also Charlie the gargoyle, all sitting together on Gunnar's bed. Crow was signaling wildly to Charlie, and Gunnar was signaling too, only at a much slower pace.

Henry looked up and saw Alex watching them. "Charlie and Crow speak the same language," he said, eyes shining. "Can you believe it? And my dad can understand Crow a little bit too!"

Alex grinned. "That's incredible," he said. "What a strange

LISA McMANN

coincidence that Charlie and Matilda would use the same sign language as the people on Warbler." He thought about that for a bit, scratching his head as he turned to leave. "Then again, that's where Mr. Today was born. Maybe he learned it there and taught it to the gargoyles." He climbed the steps, deep in thought. And then he stopped, turned around, and went back down. He peeked into the hospital ward again.

"Crow," he said, "can you tell Henry's dad what the leaders of Warbler have told you about the thorns in your neck? Did they tell you something would happen to you if you took them off?"

Crow's face turned ashen. He gripped the choker and backed away from Alex.

Alex put his hands in the air and stepped back. "Whoa, sorry. I didn't mean to scare you."

Crow watched Alex for a long minute, and then he turned to Gunnar and began to sign.

Gunnar watched Crow carefully. When Crow finished, Gunnar turned to Alex and shook his head. "I didn't get it all," Gunnar began, "but the gist of it is that if they ever escaped and tried to remove the thorns, the birds would come."

"The birds?" Alex asked.

LISA McMANN

Island of Fire » 192

Gunnar looked at Crow. Crow signed some more.

"The Warbler birds, he says," said Gunnar. "The Warbler birds will come and peck them, starting with their eyes. And then the people of Warbler would find them and kill them."

Alex stared. Henry stared. Even Charlie stared.

Crow cowered, his hands over his eyes.

Alex's mind raced. What would Mr. Today say right now to this scared little boy to soothe his fears? He put his hands in his pockets and offered a kind smile. "Well, all I know is that a *crow* can beat a warbler any day of the year."

Crow didn't move.

"And you know what else I know?"

Crow remained still.

"I know that warbler birds are friendly. I also know that the leader of Warbler told you that to scare you, and I bet I know why—they don't want you to remove the thorns so you can't talk to anyone about what they're doing over there." Alex began to wind up. "It's like Quill. Justine told everyone that the walls were there for our protection from the neighboring lands, but she was lying to us. She wanted us to be scared only so that we wouldn't dare to leave." He took a breath.

Crow let his hands slip down from his eyes.

"There's nothing special about that thorny necklace," Alex said decisively. "Its only purpose is to keep you from talking to outsiders, and to scare you into obedience."

Crow looked up at Alex, his eyes begging to be assured.

"I can prove it," Alex said. "We took Meghan's off this morning. She sat outside for hours, and no Warbler birds came. Plus, now she can talk again."

Crow's face strained with hope.

"Go find her—you'll see for yourself. And tell your sister, too. She's probably with Meghan right now."

Crow bit his lip, and then he scrambled off Haluki's bed and jumped to the floor, running at full speed to find Meghan and his sister.

Gunnar grinned at Alex. "You have a way with that boy," he said. "He trusts you."

Alex smiled. "I guess so," he said, feeling a new confidence growing inside him. And then he turned to Henry. "Now that we have our art supplies again, see if you can get Crow to draw a map of the tunnels on Warbler, will you?"

"Sure," Henry said. "He's pretty good at drawing. I showed

him my things and he drew some stuff." He got off the bed and went after Crow.

Alex looked at Gunnar Haluki. "We're doing everything we can to find Lani," he said. "She's alive, we know that much. She sent a seek spell this morning."

Gunnar smiled weakly. "I know you're doing your best, Alex. And from what little I've seen, you're doing an excellent job. Marcus would be very proud."

Alex blinked hard and looked at the floor.

Gunnar went on. "Thank you for taking care of my son. I can never repay you for that."

Alex nodded. "I'm sorry about your wife," he said.

Gunnar closed his weary eyes. "There is only one instance where living without ever expressing one's feelings seems like it could be useful, at least on the surface, and that is when someone you love dies." He took a breath. "I will never be the same person again."

Alex nodded. He thought he understood, at least a little. After a moment, thinking Gunnar was asleep, he turned to go.

"Alex," Gunnar said.

Alex stopped and looked at the man.

"I didn't want to say this in front of the boys, but Charlie is communicating with Matilda, who is in Aaron's office at the palace. She overheard a conversation. It seems Aaron has somehow managed to sentence your father to his death, but then decided to save his life again on the condition that they never support you in any way." He paused. "I thought you should know."

Alex's stomach dropped. He felt numb. He pinched the bridge of his nose as a headache threatened. And then he let out a held breath. "I see," he said. "Thank you for telling me."

"And your mother is due any day now."

Alex blinked. "She—what?"

Haluki opened his eyes. "Ahh, I'm sorry. You haven't reconnected," he mused. "According to Matilda, your mother is about to have twins."

Information
Overload

After sending out a greeting to all of Artimé by way of a very cranky blackboard, Alex retreated to the Museum of Large to search for a book that might tell him more about Warbler Island. But once he got there, he was quickly reminded of the mess that Ol' Tater had made. He picked up a few things, and then made his way to the gray shack. It was almost exactly as it had been when it stood alone on that dry plot, except for a few pieces of toppled furniture, most likely due to the Unwanteds trying to get out when they realized something was happening. He straightened it up.

LISA McMANN

Alex made a mental note to restore water to the water cabinet in case the world ended again. That had saved them. And then he bent down and looked into the cupboard where the model of the mansion was kept. He spied it and pulled it out, looking it over. "Brilliant clue, really," Alex said aloud. He smiled and pushed the miniature mansion back in its place.

"I'll fix you later, as soon as I have time," he said to the whale bones, which were scattered near and far. "Promise." And then he laughed at himself. He sounded like Mr. Today, talking to the whale as if it could hear him. "And I'll explore the rest of this room one day too," he promised himself. There were hulking things in all directions, some of them curiously covered with tarps.

On the way back to the wall of books, he patted the side of the pirate ship. It whispered unintelligibly in return.

And then he dove into the library, trying to find the W section.

There wasn't one. As he searched through piles and shelves overflowing with books, his mind turned to Sky. And to Lani. And to how awfully confused he felt. How could he even be thinking about girls when he had so much to do?

Then he thought about his parents. And Aaron. And how awful Aaron was. And about his mother having twins. Alex would be an older brother, and he'd probably never meet the children. *How coincidental,* he thought. *Twins again.*

On second thought, maybe he *would* meet one of them eventually. He gave a rueful chuckle and picked up another book, *Everything There Is to Know About Shells.* Alex opened it and just laughed. He was sure it was a great book and very useful—though not quite as useful as the vomit book, which had already provided entertainment for Alex and several of his friends—but . . .

He set it aside and dug deeper, trying to organize titles as he went through them, but ultimately giving up because the job was endless and took too much time. He searched into the night.

Finally he happened on a small book written in Mr. Today's own hand. It was a biography or a journal of sorts. Alex paged through it and then put it in his pocket to take back to his room.

When he left the Museum of Large, his mind was swimming with book titles about everything one could possibly

LISA McMANN

imagine. Books on flags, books on famous people, books on geography and cooking and war and craft making. Books on art, sculpting, music, and magic. Books of fiction, scripts, plays, and poetry. And one of the most interesting things of all was that most of the books in the library, except for the ones written by Artiméans and two piles of random titles that Alex found in pristine condition, were very old.

It was puzzling, but there was no time to wonder about it.

"Come on," Alex muttered. He was tired. He just wanted to find something that would help him. "We need to come up with a find spell," he said.

And then he spied it—a book called simply *The Islands*. It was old and tattered—well loved, Mr. Today would have said. That had to have some information about Warbler.

Alex stifled a yawn that threatened to crack his jaw, and realized he was useless without sleep. He took the two books, closed up the Museum of Large, and headed back up the not-really-secret hallway. It was late. *Late enough to be stumbling across Samheed right about now*, Alex thought. A pang ripped through him. Things weren't happening fast enough, and he couldn't seem to make anything go faster.

He squeezed his eyes shut as he emerged from the hallway, and nearly tripped over someone.

"Oh," he said, catching his balance. And then he smiled when he realized who it was. "It's you two. Sorry about that." Crow hopped to his feet. Alex blushed and held his hand out to Sky. She took it and pulled herself up, then hastily let go.

Alex looked from one to the other. And then he frowned. "You guys have rooms, don't you?"

They both nodded.

"Oh, good. I thought we forgot. I'm glad somebody took care of you," he said. "Did Meghan find you?" He tried to sound nonchalant, but it wasn't working.

The Silent girl nodded again, and then she pointed to the thorns around her neck and looked up at Alex with a solemn face.

Alex looked back at her. Just looking at her made his knees weak. "So . . . ?" He flashed a lopsided grin. "You want me to take that nasty collar off you now?"

Sky didn't smile. She just swallowed hard and nodded.

Alex took a deep breath. It was crazy how excited he was. He wondered what her voice would sound like. What if it was nothing like he expected? What if she'd had the necklace on too long and her voice didn't come back?

He'd thought about it and realized there was no need for Florence and her tools. It would be even easier removing one solid piece rather than half a dozen broken pieces. "Let's do it, then," he said gently. "All you have to do is stand there and don't move." He turned to Crow. "This would be a very, very bad time to bump me, okay? You got that?"

Crow nodded and stepped back, his eyes wide and solemn.

Alex turned back to the girl and moved her hair out of the way. "Cover your ears, Crow," he said, his eyes not leaving the girl's beautiful orange irises.

Obediently, Crow put his fingers in his ears.

Alex touched the metal thorns, careful to stay far away from her skin. "Ready?" he whispered.

Sky blinked once, not daring to nod her head. She squeezed her hands into fists so tight that her knuckles looked like they might split.

Alex closed his eyes and pictured the thorns disappearing, and then he whispered, "Dissipate."

When he opened his eyes, his fingertips were empty. In

the space in front of him, Sky stood, still as a mouse.

"It's done." A grin spread across Alex's face. "Check the mirror," he said, remembering that's what covered the wall where the secret hallway stood.

The girl put her fingers to her neck, and then ran to the mirror and stared. She traced the scars. A tear fell from the corner of her eye, and then she turned to Alex. "Alex," she half mouthed, half whispered, nearly choking as her voice struggled to make sound once again. "Thank you."

It was the most beautiful sound Alex had ever heard.

Lessons in Warblish

Every day, whenever Lani could find a moment when no one was watching, she sent out the seek spell. And every day, when no one came to rescue them, she lost a little more hope.

She was assigned to work in a fire cave, melting gold coins and making thorn necklaces. There were five or six other workers there around Lani's age, and they showed her how to use a mold to form the long, thin, sharply pointed strings of gold. While the strings were still hot, the workers loosely weaved several of them together in a curved shape, making sure the pointed ends were at the proper angles to easily be

LISA McMANN

inserted into someone's neck. It was the most horrible job Lani could think of.

The cave had a hole in the high ceiling, which let in some natural light. It also let out the smoke from the fire. It was beastly hot in there, and terribly sooty. The others talked now and then with gestures that Lani didn't understand, but most of the time everyone plodded along, making gleaming golden thorns, lost in their own thoughts. It was beyond frustrating. Lani wanted to scream, to tear the thorns from her neck and yell and stomp her feet and just *hear* something again besides the rare voice of an unthorned supervisor. She wanted the young women she worked with to be as angry as she was. But they weren't. They were complacent.

Days passed. Lani went from the women's bunkhouse to her job in the fire cave, and back to the bunkhouse. Her "leash" kept her tied to the complicated wire system above her head as she slept, bathed, and worked. Whenever she walked from one place to another, she strained her eyes, looking for any sign of Samheed, worried that he was still locked in the dark cave all alone. As much as she wanted to try to rip the wire off of her with her bare hands, she knew there was nowhere to escape to.

And she wasn't doing anything without Samheed. They were in this together, to the end.

As she worked, an empty feeling made her chest ache, and tears burned her eyes. She couldn't get the image out of her head—the man shoving Samheed to the ground, and Sam lying there, not moving, as the hulking beast dragged her away from him. She couldn't stop thinking about him. What if, after all this, she'd never see him again? What if . . . what if he was dead? She couldn't bear to think about it.

At night, his name was on her lips as she tossed and turned on her cot. She clasped her hands together and held them to her cheek, eyes closed, pretending she was holding Samheed's hand. Wishing with all her might that when she opened her eyes again, he would be there.

But of course he never was.

It was on her second week outside the dark cave, after a long day of hard work, that a woman summoned Lani and a blond-haired girl who was also tethered to the wire. Lani didn't know the girl's name, and no one knew Lani's, either—there was really no reason to learn anyone's name when you couldn't speak. The woman led them out to the main hallway and to a small room with boulders for chairs. A few people sat there. As the girls entered, they were ushered to one side of the room. Lani looked around at the others and her heart jumped to her throat. There sat Samheed, also tethered to the ceiling wire on the purple line.

His head was bowed. He hadn't seen her.

Lani stared at him, willing him to look up. After a moment, he did.

His eyes were vacant at first, but when he saw Lani, they filled with recognition and longing. Lani swallowed hard and tried to smile, but only the corner of her mouth quivered. Her heart fluttered. She hadn't really seen him since the day they'd been captured. They held one another's gaze, telling stories with their eyes, until a voice startled them from their private, silent conversation.

"I am Whimbrel," a woman said. "Your behavior has earned you all the right to learn how to speak in our island's sign language." She wore no thorn necklace, but scars marked her neck where one most certainly once had been. "The language is for communication only when necessary, not for idle

LISA McMANN

chatter. Anyone caught using the language excessively will be sent to the dark cave."

The handful of tethered people in the room didn't react. The threat of the dark cave seemed to be the punishment for everything. In their handbooks, in their instructions for their new jobs, in the dining hall. There was nothing much worse than the dark cave, it was true. But they'd all survived it, apparently.

"In a few years, if you have proved yourself loyal and worthy, Queen Eagala will consider removing your neck device, as she has obviously done for me," Whimbrel said, her voice brimming with pride. But then her face grew dark. "However, if you try to remove it yourself, you will suffer a terrible fate."

All pairs of eyes in the room opened wider. This was news.

The woman hunched over and said in a low, sinister voice, "The birds of Warbler are spies for the queen. They can track you by your thorns. If anyone but the queen removes your necklace, swarms of Warbler birds will come after you, no matter where you are." She bent farther toward the group and whispered, "And they will peck your eyes out."

Lani glanced at Samheed just as he glanced at her, and they

both had to look away quickly to keep a straight face. It was the most ridiculous thing they'd ever heard in their lives—more ridiculous than anything the High Priest Justine had told them in Quill. Besides, it was obvious the queen gave them orange eyes so they could be identified and killed if they ever escaped. It seemed pretty silly that she'd send birds to peck them out after all that effort. What good would that do? But the sad part was, everyone else in the room seemed to believe it with all their heart—even the woman speaking.

What kind of crazy place is this? Lani had asked herself over and over again. *Fear, fear, and more fear. What is Warbler so afraid of that they had to silence everyone on it? Is every island this messed up?*

"And if any strangers find their way to our shores or into our caves, you must not address them. Immediately get help. Understood?"

The small group, including Lani and Samheed, nodded.

Whimbrel seemed satisfied that she had instilled a sufficient amount of fear into the hearts and minds of the newest members of Warbler. She went on to teach them a dozen or so hand signals. Words like "come," "go," "help," "inside," "outside," "eat," "sleep," "work," "danger," "please," and "thank you."

Lani almost laughed at the last two. At least the people of Warbler were polite. She shook her head and caught Samheed looking at her. She held his gaze for a moment, a feeling of warmth flooding her chest. What a relief it was to see him—actually *see* him. It felt like a part of her that had been missing was back again. She smiled and looked down, not wanting Whimbrel to suspect they knew each other.

Once they'd learned the hand signals, Whimbrel said, "Now pair up and practice the symbols with a partner."

As the blond girl turned toward Lani, Lani pretended not to notice and instead stood up and stepped over to Samheed. He half grinned in covert delight and moved over on his boulder chair. Lani hopped on and perched cross-legged, facing him, close enough to touch. Whimbrel didn't seem to mind. She wasn't exactly the housemother type.

As Whimbrel called out each word, the language students took turns signing it to their partner. Soon the instructor told them to go ahead and work on their own. She sat down near the door, pulled a paper from her pocket, and began to study it.

Lani's eyes flew open. She shifted so that Samheed's body mostly blocked her from Whimbrel's sight, and then she reached for Samheed's hand and took it in hers. It was almost as if their blood pulsated together through their fingertips. Lani's body tingled and she took in a sharp breath. She looked up and saw Samheed swallow hard, his thorns wavering as he did so. And then he tapped gently into her hand in their own private language, "I miss you like crazy."

A Ray of Light

Lani held her breath, willing herself not to cry, because that would surely draw the attention of Whimbrel. "I miss you too," she tapped back. "I'm so glad you're okay." She studied him, his new golden-orange eyes piercing hers. His dark hair was longer than it had ever been, and the ends curled up a bit around his ears and at his neck.

They made a show of doing some of their signs in case anyone was looking. Samheed pointed to himself and then signed, "Work outside." He pointed to her, a question burning in his eyes.

"Inside," Lani signed back. "Go?" She raised an eyebrow. "Danger?"

Samheed pressed his lips into a line. He took her hand and tapped. "I make ships. Covered area so no one can see from water or sky."

Lani glanced over his shoulder and signed randomly, "Come, go, thank you, please."

She tapped. "I'm in fire cave making metal thorns."

He flashed her a look of pity and signed, "Work, sleep, eat."

She tapped again. "We have to get out of here." And then she signed, "Go, come, outside."

He nodded and tapped, "Stealing wood to make raft. Slow going. When do we get leashes off?"

Lani shrugged. She saw Whimbrel fold her paper and put it back into her pocket. Lani began signing, flashing a warning with her eyes to Samheed before wiping her face of all emotion once again.

Whimbrel stood and began walking around the room, looking at each pair and watching them sign, correcting them if they were not quite accurate. She paused at Samheed's side and watched as Lani signed beautifully, "Danger, please, help."

"Good," Whimbrel said. She smiled primly at Lani and moved on. "Tomorrow we'll learn another set."

Lani's lips parted in surprise. "Tomorrow!" she tapped into Samheed's hand.

He grinned and his face flushed. "Best news of the year," he tapped. And then he gave Lani's hand a little squeeze, and she squeezed back.

It felt right to have their fingers entwined again.

Making Plans

While Sean and Meghan rode Simber to Warbler Island to study the terrain, Alex and Florence spent their time gathering information from Sky and Crow. Crow was now free of his thornament as well, and both of the Silent children had a good deal of trouble getting their voices to work properly at first. After some practice and a little bit of magical help from Ms. Morning, Crow's voice came back, though it still squeaked from time to time. He told Alex that he'd had his necklace on for only a few weeks before he and Sky escaped on the raft.

Sky, on the other hand, had had her thornament attached

LISA McMANN

for a few years. Even with magic, her voice came back much more slowly and remained husky from that point on, which she didn't seem to mind. Alex thought she sounded quite nice indeed.

After a while they gathered in the hospital ward to talk so that Claire and Gunnar could listen as well from their beds. Alex and Florence asked them everything they could think of about Warbler. Soon, with Sky's hoarse directions, Alex was sketching a map of the underground tunnels and outlining the various workstations around the island, all hidden from the view of the shore and camouflaged with brush and trees.

"Do you have any idea where Sam and Lani would be?" Alex asked as he studied his work.

Sky leaned over the map, her hair falling forward. Absently she tucked it behind her ear and pointed to the center of the maze of caves and tunnels. "They'd be in the dark cave for quite a while," she said, her voice a husky song. "That's where they put you after they administer the thorns and the acid eye drops. I think it needs to be fairly dark for the eyes to heal." She said it without a note of bitterness. Florence studied the girl with a curious look.

"It's hard to say how long you're in there, though. It feels like a long time when you don't know when something's going to end," Sky mused. "It's pretty traumatic." She glanced at Crow. "Isn't it, buddy?"

Crow nodded. He was almost as quiet as before he'd had his thorns removed. He tilted his head and reached across the map. "That's where the boys sleep. You get chained to a wire for a while until they know you're good."

From her bed, Claire wore a stony expression. She shook her head. "I'm so sorry," she said in a quiet voice.

Sky pointed to a large cave on the opposite side. "The girls are in this one." She pointed to various caves in a clockwise pattern. "Here's where they manufacture clothing—I worked there part of the time, and also in the shipyard. This is the dining and kitchen area, which is where Crow worked. Mining is done in this cave here and throughout the island—there's an open mine hidden by rock overhangs in the center of Warbler, and there is also a waterfall with a freshwater river flowing through the middle of the island. This big cave at the south end," she said, looking at Alex, "which is the opposite side from where Meghan said she and the others anchored the boat, is where the fire cave is—they make the thorns there by melting the gold. And over here," she said, pointing to the east side of the island, "is shipbuilding."

"Ships," Alex said, tapping his lips and thinking. "Multiple ships?"

"A fleet," Crow said. "Queen Eagala wants them for the attack."

Alex turned to Crow. "What attack?"

Sky interrupted. "Let me tell this part, okay, Crow?" She smoothed his hair off his forehead. He shook his head to mess it back up again, but he looked amiable enough and was silent.

Sky hopped on a chair like she had seen Alex do when he addressed a group. She hunched over, arms reaching out in front of her as if she were imagining a new setting, and began what sounded like a story.

"Many years ago, Eagala was born on Warbler Island to the current ruling family. When she was a child, she and her older brothers and sisters created the sign language that Warbler now uses. Some of them could do magic. Today, Warbler Island is charmed with a magical silence spell created by Eagala herself. The queen and her siblings kept their magic a secret for years.

One day, when she was still a young girl, Eagala's oldest brother and sister left to explore the six other islands in our world. But they never returned. Eagala never saw them again. When she grew up she went in search of them, but found hostility at the other islands, so she made a hasty retreat back to Warbler, only to find that her father, the king, had passed away in her absence, and she was the new ruler."

Alex and the others listened, spellbound, amazed at Sky's natural ability as a storyteller, and her ability to speak so well after having been silenced for so long. He found himself admiring her even more.

Sky continued. "Fearing that her siblings had been killed by hostile enemies, she worried for her people and commissioned the residents of Warbler to dig the tunnels and caves for their own protection, which they did willingly. Soon Warbler appeared to be completely uninhabited, and she added the silent spell over the land not only so that Warblerans could work with concentration, but so no passersby would ever suspect—there is no noise from axes or hammers to be heard anywhere, and everyone was commanded to speak softly when outside. Queen Eagala credits herself for keeping Warbler from attack. But she wanted to be prepared for war, so she began to build a fleet of ships and sailing canoes." Sky looked around. "There are over a hundred ships hidden in the trees in various stages of completion," she said.

"A hundred!" Alex said, eyes wide. And then he frowned. "How many people are there on Warbler, anyway? It can't be more than a few hundred, can it?"

Sky looked at him solemnly. "Thousands of people, all hidden underground. Most of them silenced, like us, from the age of ten, and the younger children all housed far below to keep their voices from being heard. It's like an ant colony, everyone scurrying around in silence, doing their jobs, going from one place to the next."

Haluki spoke up. "Did the people also agree to wear the thorn necklaces?" He sounded incredulous.

Sky shook her head. "No. The thorns are recent within the last several years. People began to revolt against being forced to hide and whisper all the time. When other sailors found their boats drawn to our shores because of the strong current circling our island, Warblerans started sneaking away and emerging from hiding to tell the visitors of the restrictions and try to escape with them."

"So Queen Eagala found a way to silence the people completely," Alex said, wonder in his voice. "How horrible."

Sky lifted her chin high and didn't falter.

"What about the eyes?" Claire asked from her bed in a weak voice.

"It's our brand. Our mark that we belong to Warbler . . . in case we are ever discovered elsewhere," she said. This time her words were tinged with bitterness. And then she looked down. "I guess the bird thing really was just to scare us, or they wouldn't have bothered to make our eyes orange. But I think they'll come after us eventually if they believe we survived our escape. And for that I am really sorry. If you don't want us to stay here—"

Claire pushed up on her elbow in alarm and Alex stood up to protest. "Of course you'll stay here!" he said. "You—and Crow, too—helped fix Artimé. I don't care what color your eyes are. You guys are Artiméans now." Alex flushed. "If you want to be, I mean." He sat back down, feeling like he'd probably just overreacted a bit in his haste to assure them they had to stay. But the thought of them leaving now . . . He caught

LISA McMANN

Claire and Gunnar exchanging smiles and glances, which made him flush even hotter than before.

Sky flushed too.

Florence squelched an ebony smile and saved them by saying, "They'll have to get past Simber and me first. But let's turn our thoughts back to Lani and Samheed, and how we're going to find them in that maze."

"Right." Alex looked back at the map and studied it some more. "Thousands of people hidden above and under the ground," he mused, rubbing his temples. "And some of them act as guards, shooting sleep darts."

Sky and Crow nodded.

Alex frowned and shook his head—how could they possibly take on thousands of people and find the two they wanted at the same time? They'd need a whole army of Artiméans. At most, Simber could carry four on his back. Claire's boat, which was now ready and waiting, could hold at most fifteen normal-size people. . . . Florence would sink Claire's boat just by stepping into it. But Alex needed her. He needed anybody and everybody who wouldn't be harmed by sleep darts.

Slowly Alex lifted his head, and the frown washed away.

He thought for a second more, tapping his fingers on his knee, and then he turned. "Florence," he said slowly, as if the idea was still in the process of coming to him, "can you please clear the lawn, and then round up all the statues? Every last one of them, from the library to the lounge and all through the mansion, and send them to the theater?" He pushed his chair back and stood up, rolling the map into a tube. "I'll meet you there shortly. But first," he said, a slow grin spreading across his face, "we're going to need a bigger boat."

More Plans

As Florence headed outside to clear the lawn, Alex raced up the steps to the somewhat secret hallway, said the magic words "Door number one," and entered the Museum of Large. He went straight to the pirate ship and studied it, walking all the way around it, with his hand tracing the perimeter, feeling its solidness.

It had come ashore one day, Mr. Today had said. There had been just two sailors aboard, both dead. As Alex remembered Mr. Today's story, he recalled that the old mage had said that the sailors wore strange things around their necks.

"You've been to Warbler before, haven't you," Alex mur-

LISA McMANN

mured. "Perhaps you're one of the ships from Queen Eagala's fleet."

The ship whispered and whispered. Alex strained his ears, but he couldn't understand it, not even a word.

"Are you ready to have at it again?" he asked.

The ship seemed agreeable.

"I'll be right back." Alex strode out into the secret hallway and down to the end of it, to the window, and he looked out. The lawn, beach, and sea were cleared. Alex smiled, went back to the museum, and stood next to the pirate ship. He put his hands on the hull, closed his eyes, and pictured the sea in front of the mansion. He held the picture in his mind for a long moment, his hands quavering a bit, and tried not to think about what would happen if something went terribly wrong. And then, after a deep breath, he whispered, "Transport."

The ship trembled for an instant, and then it disappeared.

Alex opened his eyes, amazed at the huge space that now stood empty before him. He turned and ran back to the end of the hallway. And there, not quite all the way in the water but pretty amazingly close, was the pirate ship.

"Whew," Alex breathed. He ran back to the museum,

locked the door, and then tore back down through the teeming crowds of Artiméans who had come inside the mansion at Florence's request.

"You can all go back to whatever you were doing," he called out. "Just stay away from the ship for now, okay?" He dashed out the mansion's seaside door to make sure the ship was unharmed in its transportation process.

As he reached the ship, he saw something in the sky coming toward him. He shielded his eyes and watched as Simber, Meghan, and Sean drew closer and then landed on the lawn nearby.

Alex ran up to them as Sean and Meghan dismounted. "How did it go?" Alex asked. "Was it strange?"

"A little," Meghan said. She had formed a habit of touching the scars on her neck when she spoke. "But we were able to get in pretty close to see the tunnel that I escaped from. And we found a couple more spots where Simber could sense people nearby, only we couldn't see them." She glanced at the ship. "Um . . . explain, please?"

Alex grinned. "We made some great progress today. You left this morning before I could tell you that Crow and Sky let me take their thornaments off late last night." He shook his head. "Sky gave us a ton of information. It's pretty scary over there, and this is going to be really difficult. Come on—I'm meeting with all the statues. I'll fill you in."

Alex, Sean, and Meghan went inside and made their way to the theater via tube while Simber went through the temporary 3-D door that Ms. Octavia had put up for the larger statues. It was an odd assortment in the auditorium. Dozens upon dozens of statues of all sizes had gathered, from the enormous Simber and Florence down to a tiny porcelain kitten the size and color of a bite-size marshmallow. The kitten perched on the shoulder of a somewhat rambunctious rust-colored fox statue carved from driftwood. The fox spent most of his time playing the saxophone in the lounge band. Charlie the gargoyle was there, and even the tiki statue from the third-floor library had somehow arrived despite having no legs to walk on. The grouchy ostrich that Alex and his friends had thrown their first origami dragon at was there as well, looking quite skeptical.

Alex walked to the stage and stood next to the podium, facing them. He put his hands in his pockets and waited.

When all was silent, Alex looked earnestly at the statues.

"Thank you for coming," he said, pulling his hands from his pockets and clasping them together in front of him. "Artimé is in great need of your help, and I'm wondering if any of you are up for a bit of an adventure."

That evening, Alex gathered his most trusted instructors, friends, and mentors. He expanded the hospital wing slightly so that they all could fit inside, and they met there for the sake of Ms. Morning and Gunnar Haluki, who now had advanced to sitting up in bed.

Alex held up a handful of papers, including the map of Warbler and the books about the islands that he had found but hadn't yet had a chance to read. He looked at Ms. Morning and Gunnar first. "You know how to restore the world if anything should happen, correct?" he asked. "And are you physically able to do it if something . . . something bad should happen to me?"

"Yes," Gunnar said solemnly.

"Absolutely," Ms. Morning said.

Alex smiled. "Good. Here's a robe," he said, taking it off and handing it to Ms. Morning. "You should wear it. If you don't have a robe and Artimé disappears, you're sunk."

Ms. Morning nodded and wrapped it around her shoulders, fastening it at her neck.

Alex turned to Simber. "Does anyone in Quill know that Artimé is restored?"

"Not to my knowledge, but I'm surrre it won't be long beforrre they do."

"And the girrinos?"

"They'rrre rrready forrr anything and we have additional spies monitorrring the rrroad to Quill."

"Great." He looked down at Rufus the squirrelicorn, who stood next to him. "Do you have your team?"

"Ready and waiting, sir."

Alex smiled at the term. It felt strange to have a warrior like Rufus calling him sir, but he thought it was kind of nice and it made him feel more confident about himself, so he didn't stop the creature from saying it.

He looked at Meghan, Sean, and Henry. "You guys good?"

They all nodded.

"And you're *sure* you want to go?" Alex asked Henry. "Don't you want to stay here with your dad?"

LISA McMANN

"I'm going," Henry said. "I need to rescue my sister. And I can help with the healing spells in case anybody gets hurt. I'm getting really good."

Alex nodded. "I've noticed that. All right." Then he turned to Sky and Crow. "Can you guys help keep things rolling around here while we're gone?"

Sky's eyes narrowed. She glanced at Crow, whose face wore a look of surprise, and then she looked back at Alex. "Oh," she said. "We thought we were coming with you."

Alex's lips parted, and then he glanced at Meghan and Ms. Morning to see their reactions. "You'd be priceless in the way of helping, but I—I didn't think you'd want to," he stammered. "What if they see you?"

Sky lifted her chin and folded her arms over her chest. "Then the sight of me will be the last thing they'll ever see," she said.

Alex's heart swished. And he knew, at that very moment, that he wanted Sky on his side of any fight, anytime, anywhere, for as long as he could convince her to stay in Artimé.

And Finally, They're Off

Before dawn, Alex got up. He loaded up his component vest and filled an extra sack with more components—there was no way he was going to run out, that was for sure. And with him in charge, well, he had responsibilities now.

"I'm going away," he announced to Clive.

Clive, who was still miffed about finding out from other sources what had happened to Artimé, didn't respond.

"We're going to try and rescue Samheed and Lani," Alex said. "They're captured on another island." He looked fondly at the growing line of prototypes of the components that he

LISA McMANN

and his friends had created, thinking he'd soon need another shelf to display them all. He glanced over his shoulder and said, "It could be dangerous."

Clive pushed his silken face out of the blackboard. "I guess I'll be the last to know if it is," he said. Then he sank back and disappeared.

Alex shook his head and sighed. It bothered him more than he cared to admit that Clive was still peeved at him. But he didn't know how to explain the vast pressure that was on him. Or how much pressure had been on him the entire time that Clive and all the others were experiencing the magical equivalent of a visit to the Ancients Sector.

He turned back to the components, double- and triple-checking his quantities, counting aloud to himself, not noticing that Clive had silently resurfaced again to watch him.

Alex looked back at the line of prototypes. There was the one Lani had made for the pincushion spell. Next to it was the tiny rubber ball Samheed had altered to look like a brain for the dementia spell. He wondered if he'd ever have any more of their creations lining his shelves. Alex smiled sadly as he recalled the day they'd sent their new spells soaring at their instructors. Had it really only been a few months since then? Alex felt like he'd become an entirely different person in that time. He reached up and took the pincushion and the tiny brain, cradling them in his hand, admiring the fine detailed work his friends had done.

He wondered if Lani had changed too, like he had. She must have, he thought. He couldn't begin to imagine what she'd gone through by now. Hard stuff forces you to grow up fast—that much he knew.

But Lani was strong. "I sure hope you're okay," he whispered. He felt a pang of guilt spear through him. With all Lani must be going through, he just couldn't stop feeling guilty about . . . about . . . well, he wasn't exactly sure why he felt so guilty when he thought about her these days. Obviously because he hadn't rescued her and Sam yet, but that was hardly something he could help. Maybe it was because he didn't think about her as often as he used to. But, he argued with himself, stuff happens when your whole world disappears and you have to count on the people who are actually *there* to help you make it through.

He squeezed his eyes shut for a moment and opened them

LISA McMANN

again. He looked at the components in his hand, then slowly closed his fingers over them and put them in his pocket for good luck. "We're going to find you," he said softly. "We just have to."

And then everything will be back to normal, he told himself.

Clive slipped away once again.

Alex took a deep breath and let it out, then squared his shoulders, picked up his supplies, and carried them to the door. He opened it, glancing at his blackboard but seeing only words. "Bye," he said, and closed the door. He waited a beat, shrugged, and then he headed out to the ship.

Florence was there already, standing with an arm slung over the top of the lower deck. Beside her was a stack of crates, and she already had the gangway pulled out and resting on the ground. When she saw Alex, she nodded a greeting. "I've had a look at this," she said. "I suggest we load the humans and the lighter folks, then Sim and I will lift and push this thing out into deeper water. It'll go faster that way, rather than getting it in the water first and transporting Artiméans back and forth. I'll climb on and Sim wants to fly, which is good."

Alex felt a sense of relief wash through him. He'd been nervous, but he knew he had the best team he could possibly have. "And someone here knows how to sail this thing, right?"

"Well, I could do it in a pinch," Florence said, adjusting her bulging quiver of arrows on her back, "but Siggy found someone else in the theater supply closet with a lot more experience. He's bringing him by in a bit."

"Perfect," Alex said. "High tide is around eight. That'll help with launching this crazy ship."

"You know it whispers, right?" Florence asked.

Alex nodded. "Any idea what it's saying?"

"No," Florence said. "Hopefully nothing bad." She smiled and picked up the stack of crates, lifting them over the railing and placing them on the deck.

Before long, a strange assortment of volunteers had assembled in groups according to their assigned leaders. Alex, Sean, Meghan, Ms. Octavia, Florence, Simber, and Rufus each carried a written list of their charges, each leader responsible for counting and keeping track of their volunteers. The statues mostly stood quietly, though a few hopped around sniffing things, while the squirrelicorns circled overhead.

Soon Mr. Appleblossom arrived, walking with a marble statue. He was a man with a peg leg, and he wore the uniform and hat of a sea captain.

Mr. Appleblossom stopped in front of Alex. "A bright and lucky morn to you, my boy," he said. "Meet Captain Ahab, here to run your ship. A finer man the sea has never known." He leaned in and whispered, "Take heed, or find yourself with a fat lip."

Alex's eyes widened. "Ah, nice to meet you, Captain Ahab."

"Pirates!" exploded the statue, pointing at the sails. "Blast my skull to bits!"

Alex stared. He slid his gaze to Mr. Appleblossom, who smiled politely, almost with mischief, and said nothing.

"We-we're not pirates. We're just going to that island there, and then back again. Can you sail this thing?"

"Ransacking thieves!" he roared. "Ye ever seen the white whale?" He leaned toward Alex, leering at him.

Alex fought off a strange urge to laugh. No wonder Mr. Appleblossom kept this statue in the props closet. The captain was crazy, and Mr. Appleblossom knew it, but he was a ship captain. And, well, they really needed him. Alex decided to try a more direct approach. "Follow me," he said. He turned abruptly and started up the gangplank, hoping the captain was following him. A minute later the uneven thump of the statue's gait assured Alex he was.

"When we push off, I need you to take us there," Alex said, once they reached the main deck. He pointed to Warbler. "Okay?"

The captain peered out over the water. "Thar she blows!" he bellowed. He pointed to what looked to Alex like the next island beyond Warbler, which they could sometimes see, and sometimes not see, depending on the light and the waves. Alex looked out of sheer curiosity and thought he saw a bit of froth rising from the surface of the water, but a second later it was gone. He shrugged. Maybe this guy had a thing for whales. But that was probably just a big wave crashing against a rock wall.

"Great," Alex said. "Stay here and be ready."

"Ye blast my skull!" the captain said in return.

"You're blasting mine," Alex muttered, and then made a hasty retreat when he remembered what Mr. Appleblossom had said about avoiding a fat lip.

A glance at the waterline on the sand told him they were

LISA McMANN

237 « Island of Fire

near high tide. It was time to go. He peered over the ship's rail and called out, "All aboard!" He watched the army, pleased, as they boarded the ship in an orderly fashion. Those who could fly did so, and those who couldn't made their way to their stations on foot, the legless tiki statue again mysteriously appearing on deck, without anyone having noticed it moving.

When Mr. Appleblossom returned to the mansion to help run things, and everyone but Simber and Florence was on board, Simber braced his rippling shoulder against the stern and lifted up, taking care with the rudder. Florence gripped the sides, lifting and pushing. Together they poured all their weight into dislodging the ship from the bit of sand that remained.

Simber growled when the water lapped at his feet. He'd had enough of that lately. But he pushed on, and soon he and Florence were gliding through the water with ease. "That's enough forrr me," he said to Florence, and began to flap his wings, rising into the air. He shook his body to rid it of the awful liquid.

Florence smiled and waved him off. "Poor kitty," she said.

Simber growled again, this time playfully, and showered

Florence with droplets. "We'rrre farrr enough," he said. "Grrrab hold, I'll give you a leg up."

"Everybody to the bow!" Florence shouted. She let go of the ship and, careful to avoid Simber's wings, slung an arm around his neck. He rose slowly, bringing Florence up and out of the water, and set her gently on deck opposite everyone else to keep the ship from capsizing.

Captain Ahab gave a shout, and with that, they were sea-borne.

But then, just as they pulled away from their glorious Artimé, a figure burst from the mansion's seaside door and rushed to the shore, waving her arms and shouting, "Wait!"

Across the Sea

Simber turned his head, hearing the cry. "I'll be rrright back," he said, and soared over the ship, turning sharply toward the shore. Alex watched him, alarmed, trying to figure out who was standing at the shore. Was it Ms. Morning? What could have happened to bring her out of her bed?

Simber landed on the sand and spoke a few words to the woman, and then she climbed on his back. Soon they were heading to the ship, and within seconds the woman was dangling from Simber's neck and dropping to the deck. Alex watched, curious. The woman dusted off her clothes and looked around anxiously.

"Carina!" Alex cried. He ran over to her and picked her

up, twirling her around in a huge circle as the rest of the crew looked on, some with smiles, some with curiosity.

"Alex," she said with a wide grin, and then she grabbed his head and kissed him soundly on the cheek.

He laughed, only a little embarrassed, and happier than he could possibly explain to see Carina Fathom—or rather, Carina *Holiday*, again. "You came back!" But his delight turned to concern. "Where's your baby? Is everything okay?"

"Little Seth is fine," Carina assured him, smoothing her short locks of light brown hair. "I snuck home to Artimé during the night to see how you were all doing, and lo and behold, I found you back in business! Friends told me at break-fast that you were setting out on this adventure. They said they'd take care of Seth while I'm gone. I didn't want to miss it. I felt so bad for leaving you like that."

"Don't, please," Alex said. He gripped her arms and smiled warmly. "You needed to go, and I'm so glad to see you again. You look . . . just . . . great. Doesn't she, guys?" He turned and looked around, his eyes stopping at Sean, who was staring intensely at Carina. Alex dropped his gaze and smiled a little.

"It's good to see you," Sean said.

Carina's face nearly split, she was grinning so hard. "Sean," she said. She went to him and gave him a big hug. "I missed you."

Sean dipped his head, embarrassed. "It's . . . yeah. I— Me too."

Meghan, who had been watching the reunion, cast a glance at Alex and almost laughed. Her brother had a crush on Carina Holiday! She'd had no idea.

"Sean," Meghan said. Carina gave a look of surprise at Meghan, who could speak again. "Why don't you fill Carina in on everything that happened after she left? Alex and I have some planning to do."

"We do?" Alex looked at Meghan. "Oh. I mean, yes. We do." He let Meghan drag him by the arm to a quiet spot on deck below Simber, who only had to flap his wings every now and then to keep up with the lazy speed of the ship. From the corner of his eye, Alex saw Sky standing off to the side with Crow and Henry, watching him. But just as he was about to call out to her, she tugged Crow's shirt and headed down to a lower deck.

"Oh," Alex murmured.

"What, oh?"

"Never mind. What's up?"

Meghan tilted her head and flashed Alex a quizzical look. "What's going on with you and her?"

"Her who?"

"Sky. Duh."

"Nothing." He didn't know why he felt guilty.

"So you still like Lani?" Meghan's sharp green eyes bored into Alex's soul.

"Of course," Alex said.

Meghan looked like she didn't believe him. "You know, *if* she and Sam are alive, and *if* we are able to rescue them, it would be really bad timing to suddenly stop liking her."

"She's my friend. I'm not going to stop liking her."

"You know what I mean." Meghan narrowed her eyes.

"So?"

"So I'm telling you as your best friend that you shouldn't do anything dumb. I mean, I really like Sky. She's great. But it would be really dumb to, you know, *like* her right now. So maybe you should stop."

"I don't like Sky," Alex said, growing exasperated. "I still like Lani, okay? I'm not going to— Bah! Whatever, okay? I miss Lani. I miss her like crazy," he said, and he meant it. "You have no idea how much I miss her and Sam, or how horrible it's been for me knowing we couldn't do anything to help them. I don't even have time to like *anybody*, okay? Because this dumb job that got forced on me never, ever ends. There's always some crisis, and there's always some problem, and there's always some—"

"I'm sorry. Wow," Meghan said. "Calm down."

"No! You know what? Who am I kidding? Look at Mr. Today—he left his family to do this job, and he never seemed to have time to *like* his wife or anybody again, and I know why. It's because this job is endless. So don't even talk to me about who I should like or shouldn't like, because I'll never be able to have anything resembling . . . that. Ever." Even as he said it, he began to realize the truth in his words. He made a quick move to his feet, nearly taking a blow to the head from the tip of Simber's wing. He ducked and shuffled off to go belowdecks. "I'm not going to do anything to hurt Lani's feelings," he said over his shoulder. "But she'll figure out eventually that I'm going to pretty much be a big loner for the rest of my life."

He stepped down, barely catching sight of a familiar piece of clothing disappearing around the corner in front of him. He hurried down the step and saw Sky running at full speed toward the bow. He watched for a moment, mouth open, and then he wrinkled up his face and cursed his stupidity under his breath, pounding his forehead against the cabin wall.

A Small Problem

An hour into the journey, Alex began meeting with each group to give them a copy of the map and go over the plan. They would arrive by late afternoon and enact the plan before dark—Sky had told them that would probably be the best time. Each group would be responsible for different parts of the plan, and each leader had the authority to call off a part of the plan that wasn't working.

They had brought plenty of food along, so everyone ate a hearty lunch as they went over their directions with their leader. Alex sat quietly alone in the spot he'd been sitting in before. Meghan came up to him, apologized, and left again after

Alex apologized too. Simber flew overhead, quiet as ever, noticing everything, saying nothing, as was *his* modus operandi.

It was midafternoon, after a zillion thoughts had flown through Alex's head that kept him from concentrating, when Simber spoke.

"Alex," he said.

Alex looked up. "Yes?"

"Something's off."

Whenever Simber said those words, it was never good.

"What is it?" Alex said.

"We'rrre strrraying off courrrse. Just a little. But enough to be a concerrrn."

Alex looked up at the sails. "Is it the wind?"

Simber was quiet for a moment. "No."

"Is it the crazy captain?"

"That would be my firrrst guess."

Alex got to his feet. "Thanks. I'll go talk to him. Though I don't know what good it'll do. He doesn't exactly know how to carry on a conversation." He made his way to the ship's wheel. As he grew close, he could hear the mutterings and outbursts of Captain Ahab.

"Shred my beard and call me Ishmael!" the captain shouted. He leaned heavily on the wheel.

"Excuse me, Captain," Alex said. "It seems we're off course." He put a hand to his brow to shield the sun. "We need to go to that island over there."

"It's haunted! Teeming with ghoulies."

Alex rolled his eyes. "No, it's not. It's an island whose people have captured our friends. We need to rescue them," he said. He was beginning to get nervous. "Where are you taking us?"

"Crack ye pea-size brain! Not the island, boy, the ship. The ship! She's of a mind, and the rudder's in her ghosty grasp." Ahab grabbed Alex's shirt with a wild look, and whispered, "'Tis the doings of the white whale!"

Alex's eyes grew wide in fright, though he wasn't quite sure what he was frightened of. He tugged his shirt loose from the captain's fist. "Are you saying you can't get us to the island?"

"Blast ye to the deadly triangle's grip!" he cried. "Your words are truth. The proof lies in the wheel." He leaned hard on the wheel, but the ship didn't change course. "Haunted, sure as I'm alive. I hear the whispers like a heavy heart about to burst. But look," he said in a softer, even scarier voice. "She's tracking yonder, ever bitter, ever seeking. Revenge is in our grasp!"

Alex stared, openmouthed, not sure what to do or say. Not even sure what was happening. The captain leaned on the wheel in the opposite direction, but the ship stayed steady. Alex looked ahead to where the captain pointed, but he saw nothing but water. Warbler loomed larger to the port side, a good ways off. He knit his brow, trying to make sense of the conversation.

Finally he turned without a word and hurried back to Simber.

"We have a problem," Alex said. "It's not the captain. I don't think it is, anyway. He seems to be trying to get us to Warbler, but he thinks . . . he thinks the ship is haunted. And it's going somewhere on its own power."

Simber blinked, but showed no other clue to his thoughts until he spoke. And what he said next spread a chill through Alex's bones.

"About thrrree minutes ago," he said slowly, "as you were talking to the captain, the island beyond Warrrbler disappearrred."

Destination: Unknown

A lex scanned the horizon, and then he remembered he hadn't seen it when he was talking to the captain. "It—it should be right out here somewhere, shouldn't it? Is it hidden behind Warbler?" Alex stood on his tiptoes, but he knew that there was no way the island could be hidden at this angle. It should be right in front of them, due west, not out to the port side of the ship, where Warbler was.

Simber looked grim. "I've wonderrred in the past if therrre was something strrrange about that island. Therrre werrre times I couldn't see it, but I assumed it was because of its distance, the lighting, and the tides. . . ." He trailed off, lost in thought.

Alex watched Warbler Island as the pirate ship continued past it. His heart dropped, and he could hear people commenting about it. "I'll be right back," he said to Simber.

He ran down to the deck below. "Sky! Crow!" he called out, knowing he had to put aside what had happened earlier. "Sky? Are you down here?" He raced around the deck, frantically looking for them.

"Alex?"

Her voice always surprised him. The husky rasp remained at the edges of her words since the thorn necklace had been removed, and it somehow made her voice more beautiful. He turned, heaving from the run, and saw her eyes were puffy. He felt terrible.

"Sky," he said, "I—need you. Can you come with me?"

She lifted her chin. "Of course," she said. The words were cool, crisp enough to shatter.

Ouch. "Thanks—up a deck, to where Simber is flying."

Halfway up the stairs, he stopped suddenly and turned. Sky bumped into him.

"Oh, sorry," she said, startled. She looked up. They were alone in the stairwell.

Alex stared at her, her pretty eyes, her smooth brown skin, her hair that was bleached by the sun, and his stomach jumped and crashed around inside his ribs. He lifted his hand and it faltered, and then he swallowed hard and gently pushed a strand of her hair to the side.

"Look, I'm the one who's sorry," he whispered. "I know you heard—earlier—and I want to explain, but there's no time right now. I just . . . I kind of feel like I'm cracking apart."

Her mouth twitched.

Alex glanced at her lips, and then found her eyes again. He knew his mind had to change gears. He had a huge problem to fix. But he couldn't just toss aside this thing that consumed his thoughts more often than he wanted to admit. Still, he didn't know what else to do. "Everything is just so . . ." He breathed, she blinked, and he forgot what he was going to say.

Sky didn't speak. She stood very still, looking at him. And then she reached up, slipped her cool fingers into the hair at Alex's neck, and pulled his head toward hers. His eyes closed and he felt her mouth press against his for the briefest, weirdest moment as the world swirled around him. Her lips were cool and soft and a little bit wet, and it didn't feel anything like what he would have expected, which was strangely okay.

When he opened his eyes, his breath escaped in a tiny huff, and he stared at her, his heart still whirling. "Howowah," he said, his brain a jumbled mess.

She raised an eyebrow, a small smile curling at the corner of her lips. "Now," she said calmly, putting a hand on her hip, "what's the big dramatic emergency this time?"

They reached Simber just as Warbler began to grow smaller and move away.

"Oh," said Sky, realizing the problem. She frowned and looked to the west. "Where are we going?"

"We don't know. The ship seems to have a mind of its own." Alex sucked in a deep breath and blew it out, trying to calm his twisting insides enough to concentrate on the issue at hand. He didn't think he could look Simber in the eye for fear of breaking out into a goofy grin.

"Is there any magic you can do to stop it?"

"Not that I know of." Alex racked his brains, but he could think of nothing. "Maybe Ms. Octavia or Florence would have an idea."

"It whispers, you know," Sky said.

"We know," Alex said. "Do you know what it's saying?"

"No."

"No one does."

They stood in silence, with Simber flapping overhead now and then, gazing to the west, wondering where they were going. Florence inched toward them at a slow pace, careful not to upset the boat. "What's going on?" she asked.

Simber explained the situation with the rogue ship, and Florence tried everything she could think of to release the spell on the ship, if that was what powered it. But nothing happened.

"And then therrre's the little prrroblem of the next island," Simber said, pointing a paw.

As he said it, Alex's jaw dropped, for in the distance, water rose from the sea in a giant spout, bursting upward and frothing at the top.

"Thar she blows!" cried the captain. "The bitter white whale!"

As the water spout reached its height and began raining down again, a burst of fire exploded from the sea, unaffected by the water. Flames filled the sky, and with a shuddering roar, rocky ground erupted from below the water's surface, growing taller and wider in the space in front of them. Glowing balls of fire shot up from the center of the rising land, and soon, as the ground rose higher and grew larger, a few sodden, scraggly trees appeared on it, dotting its surface.

The rising island set in motion a giant wave that headed toward them, growing as it rolled. Captain Ahab shouted, "Batten down and hold yer hats! Whatever wears the shape of evil lies ahead!"

The Artiméans who had seen it screamed or watched in shock, some of them running below deck for cover and others hanging on to ropes or hiding inside cabinets. The squirrelicorns took flight and rose high above the wave's height.

Florence gathered Alex and several others close to her, and called out to a few small statues who didn't seem to know what to do, grabbing them in her arms.

Alex didn't dare blink in case he missed something. He glanced at Sky to see if she was okay. She was craning her neck. "Crow!" she shouted, and scrambled to her feet. "Up the ropes!" They both climbed the sail like seasoned sailors.

Alex watched in awe. "Aren't you scared?" he called.

"Only of the wave!" She and Crow held on tightly and looked down. "I've never seen it happen this close up before," she called out. "Isn't Pirate Island incredible?"

Simber, Florence, and Alex looked up at her with surprise, but they didn't have time to ask questions, for a wall of water rose up in front of the bow. The sky above it lit up with fire, silhouetting the two children who clung tightly to the top of the mast, and before anyone could take a last breath, the boat rose at a precipitous angle, crested, and headed down again, taking their stomachs with it. The next wave slammed into their faces and bodies, and everything that wasn't battened down went flying.

Pirate Island

Alex went tumbling backward and water surged up his nose and mouth, but he didn't go far before Florence grabbed his shirt once more. As soon as the giant wave passed over them, he scrambled to his feet, a sodden mess, first to see if any more waves were coming, then looking up to make sure Sky and Crow were still hanging on. He was relieved to see them high and dry.

"Leaders and volunteers to your stations!" he shouted between coughs and sputters. "Count off!" He looked up for Simber but the cat had disappeared. Alex rushed to the side of the ship and peered over, his heart in a clutch. *Not again*, he thought. *Please, no.*

LISA McMANN

But soon he spied the beast flying low to the water, plucking Artiméans from the sea as if he were picking strawberries. A moment later he returned to the ship and deposited Ms. Octavia, Henry, and the fox statue, who immediately started hopping around in a panic, shouting in a small barking voice, "Where's kitten? Where's kitten?"

"She's herrre," Simber said, opening his paw and carefully reaching out to Alex to take her. "Neverrr even hit the waterrr," he said with pride.

"Mewmewmew," said the tiny cat, in the most adorable voice Alex had ever heard.

"She says she wants to be with me," the fox said.

Simber smirked but said nothing.

Alex set the delicate white kitten on the fox's back, where he'd seen her napping earlier, and the fox settled down. "Is that everyone? Henry, Ms. Octavia, are you all right?" Henry sputtered and nodded. Alex reached a hand to Ms. Octavia and helped his instructor to her tentacles.

"It was a lovely swim," Ms. Octavia said, no stranger to the water. "Simber?"

"I was prrreparrred and watching. I got everrryone I saw."

"Great work, Simber," Alex said. "And thank you, Florence—you saved me." For the hundredth time in a matter of days, Alex was beyond grateful that Mr. Today had created such an amazing team to surround him.

"Leaders!" Alex called out. "Report. Rufus?"

"All here!" replied the squirrelicorn.

"Sean?"

"We're good!" Sean shouted from the bow.

"Meg?"

There was no answer.

Alex rushed to the stairwell and shouted down it. "Meg?"

"Everyone's here!" came the muffled shout. "But we've got a few cuts and bruises, and one of the ostrich's legs broke off. Can you send help?"

"On the way," Alex called. He turned to Ms. Octavia and Henry. "Did you get that?"

They both nodded. Henry took off sloshing in his shoes down the stairs at full speed, with Ms. Octavia swishing behind him.

Sky and Crow scrabbled down the mast

"How did you think to do that?" Alex asked, still incredulous.

LISA McMANN

Crow shrugged. "We did a lot of climbing. Trees, mostly, but Sky worked in shipbuilding for a while."

"Well, that's pretty cool. You'll have to teach me to climb like you someday," Alex said.

Crow nodded and tried to hide a grin, embarrassed by the praise. He ran downstairs to help Henry. Sky headed to the bow.

Alex went through the rest of the leader roster, finding everyone present and accounted for. "Whew," he said. And then he looked to the captain's wheel, realizing the captain wasn't on anyone's team, and he hadn't shouted in a while. "Captain?" He rushed through the maze of sopping wet humans and creatures and found Captain Ahab sitting on the deck, his head in his hands.

"Are you okay, Captain?"

The statue looked up. "My peg leg," he growled. "That treacherous whale!"

Alex looked all around. "I don't think the whale took your peg leg."

"Aye, the greedy, monstrous, insatiable thief!" He pounded the deck with his fists. "Relentless beast!"

Alex shook his head and then called out, "Attention! If anyone finds Captain Ahab's peg leg, please return it to the ship's wheel area immediately!" He turned back to the captain. "Don't worry. We'll fix you right up." He looked at the wheel, which began to turn on its own. "Is there anything I can do with this ship? Do you know where we're going?"

But the captain just shook his head. "This ship obeys a ghoulish master. I am useless to you."

"That's not true. We need you," Alex said. He patted the statue on the shoulder, trying to hide his anxiety. "Just sit tight. Ms. Octavia will take care of you soon. Are you in pain?"

"The pain of treachery festers in the darkest depths of the soul and never dies."

Alex nodded. "Okay, then. Catch you later." He turned and made his way to the bow.

Seeing Sean standing at the point with Carina, Sky, and Meghan, Alex went over to them, signaling to Simber to come along, which he did, staying far enough above to keep from disturbing the Unwanteds with his wings, but close enough to hear the conversation.

"Hey," Alex said to the others. Having Carina back made

it feel like old times on the roof of the gray shack. Alex looked out over the calm water to the island that had risen from below the surface. A burst of fire spewed up from the very top of the rocky land. He glanced at Sky, but he could feel his face flush, so he looked ahead again. "Looks like the ship is headed straight for it," he said. He cracked his knuckles and tapped his fingers on the railing. "You know, this is killing me, leaving Lani and Samheed back there."

"Me too," Meghan said. "Ms. Octavia tried everything she could think of to turn it around, but its course is set." She reached out and linked arms with Alex, resting her head on his shoulder. "Sky thinks the ship is going home."

"Home?" The others turned to look at Sky.

"It's Pirate Island. Home to pirates." Sky blushed, perhaps realizing that was obvious.

"But how could anyone live there?" Alex said. "You've seen it disappear and reappear before?"

"Yes, I've seen it from Warbler. It's a volcano island," she said. "There's something very spooky about it. No one really knows how anyone can live there, because it submerges randomly. But somehow they do."

"How do you know?" Sean asked.

"We've seen their ships—they get caught in the current sometimes around the other side of our island. Queen Eagala has added a few of them to our fleet." She paused. "Obviously, we've seen their pirates, too. Some were captured and live on Warbler now. A few escaped a couple of years ago."

Alex leaned his head forward to look at her, all memories of the kiss forgotten now in his quest to figure out what was happening. "Did they escape in a ship like this one? And did they have the thorn necklaces?"

"I think so," Sky said. "Queen Eagala tries to cover up any news of escapees, but word gets out, even though the hand signals limit conversation."

Carina tapped her chin. "I remember when this ship came ashore. The two guys inside were dead."

Alex nodded. "I bet it was them."

"So the whispers of this ship . . ."

"It wants to go home," Sky said, and she sounded convinced. She raised her hand to her forehead as a line of flames reached up from the volcano to enhance the red-gold setting sun. "Looks like we'll be there in a few hours." She turned toward the others with a very serious look on her face. "We need to hope that Pirate Island stays above the surface."

"Why?" Meghan asked. "Maybe if the island is gone, the ship will stop trying to find it."

Sky shook her head. "No. It was heading for the island when it was underwater earlier. It's homed in. But the biggest problem now is if the island sinks when we're anywhere near it. If it does, then this ship and everything on it will get sucked down into the gaping hole left by the volcano."

A Long Night

As it became increasingly clear that the pirate ship was indeed heading straight for the volcanic island, Alex called everyone to the upper deck to discuss the plan before darkness overcame them. Meghan and Ms. Octavia began to light torches around the ship so that everyone could see.

"We've hit a bit of a snag, as you can tell," Alex began. "Our ship is sailing on its own. To our extreme surprise and by no fault of our brave captain, we sailed right past Warbler and now appear to be heading for, well, that lovely-looking place." He took a deep breath, thinking fleetingly that this story would someday,

LISA McMANN

hopefully, be hilarious. But it wasn't today. "We aren't sure what will happen once we reach the island, but we'll keep you posted."

Alex cringed when he saw a wing waving in the air. It was the ostrich from the library. "Yes?"

"You're saying the boat is in control, and we might never get back to Artimé?"

Alex blinked as murmurs began chasing through the group. "No," he said quickly. "I'm not saying that. We will of course get back to Artimé, even if it means Simber carrying us back in groups. Don't worry about that."

Several of the statues began to fight over who would be first to go back to Artimé.

"Guys! Hey!" Alex said.

Simber let out a roar, which stopped all the statues mid-sentence. "Excuse me a moment, Alex," Simber said, and then he flew over to the group of complainers and growled. "Statues, let me rrremind you that you rrreprrresent me. And I am not pleased."

The statues remained quiet. Some of them nodded sheepishly. Simber returned to his spot near Alex. "Sorrry. Please continue."

Alex nodded. "Thank you." He addressed the statues. "Look. I know this is a new situation for many of you, and it's frightening, but I feel like it's better for me to tell you what's going on and admit that we're not sure, rather than try and pretend everything is okay. That's just how we do things," he said, shrugging and smiling a bit, trying to take the fear away while his insides clenched nervously.

Florence gave Alex an encouraging nod.

"So, basically, we don't have a choice. We're in for the ride. And with any luck, we'll be on track again by morning, heading back to Warbler to do the task we set out to do." He put his hands on the railing and spied Sky nearby watching him. "I just want you to know," he said, "that we're going to do everything we can to save Samheed and Lani. It's still our most pressing goal. But all of you are equally important to Artimé"—he looked at Crow and Sky—"and we all need to work together to have the best chance of all of us making it home safely." He paused, and then he said, "Are you with me?"

The response was subdued, more due to the vastness of the sea surrounding them than to lack of enthusiasm. The humans tapped their fists to their chests in support as they said, "I'm with you!" And the statues, eyeing Simber, were more enthusiastic than they'd ever been.

Later, when everyone had eaten and settled down to get some rest, and the captain had a new peg leg thanks to Ms. Octavia, Alex and his friends spread out on their backs at the bow of the ship, where the only sound was the water lapping against the hull and the soft whispers of the vessel. The vast layers of stars above reminded him of the first time he and Sky sat on top of the gray shack, after the lights of Artimé had been doused and nothing else remained. He had cried for Mr. Today, for Simber, for Lani and Samheed, and Sky had been there to comfort him. He glanced at her and saw the stars reflected in her eyes. That night seemed so long ago, but here they were, running up against yet another dead end, and Lani and Samheed were still captured.

Almost as if he and Lani were thinking in time with one another, a small ball of fire raced overhead and came to an abrupt stop in front of Alex's face. It exploded as usual, leaving the fiery outline of a drawing of Lani, with Alex's name in the corner. Alex could barely stand to look at it—it only made him more anxious and upset that they were stranded on this ship.

Carina sat up and looked at the tiny streak of light left behind, going all the way to Warbler and glowing more brightly than usual in the dark night. "What was that?"

Alex sighed, and when he didn't answer, Meghan explained.

Carina reached over and squeezed Alex's shoulder. "Poor guy," she said. "You must feel so helpless."

"Yeah," Alex said.

"At least it's comforting to know Lani is alive and well enough to send spells, though," Carina said, her voice full of hope.

Alex closed his eyes, the sudden pain in his chest making the rest of his body numb. He couldn't bear to look at Sky, or anyone else. "Yes," he managed finally. "At least there's that."

Carina squeezed once more and then lay back again with a rueful smile. "We'll find them," she said.

Alex couldn't respond. His mind was whirling with confusion, and his stupid feelings kept messing everything up. Oh, what he would give for this moment to be in Quill again, where feelings weren't allowed.

Finally he got up and stood in awe as Pirate Island loomed

large and tall before them. It hadn't spewed any fire since sunset, and by the light of the night sky, Alex could see a few patches of bushes and scraggly trees growing sideways from the rocky volcano's shaft, with large blankets of seaweed draped over craggy points.

The ship skirted around a shoal as if it knew it was there, and headed for the calm, deep water of a lagoon. With a startling clap the sails dropped all at once and the ship glided, slowing to a stop not more than twenty feet from the rocky shore of Pirate Island.

"We're here," Alex whispered. It felt sacred and spooky, the only sounds the whispers of the ship and the squeaky reel and splash of the anchor chain eerily releasing of its own accord.

Alex looked around, finding Simber in his usual spot near the stern. He lifted his hand and drew a circle in the air with his finger. Simber nodded and flew toward the base of the volcanic island, weaving around rocks and clearing small juts and peaks, searching for signs of life.

By now the others had stood too, and they all watched in silence, looking down into the murky water and up at the volcano, hoping it was tired of shooting fire for now, because they were uncomfortably close.

» » « «

It was a long, anxious thirty minutes before Simber came back into view again, and half the ship let out a sigh of relief to see him, backlit by the moon. He drew close and landed on the nearby shoal, resting his wings for the first time since that morning, though he didn't need to. Alex moved to the side of the ship nearest Simber and leaned over the railing.

"Did you find anything?"

Simber folded his wings and licked his shoulder where some water had splashed on it, and then he turned his attention to Alex and the dozens of others who had tuned in to listen. "No signs of life, not human, crrreature, or anything else, that I could detect," he said. "It's completely deserrrted."

Still Stuck

Alex and Simber decided it was safer being on the ship than on the island, and there wasn't much they could do in the dark, so everyone tried to settle in for the night.

Alex stayed on the deck near Simber. He lay on his back staring up at the sky, his arms propping up his head. He couldn't sleep knowing that at any second, without warning, the volcano could sink back into the sea, creating a vortex that would pull millions of gallons of seawater and their boat into its mouth and swallow them up.

The ship's whispers grew stronger, or maybe it was the quiet night that made the whispers seem louder; Alex wasn't sure. He could hear a soft purr somewhere nearby, more kittenlike than Simber-like. It was a comforting sound, and Alex was glad someone was feeling comfortable. He couldn't stop thinking about being responsible for all these lives. He couldn't stop thinking about Gunnar Haluki losing Henry and Lani. About Carina's son growing up an orphan, never really having a chance to know either of his parents. About Artimé losing so many great leaders. Maybe it had been a bad idea to bring so many of them with him.

But he needed them. If they could ever get out of this lagoon, Alex would need them desperately. He fell into a fitful sleep, waking at every sound, expecting to be swallowed by the volcano at any moment.

When at last the sun rose, Alex stood up, shivering a little in the cool morning air, waiting for the rays to warm him. He could see Quill, a dot in the east just this side of the sun, and Warbler, a large lump on the horizon with its rocks jutting out.

In front of him the volcanic Pirate Island loomed blue-black and craggy and ominous, throwing spooky shadows everywhere. As far as Alex could tell, the fiery outburst had subsided completely.

Alex peered beyond Pirate Island to the west, knowing there was one more island out there somewhere. He thought he spied something rising up from the water, but it wavered and moved, the sea playing tricks on his tired eyes.

Simber stretched his hind legs, first one, then the other, and then arched his back and yawned.

Alex leaned over the side. "I want to explore," he whispered, not wanting to wake anyone. "Maybe there's a clue somewhere about how to deprogram the ship."

Simber nodded. "Just you?"

Alex thought for a moment. He shook his head. "Be right back," he said. He picked his way over sleeping bodies on the deck, making his way to the bow, where his friends had camped out for the night. He bent down next to Carina and shook her shoulder.

She roused and was wide awake in an instant. "What's wrong?" she asked. She smoothed her pixie-cut hair, but it still stood up in one spot.

"Will you come explore the island with Simber and me?"

"Sure," Carina said. She got nimbly to her feet.

Alex grinned. He stepped over to Sky and found her already awake. "Want to explore?" Alex whispered.

Sky nodded once, and then she said, "But not without Crow."

Alex flashed her a puzzled look. "Okay," he said. "He can come too. No problem."

Sky stood up and woke Crow, and then the four went back to the side of the ship nearest to Simber. Crow rubbed his eyes sleepily as he stumbled along.

Alex signaled to Simber and the great cat unfurled his wings, making a bridge to the ship. Alex hoisted Crow up on the wing first, and the boy crawled along it to Simber's back without fear. Sky went next, and then Carina, and finally Alex.

"Hang on," Simber said quietly, then loped along the shoal and flapped his powerful wings. Soon they were soaring toward the rocky shore, and then the short journey was over. Simber landed and everyone got down.

"Stay close. If anything begins to move, jump onto my back," Simber said.

Alex hesitated. He glanced back at the ship, realizing that

LISA McMANN

275 « Island of Fire

thanks to Simber, the four of them were probably safer here on the base of the sinking volcano than the others were in the boat.

"That's why," Sky said softly, reading Alex's mind. "I can't leave Crow. We live and die together. I took that oath when I took him with me from Warbler."

Alex and Sky followed behind Simber, Carina, and Crow. Alex glanced at Sky with admiration. "That's pretty noble of you," he said.

"He's the only family I have now."

Alex wondered what she meant, but he didn't dare ask. It felt personal.

She touched his elbow. "I'm sorry I kissed you," she said softly. "That was . . . weird. I know that you and Lani are . . . whatever. It was just—I wanted to feel like—" She sighed. "Oh, never mind. I know you and Lani . . . you know. And not me, and that's okay, because I'm not sure about . . . things . . . either. So you don't have to, like, feel bad." She blushed, fingering the scars at her throat.

Alex looked down, feeling strange and empty inside. A sort of airy rushing sound batted him around his ears, almost making him dizzy. But when he remembered to breathe, his brain went back to Mr. Today and how he'd seemed destined to be alone. "Don't worry," Alex said, trying to sound cheerful. "I already forgot about it." But it was the biggest lie he'd ever told. So big that saying it made his skin hurt.

"Oh," Sky said. "Good." Then she added, "Me too." And she was silent.

They climbed over rocks and globs of seaweed and tiny pools of water, looking for any clues that would indicate why a ship would want to come here. After a quarter of an hour they reached a long, flat piece of land with some vegetation and wet sand. Several planks of rotting wood stuck out of the dirt.

Alex pointed to it. "Could someone have lived here once? It looks like the frame of a house."

"That's what I was thinking," Carina said.

There was a rivulet coming off the side of the mountain, washing away some of the sand. Alex put his finger in it and tasted. "This is freshwater," he mused. He didn't understand where it could possibly have come from.

Crow ran ahead, climbing some of the rocks to see if he could find the origin of the stream.

"Stay close," Sky warned.

LISA McMANN

"I'm just going right here," Crow said. "There's a flat spot and a little pond." He hopped up and looked around. Carina followed him.

Alex frowned. He wasn't sure they'd find any clues about ships in a place where ships couldn't get to. He gazed around the flat area, and then went to the edge of it, where waves lapped the shore, and peered into the water.

A fish jumped almost under his nose. "Whoa," he said, and he stepped back, laughing at himself. It jumped again in almost the same place, which was strange, and then Alex saw it had a hook in its mouth attached to a line of fishing wire. The fish sank straight down, as if it was being pulled, and disappeared.

He whirled around to tell the others, but before he could say anything, Carina gave a shout and Crow gasped.

A Face in the
Pool

What's happening?" Alex said, and he ran for the rocks where everyone else had already gathered.

"A person!" Crow said. "I saw a person!"

"Are you sure it wasn't your reflection?" Sky asked him.

"*I'm* sure it wasn't his reflection. I saw it too," Carina said. She knelt down at the edge of the shallow pool of water, stuck her arm in, and pushed the wet sand away from the bottom. Sky and Alex stood behind her, looking over her shoulder. Simber opted to watch from above.

As Carina slid the sand to the side, she revealed the water's

LISA McMANN

bed. It wasn't the black rock that made up almost the entire island. Not this part. The bottom of the pool was clear, like a window.

Crow put his face near the water. "I can see down in there!" he said with a loud whisper. "There are people moving around, way down at the bottom!"

Carina made room for Alex and Sky. It was like they were standing on top of a glass box, or a skylight on the roof of a tall building. They could look through this window and see the glass walls with fish swimming outside the sides.

"It's like an aquarium," Alex said, breathless. "Only the water is on the outside, and the glass encases a dry world." He looked up at Simber. "It's a *reverse* aquarium."

"Look," Sky said, pointing. "Here, on an upper level. There's a garden."

"And there's a playground at the bottom too," Crow said. "See the little kids jumping around?"

"It's really light down there," Carina mused, "so there must be more skylights like this one. And there are walkways and little rooms on this upper level too. But look—see how the volcano runs down the center of it all?"

"That must be theirrr sourrrce of heat," Simber said. "And the sun, I suppose."

The five watched the people, oblivious to the ceiling visitors in their busyness, scurry around far below.

Alex pointed wordlessly to the floor directly beneath them as a sliding glass door opened, making a sheet of water pour into the reverse aquarium. Someone walked in through the water wearing a strange mask. The door slid shut again. All the water that had come in disappeared through a grate in the floor, none of it flowing to the floors below.

The person was carrying a string of fish on a hook. He took his mask off and placed it on a shelf, and then walked around a corner with the fish. "That hook is his hand," Alex said, intrigued. "He caught the fish right where I was standing, there." He pointed.

It was Crow who noticed the creatures. In a real aquarium attached to the reverse aquarium, Crow could just barely see things swimming around. "I can't see what those things are, but they don't look fish-shaped," he reported.

"I wonder if anyone down there can help us," Alex said. "I suppose we could dive down and see if they notice us through the glass wall."

LISA McMANN

Everyone was quiet, wondering if these people were friendly, or if being seen would only get them into more trouble.

"They seem . . . normal," Carina said weakly. She looked over her shoulder at Alex. "I think we have to try. We don't have a choice."

Alex nodded. "I can try right here, I suppose." He scratched his head, thinking. "No, this spot is where the guy was fishing. It didn't look like anyone else was over there."

"The ship took us to a cerrrtain spot," Simber said. "Perrrhaps forrr a rrreason."

"Good point," Alex said. "Let's go back there. And then we'll have help from our army in case we need it."

While Carina, Alex, and Simber plotted, Sky stared through the glass, frowning. She nudged her brother and pointed. He turned to look, and then he gasped. Before anyone could stop him, Crow began pounding on the glass with all his might.

Sky whipped her hair out of her eyes with her hand and stared, then grabbed Crow's arm to stop him from pounding. "No," she said. "We don't want them all to see us. Watch."

When a woman walked on the floor nearest them, not

twenty feet away, Sky leaned over the glass, stretching her shirt wide to block the sun. "Watch," she whispered again, "I'm a cloud." Her heart thumped.

The woman, in a sudden shadow, looked up. She frowned, and then her mouth slacked and her orange eyes grew wide.

Sky choked on a sob, which caused the others to turn and see what was happening. Immediately, through her tears, Sky's hands flew through the air, speaking a language few of the others knew.

The woman held a finger to her lips and looked all around. Alex went to Sky's side and put his hand on her shoulder, feeling it quake. Crow simply clutched the rocks on the edge of the pool and stared, a look of agony on his face.

Then the woman signed something very quickly and scurried away to a set of stairs. When she disappeared, Sky slumped back into Alex's arms and sobbed.

He pulled her to him and patted her back, unsure what to do.

Carina knelt next to Crow. "What's wrong?"

Crow's face crumbled. "That stupid creep told us she was dead!" he cried, his face hot with anger.

"Who is that woman?" Alex whispered into Sky's hair, though he thought he knew.

She took a deep breath and pulled back, still clutching Alex's shirt. "Our mother," she said.

Waiting

I told her about the ship," Sky said. She let go of Alex, wiped her eyes with the back of her hand, and sniffed a few times. She slid back to the edge of the glass so she could see. "She said don't dive down. Don't let anyone see us."

The others stared at her.

"She's going to try to find out how to disenchant the ship so we can get away, but she's only—she's a—" Sky pounded her forehead and took a few deep breaths, blowing them out. "Come on, Sky," she muttered.

Alex had never seen her so upset before.

LISA McMANN

"She's a slave to the pirates," Crow said. His fiery eyes narrowed into slits.

Carina put her hand on Crow's shoulder, and he let her leave it there. "I'm sorry," she said. "And I'm sorry someone told you she was dead. What a horrible thing to do."

"It was Queen Eagala." He nearly spat the words out.

Carina said nothing. She only lowered her head and rested it on her free hand, closing her eyes.

Simber perched on a nearby rock, not wanting to be seen through the glass. "Did yourrr motherrr say how much time the volcano stays above the surrrface?" he asked in a rare gentle voice.

Sky shook her head. "There wasn't time to ask. She had to hurry."

"That's okay," Alex said. "We'll wait. And then, once we've got Sam and Lani, we'll figure out how to get her out of here." His stomach felt like he'd just swallowed a dozen lead milk shakes. *One more impossible thing.*

Sky looked up at him, her bottom lip quivering.

He read the question in her eyes. "I mean it," he said.

The look she gave him was enough to warm Alex through.

LISA McMANN

He glanced at Carina, who was watching them curiously with a little smile. Alex bit his lip. It didn't matter what anyone thought. He would be the same as before with Lani until Lani figured out that he was never around to hang out with anymore, which wouldn't take long because Lani was pretty brilliant. And even if he wanted to, there was no way Alex could go running to spend all his free time with Sky after that—it would hurt Lani's feelings and make him seem like a total flake. Not a good look for a leader. Maybe that's why Mr. Today had stayed alone for so long.

Alex felt his face growing warm with all the staring. "Look," he said, "is that her coming back?"

But it was someone else—a woman in an enormous, flouncy, feathery dress. At least Alex had turned the attention away from him. He got to his feet and stretched out a cramp in his leg, then went to join Simber, who had found a place to perch on a cliff above. "I don't know what else to do but wait," Alex said. "Do you?"

Simber sampled the air. "Florrrence knows we'rrre herrre. She can send Rrrufus if they need us. I don't think therrre's anything else we can do."

Alex's stomach growled. "We should have eaten breakfast."

Simber yawned and closed his eyes. Alex shrugged and sat down, leaning against the beast.

Carina, Crow, and Sky waited by the pool of water.

All of them desperately hoped the volcano would remain above the surface.

Crow's harsh whisper startled Alex awake. He scrambled down the rocks as Sky spoke with her hands at top speed, and then he peered over the edge and watched the woman hold up a piece of paper with strange words on it.

"Memorize it!" Sky said. "Hurry!"

"I'll take the last line," Alex said.

"I've got the third," Carina said.

"First," Crow said.

"Second," Sky said.

They all stared, trying to think of tricks that would help them remember the strange words. Alex suddenly remembered that he had his notepad with him, and he pulled it from his pocket. He tapped it, making a pencil drop out of nowhere. He began scribbling the words. Too soon, the woman snatched the paper down and shoved it in her meager peasant dress.

They each recited their lines, and Alex wrote down the words, correcting the spelling as the others told him to. When he finished, he held the notepad facedown just above the water.

Sky's mother squinted, trying to see it, and then she nodded and began speaking to Sky once again. Sky replied, and they went back and forth for several seconds, almost as if they were arguing.

Then Sky gasped. Her mother whipped around. A rugged man in a billowy shirt with gold bars on the shoulders approached her. She shook her head vehemently, but he grabbed her by the arm and pulled her away. The last thing Alex saw was Sky's mother turning back and mouthing the word "Go."

Sky held her fingers to her lips and sent a kiss, but it was too late. Her mother didn't see it.

The Death Enchantment

Sky scrambled down the rocks with the others right behind her, and she told them everything as they hopped back onto Simber and headed to the ship.

"She said the pirate ships are ancient and enchanted with a lost language, the original language of their owners, which is why we can't understand what it's whispering," Sky explained. "My mother said this saying is carved into the wall of the volcano, and she's seen her master disenchant ships before when they've returned to the lagoon. I guess when someone dies aboard the ship, the ship immediately whispers its wishes to turn back home, and steers itself there."

"Weird," Alex remarked. "It must have run aground on our island as the sailors were dying. It never had a chance to go home."

"So it's been whispering ever since," Carina mused. "Yes, as I recall, Mr. Today thought the sailors might be able to be revived, and he tried, but it was too late."

"Did your mother say anything else?"

Sky was silent for a minute. And then she said in a softer voice, "Mother said we should go quickly and never come back. There's no way to save her." She bit her lip hard. "Everyone from the outside who has tried to get in has drowned."

Alex looked at her, feeling a rush of courage. "Then we'll have to figure out how not to drown."

Sky looked down. "You mean it," she said. It wasn't a question.

"Yes. But we're not prepared today. We'll have to come back. After."

"Of course," she whispered. "After we get the others home safely."

Home, Alex thought. *She called it home.*

The conversation weighed heavily on all of them as Simber

291 « Island of Fire

dropped the four aboard the ship. As he did so, the volcano rumbled and a belch of flames shot from its mouth. Bits of glowing lava dropped down and sizzled in the lagoon, and a small glob landed on the ship's deck. Sean jumped to attention and stamped the fire out.

"Sheesh," Alex said, eyeing the volcano. "Let's get out of here." Alex and the others placed their hands on the ship's railing. He nodded to Sky. "You want to do it?"

She looked startled. "Me?"

"Why not?"

"Just hurrry, please," Simber said from the shoal. "We'rrre still in grrrave dangerrr."

Sky nodded. "Okay." She read the words in a slightly faltering voice, not knowing if she had the accent right. When she finished, they all craned their necks and strained their ears, listening to the whispers.

When nothing happened, Alex nudged her. "It's okay. Try again." He knew more than anybody that things didn't always work right the first time.

Sky took a deep breath, and she and Alex shared a quick, private smile. She had to remember to breathe too sometimes.

And then she read the words once more, louder this time.

Everyone waited.

After a moment, the ship's whispers grew faint, and soon they were gone completely. With a startling snap, the sails flew up and the anchor chain groaned as it wound itself. The Artiméans cheered.

"Captain Ahab!" Alex shouted. "The ship is now yours. Can you get us out of here?"

"Blast my skull!" came the muffled reply.

The ship's sails had already picked up the breeze, and the vessel began to move as the captain clumped to the wheel. He shouted orders to some statues he'd trained on the sails, and with help from Florence and Simber, they managed to turn the ship around, moving nimbly around the shoal as if the captain had done it a million times before.

When they were on the open water once again, Alex grabbed a few sandwiches from below and brought them to the upper deck. He found Sky, Crow, and Henry at the stern, glumly watching Pirate Island grow smaller.

"Sandwich?" he asked, holding them out.

"Thanks," they said, each taking one. Alex sat next to Henry.

The four ate together in silence, with Simber, as always, overhead.

"I'm really sorry about your mother being there," Alex said. He knew he could never understand what they were feeling because his experience with his mother was so different, so . . . clinical. But he thought she might feel something like he had when Mr. Today died. That overwhelming pain and grief. He knew a sandwich couldn't fix it. And he knew he really couldn't make it better for them. It was going to be hard no matter what. But he also knew that when he was having his darkest moments, Sky was there, and Alex would try to be there for her too.

Sky picked at her sandwich, not really eating it. Crow took a bite and chewed it forever before he could swallow it.

Alex looked at Henry, who had lost his mother, and he just shook his head. "So much stupid grief," he muttered. "Every day brings another broken heart." He stood up abruptly, a little embarrassed at his poetic sentiment, but no one seemed to think it was a silly thing to say. Alex gave each of his friends a quick squeeze on the shoulder, and walked through the crowd to the bow, feeling completely beside himself. As he stood there, wind in his hair, he realized how much he ached to make something again—something creative. Something useful. Something beautiful or meaningful. It seemed like forever since he'd had a chance to just sit and create something.

He thought about Mr. Today and the Museum of Large. How the old mage had worked out his private thoughts by fixing up this ship, and how he'd created so many amazing creatures and statues. "If we ever make it home," he said to the wind, "I'm going to build something beautiful."

Gondoleery Rising

S ecretary!" Aaron barked.

Eva Fathom rushed to Aaron's office, finding him standing at the window yet again, staring out at the water. "Yes, High Priest Aaron?"

Aaron turned slightly toward her, acknowledging her presence but not taking his eyes off the sea. "Who are my enemies?" he asked.

Eva's eyes widened. She hesitated, not sure what Aaron wanted to hear. "Artimé, of course," she said.

Aaron scowled. "Here in Quill, I mean."

"You have none that I know of," Eva said smoothly.

"Of course I do. Every leader has enemies. I need you to find out who mine are, and then round up the Restorers for a meeting here at the palace this evening." Aaron picked his teeth with a thin stick he kept in his breast pocket.

"I'll begin right away," Eva said, her voice even, though she was quite disgusted by the task, which would take a normal person more than a day to complete.

Eva set out with a driver, studying her list of Restorers, many of whom she hadn't seen since the attack on Artimé. Most of the people on the list were Wanteds, so she directed the guard to stop at their homes, which was the likeliest place to find them in the middle of the day. Eva hurriedly approached each door and spoke to the Restorers, taking care not to expose anyone who was keeping his affiliation a secret, and asking, when appropriate, who they thought Aaron's enemies might be. She made the rounds as the day drew on, making her last stop the home of Gondoleery Rattrapp just as the sun was disappearing over the wall.

Eva strode up the walk and glanced into the window of Gondoleery's living quarters, noticing that the curtains were drawn and light behind them seemed to make them glow. The curtains weren't completely closed, and a dagger of brightness stabbed through them. Eva stopped walking and puzzled over it for a moment. And then, instead of going to the door, Eva snuck up to the window and peered in.

Her heart clutched. Gondoleery's living quarters had been transformed into something so incredible that Eva had to turn around and look at Quill to make sure she wasn't going senile. She turned back to the slit in the curtain and drank in the sight.

The entire room was covered in ice.

Stalactites of ice came down from the ceiling and stalagmites grew up from the floor, and all of it glowed a bright blue-white. The furniture was encased in it. And in the middle of the room, atop a chair that had bloated to twice its size due to the layers of ice that had built up on it, sat Gondoleery Rattrapp, wearing dark glasses and a patchwork coat adorned with—Eva had to look twice to make sure—chicken feathers.

Eva didn't quite know what to make of it. How could the ice even exist in the heat of Quill? There was something vaguely familiar about it. Something that tugged at her memory. But right now, Eva had a new question on her mind.

She faithfully went to the door and knocked. She waited a few minutes and knocked again. Just as she decided that Gondoleery was going to ignore her, the door flew open.

"Oh, hello," Gondoleery said. She now wore her regular clothing, and there was no sign of the dark glasses.

"Greetings," Eva said. She slid over to one side of the doorway, trying to see inside the house. "Aaron wanted me to ask you if you could come to a Restorers meeting at the palace in about an hour." She managed a glance into the living quarters and saw that it looked just like every other Wanted house in Quill. There was no ice anywhere.

Gondoleery didn't seem anxious at all about Eva standing there, and she didn't seem to be hiding anything either. "The Restorers?" she said with a laugh. "I thought we had disbanded."

Eva smiled. "Seems that way, doesn't it?" she mused. "I guess Aaron wants to see who of the former Restorers is still on his side and perhaps find out if he has any enemies."

Gondoleery laughed out loud, which was something the people of Quill never did, so it was all the more shocking to Eva. "Aaron? Enemies? Ohhh, well, of course not. How could anyone be against that boy?" Gondoleery looked hard at Eva.

Eva lifted her chin ever so slightly, her lips set in a line. "Exactly," she said, her voice thin but not without a hint of accusation as well.

They stood for a moment, regarding each other through narrowed eyes. Finally Gondoleery broke the strained silence. "Please tell the high priest I can't make the meeting."

Eva nodded slightly. "I will deliver the message."

As the Quillitary vehicle carried Eva back to the palace at a snail's pace, Eva Fathom gazed out the window, lost in thought.

Warbler Calls

Inspiration struck, and as the ship traveled toward Warbler, Alex took out his notebook and drew tiny pictures of each member of his army. He tapped them with a little bit of rubber, affixing the magical coating that would keep it from being destroyed under most circumstances. By late afternoon the pirate ship was drawing near to Warbler again, and this time it was heading straight for it. Alex was relieved, but still jittery. It was a dangerous mission—the evidence of which was found in the fresh scars around Meghan's neck.

As they drew close to the island, Alex gathered all the

Artiméans together again to discuss the mission and go over the plan. He held up the map, reminded everyone of their routes, and then he handed out the pictures he'd drawn earlier. "Even if you've never tried magic, you should be able to do this. If you are captured or in trouble, close your eyes and touch this drawing, and think or say the word 'seek.' It will send out a ball of fire, show me your picture, and guide me to your location. We will come for you. Don't be afraid." He paused, a lump in his throat, while he waited for everyone to either pocket their picture if they had pockets, or for Meghan to stick it to their bellies if they were statues or creatures.

"Now would be a good time to get some water and food if you can stand to eat," he said. "I sure can't," he added with a grin, which brought a round of nervous laughs. "I'll see you back at your stations in twenty minutes, ready to go."

They all dispersed, leaving Alex alone with his thoughts again. He bounced on the balls of his feet, focused but anxious, and took a few deep breaths. Simber flew over to him.

"And what if *you'rrre* capturrred or in trrrouble?"

Alex looked up. "What?"

"You gave everrryone a way to call for help but yourrrself.

LISA McMANN

Don't tell me I'm going to have to rrransack the whole island searrrching forrr you," he said.

"Oh—I—" he started. "I guess I didn't think of that." He paused, and then said, "But I can't give a drawing to myself, because the seek spell wouldn't go anywhere."

"I'm awarrre of that," Simber said. He held the side of his paw to a burning torch for a few moments, brought it to his mouth, and bit down hard, making a cracking noise. He turned his paw up and let something slide from his mouth into it. "Somebody's got to take carrre of you, I suppose," he said gruffly. He tossed it to Alex.

Alex caught it and opened his hand. It was the stone dewclaw from Simber's paw.

"Oh, Simber," Alex said. "You didn't have to ruin yourself."

"Well, I can't drrraw. Besides, I don't use that claw anyway. I didn't exactly make it, but it grrrew afterrr Marrrcus made me, so I'm hoping it counts as something I crrreated. It's all I have. Just stick it in yourrr pocket and be quiet about it." Simber frowned, which was an even surer sign that he cared.

Alex could hardly speak. "Thank you," he said in a quiet voice.

Simber nodded and went back to his post.

Alex put the stone claw into his pocket, and it clinked against something. Alex reached farther and pulled out the two spell prototypes that Lani and Samheed had made.

"Oh yeah," he said, smiling. He closed his hand over them and wished on them. And then slowly he opened his hand and stared at them, thinking hard. "Wait a second," he whispered. His lips parted and he sucked in a short breath. And then he closed his hand over them tightly and pumped his fist. "Yeah," he said. "That's a bonus."

As he slipped them back into his pocket, the captain called out, "Blast my skull! It's land!"

The Front Line

From the deck, the Unwanteds could see no sign of
life on the shores of Warbler. "It's just like last time,"
Meghan said in a soft voice to the first group. "Don't
be fooled. Right, guys?" she looked at Sky and Crow.

They nodded. "There are eight or ten guards in the trees,"
Sky said softly. "They know we're here, but they won't alert
anybody yet—they don't want to be seen, and they don't know
we know they're there. They are experts with the sleep darts,
so they feel very confident right now."

"Do you know how many darts they have?" Alex asked.

"At least a dozen each, I'd guess." Sky lifted her chin in

LISA McMANN

defiance as she gazed at the island. "They're very accurate, though, so they never expect to use them all."

Alex nodded. He checked the sun, which hung low over Pirate Island. "We've got about an hour of daylight left," he said. He turned to get reassurance from Simber as his stomach started flipping like a fish on the sand. Simber nodded.

"First wave," Alex said, trying to make his voice sound commanding, "you're up. Be careful." He turned to the fox and kitten. "You know what to do."

They both nodded. Fox's hind legs jittered with excitement, and Kitten stood up on Fox's head. With a nimble leap, the driftwood fox jumped over the side of the ship and splashed in the water, bobbing immediately to the surface. He began swimming with all his might. Kitten rode high and dry—except for the initial splash, of course. Florence followed, stepping carefully off the ship as Simber put his weight on the other end to balance it. She gathered up the rest of the statues in her arms like a bundle of sticks and made her way to the shore in a few long strides, just barely beating Fox and Kitten. Everyone else stayed on the ship.

Meghan gripped Alex's arm as Florence set everyone down

on the sand. "Just when you think you're safe," she whispered. "Bam!"

Right on cue, the first round of sleep darts soared through the air. The tiki statue remained on board to count darts with its three sets of eyes, and Simber hovered above the ship, waiting.

When the darts bounced off the statues, Captain Ahab hobbled around, picking them up and putting them inside his hollow peg leg, and the statues, unaffected, kept walking. There was a moment when no darts flew. "They're shocked," Sky said. "But now they're recovering and reloading."

A moment later the darts began again, pelting the statues like a freak desert hailstorm. In the flurry, the fox and the kitten darted into the trees and disappeared. Charlie loped after them.

"Magicians ready?" Alex called. He pulled out a component in each hand and held them. When the darts thinned out and the tiki statue had counted one hundred and fifty, he said, "Go!"

"Attack dart throwers!" the magicians commanded, each launching two origami dragons. The flaming dragons soared toward the trees, seeking out their invisible targets.

"Okay, Simber. You're up." Alex said.

Simber beat the wind and flew through the air just as the dragons began to explode, pointing out the hidden dart throwers. Florence and the other statues grabbed the ones who fell from their posts attempting to escape the fierce fiery dragons, and Simber plucked all the other dart throwers from the trees. From the ship, Ms. Octavia was the best long-distance shot, and she froze any of them who tried to get away, while Florence cast spells on the ones within their grasp on the beach.

Soon all the orange-eyed dart throwers were contained and placed in a neat stack on the beach, frozen. Simber and Florence checked the trees once more, finding no one else. Florence turned to the ship and gave Alex a thumbs-up that all was clear. Then she barked out an order and most of the statues began to move along the perimeter of the island, staying close to the trees to guide any stray, fleeing, or lost Artiméans to safety. Florence disappeared, making her way to the other side of the island, where the entrance nearest Queen Eagala's cave was, in case any problems arose there.

"Rufus, your team is clear to go," Alex said. "Be safe up there."

The small army of squirrelicorns took off flying for the center of the island.

Alex turned to the humans. "Meg, if there are any problems, send me a seek spell. And if Lani and Sam both make it back here, send out Lani's so I know. The squirrelicorns are monitoring above and will alert Florence to any activity. Once things move this way according to plan, she'll head back here to get the statues loaded on the ship."

Meghan nodded. He face was white and she gripped the railing. This was a little too real for her.

Alex glanced at the setting sun once more. "How long has it been?"

"Eight minutes since Fox and Kitten made a break for it," Sean said.

Alex set his jaw. "I can't stand this."

"You have to give them time," Sky said.

"I know." He stared at the island, unable to see anyone at all.

The agonizing minutes crawled by. Alex fingered Lani and Samheed's spell components in his pocket, waiting. "Time?" he asked after a while.

"Twelve minutes."

"Sheesh." Alex dropped his head in his hands and wiped away the sweat.

Everyone else paced, or wriggled a foot nervously.

Finally Sean touched Alex's shoulder. "Fifteen, my friend," he said. "Let's do this."

"Okay." Alex sucked in a breath and pulled the two proto-type components out of his pocket. He clenched them in his fist and held his hand in front of him. He let out the breath, concentrating on the items in his hand, and whispered, "Seek."

Two flaming balls whooshed out of Alex's hand and raced to the shore, going in different directions, and soon they were hidden by trees. "Come on," Alex whispered. He blew out another nervous breath and gave a grim smile to his friends. "Okay," he said. He looked at Crow, Henry, and Sky, and then at Sean and Carina. "Ready?"

They nodded.

Alex turned back to Sky and Crow. "Are you sure you want to do this?"

Both of them looked sure. "Yes," they said, breathless.

Alex nodded, and then he took out two invisibility paintbrushes from his vest and addressed Crow and Sky. "We'll leave one of your arms unpainted so that we can see where you are, but this way no one will recognize you. But we need to hurry—it'll wear off in fifteen or twenty minutes."

They held an arm out and Alex painted the rest of them quickly.

"Why aren't you painting all of us?" Henry asked.

"Because we don't want to have to call out to find each other—we'd be discovered for sure. And we will lose each other if we're all invisible. Plus Lani and Sam won't be able to see us then either, and they won't understand what's happening. We can't risk them not believing we are who we say we are."

Henry shrugged. "Guess that makes sense." He wanted Lani to see him, that was for sure.

Everyone but Meghan removed their vests and held them high above their heads with one hand as they climbed down a rope to the water, careful not to get their vests too wet. Then Sean and Alex loaded the nearly invisible Sky and Crow on their shoulders to make sure they didn't lose sight of them completely in the water.

"Be safe," Meghan called out as the six made for the shore.

She stood by Ms. Octavia and the tiki statue and nibbled on her fingernails, the giant bag of spell components in reach so that she could defend the ship if she needed to.

Alex glanced back. "Don't worry, Meg. We've got this. Sean and Carina will be right here on the beach in sight at all times to fight off attackers and get the team home."

As they reached shallower water, all six now walking independently toward the beach, a ball of fire came whizzing through the trees and stopped in front of Alex. It exploded, but this time it wasn't Lani's face looking back at him.

Alex gasped. It was the fiery outline of a tiny porcelain kitten.

Hope at Last

It was the end of Samheed's second week of work on Warbler, but there were no days off here. He swung his dulled ax over and over, silently splitting logs for ships. It was crazy how much his muscles ached and burned, and there was no satisfying crash of the ax breaking the wood to go with it. He didn't dare slow his pace, though, or attempt to sever the leash—there were at least ten other young men and women out here who would report him in an instant, including the project manager, who'd had his thorns removed recently and liked to remind everyone how hard he worked to get that privilege.

The only thing Samheed could think about to get him

LISA McMANN

through each day was the sign language class with Lani. That was the only time he was certain he'd see her, though they were slowly exchanging information about where they regularly were at certain times of the day, and they tried to catch glimpses of each other in passing.

He'd seen her this morning, just for a second, her long black hair disappearing around a corner. That moment made his throat ache on and off all day, but it kept him going, kept him working hard. The harder he worked and the more obedient he was, the sooner he'd be off this chain, and then he'd be able to move about a bit more freely. He'd even be allowed to eat dinner with Lani. Everything he did was motivated by a chance to see her, and their chance to escape.

And when he thought of escape, his mouth soured, because certainly by now someone from Artimé would have done something to rescue them. Lani's father, for sure, if no one else cared enough—he was the high priest, after all. He could do anything. That Gunnar hadn't come was the one thing that still gave Samheed pause—perhaps there was some horrible reason why no one had rescued them even though Lani's seek spells seemed to be going through and she sent them as often as she could. Maybe the spell couldn't find Alex, or something had happened to him. Or maybe Artimé was too far away and the spell couldn't get there. He wanted to believe that his friend Alex would do anything for him. But he was beginning to lose hope.

There was only one good thing that had come out of this, and it was the one thing that kept Samheed from giving up. Lani. He knew she must still be very fond of Alex, though she seemed to enjoy holding Sam's hand a lot even when she didn't need to. But if Alex ever showed up to help them, Lani would surely go back to liking him. It hurt Sam's stomach to think about it.

But Alex wasn't coming. And Lani was all Samheed had. So he was going to let his heart do whatever it had to do to keep him from losing his mind, stuck here in this horrible place.

The project manager startled him out of his thoughts, calling for a five-minute break. Samheed knew that he could take the break with the others, but if he kept working, the project manager would be impressed. So Samheed waved off the others and doggedly continued as they headed to the water area.

And then the strangest thing happened. Just as Samheed

began to swing, a tiny, shiny white *thing* jumped on the log in front of him. Samheed pulled the swing just in time and wiped the sweat from his eyes, thinking he might be seeing things. He looked closer and saw it was a porcelain kitten.

Where in the world did you come from? he wondered. He looked all around, making sure no one was watching, and then he knelt down next to the log. The kitten moved. And then Samheed heard a sound. "Mewmewmew," it said in a tiny voice. It hopped up and down on the log, and then it jumped and tumbled down and ran over toward Sam's giant pile of wood. It looked back at Samheed as if it were waiting.

Samheed looked around again. Was this a trick to see if he'd just keep working? But he'd never seen anything like a living statue on Warbler before. They didn't exist here. He took a step toward it. The kitten hopped up and down excitedly, then ran back to Samheed and turned around and pranced back to the woodpile, its little tail swishing. "Mewmewmew!" it said. It had to be enchanted for its nonhuman voice to be heard over the island's silence spell, Samheed decided.

The noise made Samheed nervous. What if someone heard? He put a finger to his lips, and the kitten bounded around to the other side of the woodpile and disappeared. At the same time, a ball of light zipped through the trees and stopped in front of him. Samheed froze. It exploded, showing him a picture that puzzled him. It was a brain floating in the air. It fizzled and disappeared, leaving only a silvery trail of light weaving through the woods.

What the—? he thought. And then he remembered. It was his dementia spell. His heart leaped into his throat. He'd given the prototype to Alex for his collection. . . . Could he possibly be here? After all this time?

Samheed's blood pulsed and pounded. He strode toward the woodpile, forgetting about his leash, and with a yank that almost took his feet out from under him, he came to an abrupt stop. The thorn necklace jabbed deeper into his skin, sending pain searing through him. He couldn't go any farther.

After a moment, the kitten reappeared. Sam pointed to his neck and to the leash, trying to explain. The kitten watched, tilting her head. And then she darted around the woodpile a second time.

Samheed had to keep swinging his ax or someone would notice he was just standing there. He pounded the log halfheartedly, glancing at the woodpile now and then. After a minute, he looked again, and the ax nearly fell out of his hands, for there, peeking around the edge of the logs, was the ugliest, yet most adorable gargoyle face Samheed had ever seen.

"Hello," Charlie signed. He waved his two-thumbed hand.

Samheed ducked down and signed a greeting back to Charlie, wondering, *Does Warbler use the same hand signals as the gargoyles?*

Charlie confirmed it in an instant. Samheed couldn't understand everything the statue was saying, but he got enough of the message to figure out that help had finally, finally come.

But he had no idea how they were going to get him out of there. And he certainly wasn't going anywhere without Lani.

A second later, the kitten and Charlie disappeared behind the logs, and Samheed saw a brief flash of light and a seek ball skirting around the ships and disappearing. Samheed stood on his tiptoes, trying to see where the statues went, hoping they understood he couldn't follow. And then he felt a hand on his shoulder.

"Looking for something?" the project manager asked, his eyes like slits.

Finally, the Beginning of the Third Rescue

S amheed shook his head, pretending to be bewildered. He began signing random words. "Water, left, chicken," he said. He panicked, wishing he hadn't said "chicken," or any kind of animal that might make the manager think of living statues. "Morning, rain," he added.

The manager gave him a puzzled stare. "You're not very smart, but at least you can swing an ax," he muttered. "Back to work."

Samheed began swinging his ax again, chopping with all

LISA McMANN

his might. The dull edge of the ax made it bounce back hard without splitting much. His arms reverberated with the hit, making his fingers and wrists ache, but he kept going, thinking over and over to himself, *Please, please, please.*

From the corner of his eye he thought he saw a fox slinking away, and then he was sure he saw Charlie running back to the woods. Charlie inched his way up a tree in the distance, near a clearing, until Samheed could see him. Charlie waved again and pointed. He signed something quickly with one hand, the other holding tightly to the tree.

Samheed didn't understand, but he also didn't dare ask questions of the gargoyle. He hoped it wasn't important. Soon enough, the gargoyle slid back down the tree and disappeared, and Samheed kept his head down, not noticing the long shadows of squirrelicorns circling on the ground in the open area around the covered work space. Soon it would be dark and his workday would be over. Then how would they find him? And what about Lani?

Lani tried to shrug her hair from her cheek, but it had stuck fast to her skin with sweat and grime from the melding fires.

In less than an hour and she'd be free of this cave for the day. She paused as she worked, and asked herself for the hundredth time how it was possible that her life had become like this.

She slid the still-glowing thorns into a tub of water to help them cool, and then she went back to the fire, loaded her mold with gold coins, and pushed it into the flames, holding it by its long handle until she could bear the heat no longer. Her face felt like it was about to melt. She closed her eyes and willed herself to stay there a minute more.

And so it was that when a ball of fire streaked into the room and exploded in front of her, she didn't even see it.

On the beach, four visible Unwanteds and their two almost invisible friends stared at the seek spell's burning portrait of the kitten. Alex watched it sputter out and disappear. "She did it," he whispered. "Do you think she's in trouble already?"

"I don't think she did it for fun," Sean pointed out. "Though she is kind of a silly kitten."

"Crud," Alex muttered. Had he been too ambitious to think they would all come out of this easily? He looked at Sean and Carina. "Okay, well, let's proceed as planned. You guys

LISA McMANN

stick with assisting anybody heading back this way and help Meghan and Ms. Octavia defend the ship if the Warblerans come to attack. We'll see you soon. I hope." Alex's voice faltered, and he felt an invisible hand on his arm. He brightened with courage he didn't really have and said, "Come on, Henry. Lead the way, Sky and Crow."

Sky grabbed hands with the younger boys, and Alex followed behind as Sky led them on a stealthy journey off-path.

What they didn't see was Sean and Carina flinch, one after the other, and crumple to the sand. A single remaining guard skittered down his tree and ran as fast as his legs could carry him to the other side of the island.

Sky moved swiftly, leading the way. "I've been thinking a lot about how much time has passed, and about where the new captures like Sam and Lani would be stationed," she said in a low voice as her feet flew expertly over the brush. "They're probably still tethered to a wire—it's like a wire leash. It helps them find their way around the tunnels, and it also keeps them from trying to escape. They don't usually get that taken off of them for a few months, until they can be trusted."

"Great," Alex muttered. He wondered if there was a wire cutter on the ship that they could use. But it was too late now to go back. Darkness was threatening. He fingered his spell components, keeping something in his hand at all times in case they were surprised, and changing his mind every other second on what would be the best spells to have in hand.

After several minutes of following the kitten's seek line, Sky whispered, "It's leading us to the shipbuilding yard by the water. Be careful now. Stay low and don't speak. This place is teeming with brutes."

They neared an area of trees that had been freshly cleared. In the distance Alex could see dozens of men and women working silently on various types of watercraft. Sky stopped and pointed to where the string of light was leading. Alex peered through the trees, looking for signs of the fox and Charlie, knowing the kitten would be hard to spot.

As he stood there looking all around for anyone or anything that was remotely familiar, the hair on the back of his neck started prickling. Alex whirled around as someone—or something—came flying at him, hitting him square in the chest. It knocked him down, and before Alex could get a shot

LISA McMANN

323 « Island of Fire

off, Henry had the creature frozen in a crunchy chocolate shell. It rolled off Alex.

"Oh no!" Henry whispered. He released the spell immediately, and the fox sprang to life again, hopping about. On his back was the kitten, and standing ten feet away was Charlie, waving.

"Sheesh," Alex said. "I'm glad Kitten is okay, but please don't do that again. This is a *stealth* mission, okay?" He scrambled to his feet and wiped the dead leaves and dirt from his clothes.

"Mewmewmew!" the kitten said.

Alex looked at the fox. "What did she say?"

"She said Samheed is working on the other side of that ship and he knows we're here, but he has a leash stuck to his neck thing and there are lots of others about. Also, she heard the manager say it was nearly time to quit for the day."

Alex looked skeptical. "She said all that with three tiny mews?"

The fox nodded. His face was very serious. "And Charlie can talk to Samheed in the sign language."

Alex didn't want to know how the fox found that out, but

he was glad. "Okay. Kitten, you did good to send out the alert."

The kitten hopped up and down on the fox's back.

"Let's move around so we can see him," Alex said.

The fox tilted his head when he noticed the two arms float-ing in midair. He sniffed, and then followed them, along with Alex and Henry. They got down on their hands and knees and snuck around to the back of the woodpile where the statues had been before. In front of them was an enormous covered pavilion, where a dozen young men and women chopped logs. A large shadow passed over the trees, and Alex looked up to see Simber, who had spied them as well. Alex signaled to Simber and whis-pered, knowing the cat had amazing hearing. "There's no open place for you to land without everybody noticing. Can you go and tell Sean and Carina that we've found Samheed? Then come right back and see if we need help."

The cat circled and flew off.

"Psst," someone said.

Alex looked all around. Up in the trees he saw them—a dozen squirrelicorns, including Rufus. Alex flashed a shaky grin. He was suddenly feeling better about this.

"Okay, team. You run and fly out there and distract them

LISA McMANN

325 « Island of Fire

while I get Samheed off his leash. Henry, as soon as you're close enough, hit everyone else with everything you've got. I'll help as much as I can. Ready, everyone?"

They all nodded, and Rufus circled a paw in the air, commanding his team.

"Go!" Alex said.

Like a disturbed beehive, the shipbuilding area was suddenly swarmed with screaming squirrelicorns and a few hopping, yelling statues. The Warblerans dropped their axes in fright as Samheed started throwing punches at anyone within reach.

Waiting for his cue from behind the woodpile, Alex grinned as he watched Samheed fight with every ounce of energy he had. "Man, have I missed you," he whispered.

grabbed a squirrelicorn from the air and threw her at Alex. The squirrelicorn's horn hit Samheed's neck, jolting them all. And as the thorns vanished, so did the creature.

Alex pulled his hand away with a gasp. "No!" He looked all around, as if the squirrelicorn might be hiding somewhere, but she was gone. The leash dangled from the overhead wire, and Samheed was free.

"Alex!" Rufus cried out. "Let it go and carry on!"

That brought Alex to his senses. He shrugged off his vest and shoved it at Samheed. "You can speak now, or at least whisper," he said. "Fire away!"

Samheed wore a dazed expression, not sure what had just happened, but at Alex's words he came back to life and shoved his arms through the vest. He brought a hand to his neck, feeling the dents and holes in his skin. And then he grabbed components and started fighting.

Alex, who had padded his other pockets, began pelting Warblerans with spells. But when he heard a cry, he turned, finding Henry dangling from the arms of an enormous man, who held the boy out in front of him like a shield as he ran for a tunnel. "Alex!" Henry screamed.

The First Loss

A lex leaped over the end of the woodpile, casting blinding highlights on his way to Samheed. "Sam!" he said as he ran up. "Stand still now, don't move an inch." Samheed dropped his fists and began to shake, overflowing with adrenaline. The Warblerans he'd punched came to their senses and began to fight off the winged, horned creatures that stabbed at them.

Alex shot off a few more spells, and when it looked like he had a few seconds, he touched Samheed's thorns. "Hold very still," he whispered. He took a breath, and whispered, "Dissipate."

Just as he breathed the dangerous magical word, a Warbleran

LISA McMANN

Alex didn't have a clear shot at the man. He whirled around frantically, searching the area. Finally his eyes alighted on the one he was seeking. "Kitten!" he cried. "Go!"

The kitten didn't need any more instruction. She tore after the man, climbed up his leg, and wriggled her way into Henry's pocket. Alex shot off a round of shackles at the man's feet, but the man was running in a zigzag pattern. The spell missed and bounced off the ground. There was nothing else Alex could do without risking Henry. Then he thought of one thing. "Freeze," he called out, holding his hand in the direction of the escaping man. But the man ducked down a hole in the ground and disappeared, and the freeze spell hit the side of a ship and shattered like ice to the ground. Alex grabbed a few more spells from Samheed's vest and chased after them.

Meanwhile, Samheed found his whispery voice and began casting spells with gusto. He was a little rusty with his aim, but he soon got back into the rhythm. He mounted the log pile for a better view of his attackers. As more Warblerans came running, Samheed blinded, shackled, scatterclipped, and froze them before they had any time to fight back. It was a bizarre,

LISA McMANN

quiet fight, the only sound coming from the very few who had voices. When at last Simber returned, Samheed had polished off everyone in the area.

Samheed ran up to the giant cat.

"Had a minorrr incident to clearrr up at the beach with some of our fighters," Simber told him. "Climb aboarrrd," he said. "We'll get you to the ship."

Samheed shook his head violently, and then remembered he could speak. "Not without Lani," he rasped, his voice trying hard to come back. He coughed a few times, attempting to clear his throat, and wished he could get his body to stop shaking. "I'm not going anywhere without her."

Simber frowned, but then he nodded. "Do you know where she is?"

"Fire cave. Deep down below. But I'm sure word is spreading that you're here. We have to hurry." He thought for a moment. "Oh—but you can't fit down the tunnels. If you can find the exit hole on the south side of the island by the lagoon, I'll try my best to bring her out there."

Simber nodded. "I will be therrre if I am not needed else-wherrre. Otherrrwise head straight to the lagoon wherrre you

L I S A   M c M A N N

arrrived a month ago. Do you know how to get therrre? The pirrrate ship belongs to us."

"I'll find it." Samheed started to run, and then he turned back. "Is Meghan . . . ?"

"She's waiting forrr you on the ship."

Samheed sighed heavily. "Thanks. Thanks for coming back for us."

Simber nodded. "Go."

Samheed grabbed spell components in both hands and jumped down the entry hole, sliding on his back and landing on his feet. He ran down the tunnel, seeing frozen and shackled Warblerans everywhere, no doubt thanks to Alex. He saw Warblerans huddled in caves, peering out, and ducking when they saw him wearing the strange vest. Some of them signaled to him as he passed, pleading, "Save me." "Let me come with you." It was heartbreaking. But Samheed couldn't risk saving anyone else right now. He had to get to Lani.

Alex chased after the man and Henry, getting farther and farther behind as Warblerans tried to stop him. He shot spells left and right and pressed his way through the crowds, closing off caves with glass spells and locking the people inside when he started running out of components. He felt terrible about it, but it was the only way to keep up.

But in the maze he lost them. He kept running, unsure of where to go. "Kitten!" he yelled. He waited at a circle where several tunnels came together, having no idea what to do, which way to go, and constantly turning to make sure no one was coming up behind him. He was starting to panic.

And then the ball of light arrived. Kitten again, this time to save the day.

Alex sped down the proper tunnel, eventually hearing Henry's screams once again. He snuck up to the entrance of a cave, finding himself in a hospital room of sorts. The brute held Henry down on a table, and another Warbleran reached into a cupboard, pulling out a handful of braided thorns.

Alex's eyes widened. "Get your hands off him!" Alex yelled, furious. He blasted the brute with an encasement spell and hit the other with a dog collar shackle that stuck her to the wall, her feet dangling off the floor. Henry scrambled off the table, a look of terror in his eyes. Alex grabbed him by the arm and ran to the nearest opening, having no idea where on the island they were but hoping one of the statues would be around to help. They emerged to find Florence stacking frozen bodies like logs.

"Don't shoot!" Alex cried. "It's us. Get Henry to the ship, fast! I'm going back down."

"Good luck!" Florence picked up the boy and ran, her steps shaking the earth, while Alex dove back underground.

Finding Lani

Finally it was time. Lani cleaned up her thorn station for the day with the other melters. She was running behind because at the last minute she'd decided to get one more mold of thorns made, hoping her manager would notice. Maybe then she'd get the leash off sooner. If anyone could fake being the model of good behavior, it was Lani, and she was doing everything she could to get the leaders of Warbler to trust her.

The others finished up, and one by one they left, until finally Lani was alone. She jiggled her sizzling mold, trying to get the stupid thorns to solidify and come loose without burning her hand off. While she waited for it to cool, she wiped up her table and scrubbed it with her scraper to get the tiny drips of gold off before they stuck there for good.

When she heard a voice coming from the tunnel outside the cave, her heart raced. She hoped it was one of the leaders, who would see that she was still hard at work. She began scraping harder.

Then she heard the voice again. "Glass," it said. The voice was familiar, but she couldn't quite figure out which of the leaders it could be. She picked up her thorn mold and went to swish it in the water to help it cool and loosen from the mold. And then, from the doorway, she heard her name.

"Lani." It was a whisper.

She looked up. Her fingers trembled and went to her mouth. The mold slipped from her other hand and hit the floor without a sound, thorns popping out like toothpicks and scattering on the floor. And then she ran to him and jumped into his arms, her lips mouthing his name as her heart screamed it.

Alex.

He held her, laughing and crying as she sobbed silently into his neck. He twirled her around in the doorway, knowing they had to hurry and wanting to get her neck thorns off, but she clung to him and wouldn't let go. He closed his eyes and wrapped his arms around her waist, feeling her shuddering breaths against him, wishing he could fix it all so this had never happened. He smoothed his fingers over her hair as her sobbing slowed, and then he opened his eyes and whispered, "We have to hurry."

He turned to look down the tunnel, hoping none of the spells had worn off, and then his jaw dropped as he saw two arms on the other side of the glass barrier, with other body parts of Sky and Crow beginning to appear as their invisibility spells wore off, including Sky's face. Clearly, she didn't know he could see her.

He set Lani down hastily. "Let's get this thing off you. Please don't move, not even a fraction. This will only take a few seconds."

Lani obeyed, tears still washing down her streaky, sooty face, and soon—without any casualties this time—her thornament was gone.

"You can speak now," Alex said. He handed her most of the spell components he had left, and then he hurriedly released the glass spell. In a low voice he said, "This is Sky and Crow from the raft, remember? They can speak now too."

He turned to Sky as they began moving for the exit. "Boy, am I glad to see you," he said. "I was afraid I wouldn't be able to find my way out of here." He hugged Sky's shoulders and they started jogging through the tunnel, past an occasional frozen person.

Lani cleared her throat. "Where's Sam?" she whispered. "We have to find him."

"We found him once, but then I had to go after Henry. . . ."

"Henry—is he okay?" Her voice was a rasp.

"He is now."

"This way," Sky said, taking her brother by the arm and turning sharply. "This leads away from the queen's throne room."

"I'm not leaving without Sam," Lani said defiantly.

"Well, duh," Alex said. He grinned at Lani, and she gave a reluctant smile in return.

As they passed various caves, Alex threw more glass spells, locking in as many Warblerans as possible to keep them out of their way. He was glad that spell didn't require a component. Sky made them turn once more, and they could see the end of

LISA McMANN

the tunnel. "Almost there," Sky said under her breath. They broke out into a full run.

They saw the ostrich down one stretch of a tunnel. "What is she doing down here?" Alex wondered, puzzled. "Never mind," he added hastily and called to her to follow.

"You brought the ostrich?" Lani said. "She hates us."

"I know, right?" Alex chuckled. "We have a lot to tell you." His laugh died in his throat when he realized just how much Lani and Sam didn't know. He wasn't sure if he could tell that story again.

They reached the end of the tunnel. Sky, then Crow, lunged for the ladder and scaled it like they'd done a thousand times. Lani tried the same thing and struggled, but made it up, and then Alex held out his hand to help boost the ostrich. "Are there any more of you in the tunnels?" Alex asked.

"No, I'm the only one," she said with no evidence of grouchiness whatsoever. "Florence sent me to look for you."

"Perfect," Alex said. He helped the ostrich up and out. He sealed off the tunnel behind him with another glass spell in case anybody was coming after them. And then he bounded halfway up the ladder, and just as his head emerged, he froze.

In his face was a saber, held by a stately woman with long silver hair. He gasped, his eyes darting around the hole, where Lani, Sky, Crow, and the ostrich were being held by four brutes, each holding a saber to the Artiméans' necks.

"Hello, you annoying little man," the woman said, drawing her words out in a sickly sweet voice. "I am Queen Eagala. I think you need to turn back around. We'll get a collar and chain on you right away so you can stop stealing my people." Her voice was eerily familiar, and so were her looks. In an instant, it dawned on him. He knew exactly who she must be.

Alex hesitated, inching his fingers toward his pocket. He didn't dare slide his eyes toward Lani, but he knew she'd be ready. "I'm not stealing your people, I'm rescuing mine," Alex said in as calm a voice as he could muster. Against the ladder his fingers slid into his pocket, where the prototypes were. "They want to leave, don't you, guys?"

"Yep," Lani said.

Sky followed suit. "Mm-hmm."

"Sure do," said Crow.

The ostrich rolled her eyes.

"They can't leave. They're on my property, they're branded,

LISA McMANN

and they work for me now," said the icy woman. A smile played on her lips as if she was enjoying the little game.

"Maybe you could *fire* them," Alex suggested. He put extra emphasis on the word "fire" and glanced at the ostrich, who couldn't possibly be hurt by the blade on her neck but was playing along beautifully so far.

His fingers felt the sandpapery stone claw, and he tried not to be too distracted as he thought the word: *Seek.*

"Oh, they're much too good at working for me to do that," Queen Eagala said.

Nothing happened, and for a moment Alex feared the worst—that somehow Artimé was gone. But then he remembered what Simber had said, that his claw might not work because he hadn't created it artistically.

Alex was starting to panic, but he forced himself to remain calm. A drop of sweat rolled down his back as he moved his other hand to grab more spells, but he didn't have much choice. He clutched the dewclaw harder and said, "So, you *seek* to hire more people, is that it?"

With that, a ball of fire burst from Alex's pocket and shot straight up into the air, and everybody reacted. The ostrich slammed back the foot she wasn't standing on, straight into the man's kneecap. Then the bird launched her stone head backward into the brute's face as hard as she could, dropping the guy. The ostrich flapped her stone wings, knocking Crow's guard in the side of the head. Teeth flew from the man's mouth. He dropped his saber, staggered a few steps, and fell to the ground on top of the first guy.

At the same time, Lani stuck a pincushion component into her guard's thigh with one hand and tossed a handful of scatterclips at Queen Eagala, pinning her to the tree behind her. The queen screeched, furious, unable to move.

Lani's guard, feeling a thousand pins pricking his skin, began dancing around in agony, but still took a swipe with his saber at Lani as she searched for more components. The long, sharp blade caught Lani in the thigh, slicing through the fabric of her pants and deep into the skin. She gritted her teeth, unwilling to show how much it hurt. Seconds later, blood soaked through the fabric and spread in a growing circle around the wound. She whirled around and managed to dodge the next swing, wondering where Samheed could possibly be. Was he already on the ship? She didn't know, and there was no time to go back through the tunnels now. It was too late. "Samheed!" she screamed, frantic. She couldn't leave without him.

With his last component, Alex blinded the guard holding Sky, who scooted out from under the knife and grabbed Crow. "Run!" Alex shouted to them, and they went a short distance, but Sky turned back.

Alex jumped up the ladder the rest of the way and slammed a fist into the blinded guard's gut, almost breaking his fingers. But the guard was expecting it. He picked Alex up like a toy and shook him until his eyes and teeth rattled, and then threw him through the air. Alex slammed back-first into a tree trunk, his head ricocheting into the tree bark without a sound. He flopped to the ground, face-first in the sand, and didn't move.

"Alex!" Sky screamed as Simber, without a sound, arrived, diving through the trees, knocking them down left and right. "Rrrun forrr the ship!" he growled. He picked up the guard who had tossed Alex like a sack of beans and roared in the man's face until it turned white and his eyes rolled back in his head. Then Simber grabbed the man, flew straight up, and deposited the guard in the top of the tallest tree, leaving him there. He came back down and dive-bombed the pincushioned guard as

LISA McMANN

the creep started toward Alex's motionless body. Simber picked the man up with his claws and hurtled him with all his might, sending him soaring far across the island. The man crashed through the palm fronds that made up the shipyard roof.

Samheed had been ambushed on his way to find Lani by some rather ugly guards, but he managed to fight his way out of their grasps and went back to his initial plan. He raced to the fire cave, but by then he could tell he was too late. It was empty. He turned back and raced for the south exit, not exactly sure how to get there in the maze of tunnels. "Lani!" he yelled as he ran past glassed-in caves with Warblerans peering out.

A squirrelicorn darted past his head. "I'm Rufus. Are you Samheed?"

Samheed took one look and blew out a breath of relief. "Yes."

"I had a feeling you were still down here," Rufus said. "Follow me." He buzzed through the tunnels as if he'd lived there all his life, Samheed on his heels. Two Warblerans came out of nowhere and began to chase him, and after working hard all day, Samheed wasn't as fast as he wanted to be. "Call horse!"

LISA McMANN

Samheed cried, and an invisible steed shot up under him, running at full speed for the exit. Samheed hung on.

Just before they reached the exit hole, Rufus shouted, "Whoa!" He dove into a hairpin turn and the steed slammed on the brakes and skidded to a halt. With no time to react, Samheed wasn't so lucky. He flew forward off the steed, clanged against the glass wall Alex had left, and bounced to the floor of the tunnel.

"Ooof," he gasped.

Rufus came back around more slowly and began ramming the glass spell in the hallway with his horn. "We need—to get—through here," Rufus said between jabs, but he was getting nowhere.

At first Samheed didn't know what had hit him—or what he'd hit. And then he reached his hand out and moved it across the glass. "Dang it, Stowe," he muttered, rubbing his shoulder, and he would have laughed if it hadn't hurt so much. Quickly he got back up. The men were on his tail.

He released Alex's glass wall spell and cast a new one between him and the approaching guards. Then he dispelled the steed and crawled up the ladder as fast as he could go. He was free! Rufus zoomed up and out the hole past him to make sure the coast was clear.

"Lani!" Samheed yelled at the top of his voice, not caring about anything else. He was free, but was she? He thought so, based on the glass walls. But he wasn't going anywhere without being sure.

He looked around and nearly fell back into the hole. The queen faced him just a few feet away, and at first he didn't real-ize she was stuck to a tree.

"Release me!" she screamed, but no one came to her aid. Certainly not Samheed. To his right he saw two enormous guards lying in a heap—probably one of them was the one who had dragged them out of the dark cave.

He heard Simber roaring somewhere nearby but couldn't see him. Samheed blasted the queen with a silence spell, which was a relief, and tossed shackles on the two guards, who weren't moving. Then he shot another round of scatterclips at the queen just to make sure she was stuck fast. He ran down the path.

"Lani!" he shouted again.

Simber landed on the ground in front of him and raced past

Samheed to a tree in the woods just as an orange-eyed girl ran up to him. Samheed whirled in alarm.

"No—Samheed, it's me. From the raft. I'm Sky. You need to come with me. Hurry!"

It took him a second to recognize her as the Silent girl. He hadn't even seen her with her eyes open before. "Oh. Sorry. You look like . . ."

"Everyone else here. I know. Come."

He followed her, wiping the sweat from his forehead. "Have you seen Lani?"

Sky nodded. "She's hurt."

The look on Samheed's face startled Sky. "Where!" he cried. "Where is she?"

She grabbed his arm. "This way. I'm trying to take you to her. She can't walk." She ran in the direction of the lagoon, where Lani lay off the path. It was as far as she had been able to go. Her eyes were open but she was breathing hard, her face telling everything.

"Sam," she said, reaching for him.

He ran to her and knelt down. She wrapped her arms around his neck and he lifted her up. She stared at him, and he stared at her. Sky watched, a little puzzled, and then her lips parted. A second later she snapped her lips shut and tugged on Samheed's sleeve again. "We need to hurry," she said.

Sky led Samheed as fast as he could go to the lagoon, where Florence stood. She paced, looking around anxiously. The ground shook slightly around her. "Ah, there you are." She took a giant step to reach Sam and Lani and picked them both up like they were a sack of arrows. "Thank you, Sky," Florence said over her shoulder as she walked Sam and Lani to the ship, where a cheer rose up at the sight of the rescued Unwanteds.

But Sky was not there to hear it. Instead she raced back to the trees as Simber gently nudged the young mage of Artimé into his jaws.

Simber looked up when he sensed Sky standing there. His eyes were sad. He unfurled his wings, letting one come to rest at her feet, and tipped his head, indicating she should climb on. She scurried up his wing and settled on, grasping him tightly around the neck, pressing her face against the cool stone.

Just then a silent army of Warblerans, unstuck from their temporary spells, melted out from the cover of the trees and spread like lava, surrounding them.

Simber flashed them a disgusted look as he bolted down the path and leaped into the air, pumping his mighty wings. The Warblerans' spears, rocks, and sabers only fell back to the ground, harming no one but themselves.

A Somber Ride

S imber lowered his hindquarters into the water at the edge of the ship and folded his wings to give the Artiméans a better chance to remove Alex safely from his jaws. Once Alex had been brought to their temporary triage area, Simber made a bridge of his wing for Sky, who crawled across it and waited anxiously, watching as Henry came running with Ms. Octavia to see how they could help.

"Wherrre's Carrrina?" the cheetah growled. "She has some healing experrrience, doesn't she?"

"She's over there where you left her, still out from the sleep

LISA McMANN

dart, Sim," Ms. Octavia said. "I'll do my best, and Henry's here. He's been studying."

Simber frowned. There was nothing else they could do. He glanced back at the shore and then turned to the ship. "Lead-errrs," he roared, sounding fiercer than they'd ever heard him. "Is everrryone accounted forrr? Sound off, just as yourrr mage would have you do!"

Those who could, did, and Florence covered the rest. "You're the last ones in, Simber," Florence said gently. "Unless we want to try to rescue some of the other people of Warbler."

Simber glanced over his shoulder once more as the army of Warblerans reached the beach, but they didn't enter the water—at least not yet. And then he looked at Alex. "We can't," he said, defeated. "We arrren't strrrong enough to go back now. And we've rrrisked enough alrrready." He turned sharply. "Captain," he called, silencing the muttering statue, "We *must* hurrry."

The captain commanded the statues to raise the sails, and he took the wheel. "Ye can't escape, thou treacherous beast!" he cried, shaking his fist toward the nebulous east. There was little wind to take the sails. "A longer night no man or beast

LISA McMANN

has likely seen," he added, but no one was really listening.

Simber pushed the ship farther out until he could reach the sea's floor no longer, and then he rose into the air as darkness settled.

Suddenly the fox came tearing up the stairs and jumped up and down next to Florence. "Hey," he said. "Hey. Hey. Kitten is missing! Kitten isn't here!"

"What?" Florence asked, alarmed. "You're serious? No, I'm sure I counted her. Or maybe I counted you and assumed she was on your back." The ebony statue cringed. She looked over to the shore as if she might be able to see the tiny kitten in the dark. She looked up at Simber.

"We can't go back," Simber said gruffly, reading her mind. "Not now. I'll come back forrr herrr laterrr. She's a cat. She'll be fine."

The fox hopped, anxious, and then he flopped to the deck dramatically and buried his face under his paws, sobbing.

Florence looked around the ship. "Has anyone seen the kitten?" she bellowed. Immediately all the statues and creatures who weren't busy with other things began to search, for their brave kitten was a hero, having helped save Henry.

LISA McMANN

"Kitten!" they began calling. "Here, Kitten!"

Henry looked up from leaning over Alex. "What's going on?" he asked Ms. Octavia, having been fully concentrating on Alex. "Kitten's not missing." Something wriggled in his pocket. "She's right here," he called. "She was taking a nap in my pocket. She's fine!" He fished the kitten out as the fox bounded over. Kitten stretched adorably in Henry's hand and squeaked, "Mewmewmew!"

"She says that she is very sorry to have worried everyone by accidentally falling asleep in Henry's pocket instead of on my back, which is where she prefers to be, and that she's just fine, and she loves you all—"

"Shut up," Simber growled.

The fox froze, looking at Simber in surprise. Then he snapped his jaw shut again and lay down, resting his chin on his front paws. His eyes pooled. The kitten climbed on his back and nestled in.

Simber frowned, muttering something only Florence could hear, and despite the seriousness of their situation, Florence had trouble keeping a straight face. But then she caught herself and looked over to the covered deck, which had become the triage area. Lit torches marked the boundary.

Henry, Meghan, Sky, and Crow hovered over the injured. Sean and Carina lay completely still, eyes closed, but Sky assured the others that they would be fine—they were just getting a nice rest. But Alex was still and gray. And Lani lay on her side, eyes glazed with pain, squeezing Samheed's hand as Meg and Henry cut her pant leg open and treated the wound.

Ms. Octavia lifted Alex's head and poured a small vial of liquid between his lips. He choked and coughed. Henry turned sharply, then reached over to touch Alex's forehead and utter a spell.

"Was it bad that he coughed?" Sky whispered. She could hardly stand watching, but she couldn't leave Alex's side.

"No, it was good," Henry said. "I read it in a book." He turned to Lani and smiled. "And now I get to try magic stitches for the first time on my sister," he said in a mildly wicked voice. Samheed lifted his head and shot the boy a quick grin.

"Great, can't wait," Lani whispered. She tried to smile too, but she was very weak from losing so much blood. "How's Alex?" she rasped.

"Well," Henry said, almost chipper as he basked in being in

LISA McMANN

353 « Island of Fire

his element, "if you think about the worst headache you've ever had, multiply times a hundred or so, that's probably what Alex is going to have when he wakes up. Plus his back probably hurts pretty bad."

Sky swallowed hard. "When . . ." She cleared her throat. "Uh, I mean, when do you think he'll wake up?" Her fingers worked over each other, unable to keep still.

"I'm not really sure about that," Henry said. "Could be anytime. Could be a while." He took out his magnifying glass and examined Lani's gaping wound. "Wow," he said, impressed.

Sky looked down, squelching her disappointment. When she turned, she caught Samheed watching her.

He looked away, only a little embarrassed to be caught. It was weird for him, seeing Sky and her little brother acting so alive and normal, and Meghan treating Sky like she was one of their close friends. It almost felt like . . . like Alex and Meghan and everybody else had been too busy making friends with the new kids to be bothered to come rescue him and Lani.

He lifted his head and sucked in a sharp breath, disgusted with himself for thinking such a thing. They'd risked their lives for them. "Don't be stupid," he muttered.

Sky slid across the wooden plank deck to the starboard side of the ship, knowing she was probably just in the way. She took a long drink from a tiny magical fountain Ms. Octavia had sculpted while she'd anxiously waited for everyone to return to the ship. The water was cold and pure and delicious—the best water she'd ever tasted. But all she could focus on was Alex, and in between thoughts of Alex her mind went back to her mother stuck inside that strange underwater glass case. She pressed the heels of her hands to her eyes. As happy as she was that they'd rescued Sam and Lani, somehow she felt like everything had gotten worse instead of better.

Once everyone had settled in and had something to eat and drink, Florence carefully stood up midship and beckoned to Simber. He moved directly above her to keep his wings from knocking her head clean off, and they held a private meeting far above the others.

"We're going to need to tell them soon," Florence said in a soft voice.

Simber stared stonily ahead.

"We have to tell them before we get to Artimé, Simber. Or

LISA McMANN

355 « Island of Fire

they'll wonder where *he* is, and why he isn't there to greet them. And then we'll have chaos. This is at least a semicontrolled environment."

Simber still said nothing.

"I don't want somebody saying something accidentally, either, and the longer we wait, the more likely that is to happen," Florence said.

Silence.

Florence sighed. She tried once more. "I know you're worried about Alex, but think how they'll feel if we wait. They'll feel betrayed. That's not what Artimé's about."

Simber growled low and long. Finally he said, "Alex is the only one who saw it all. They need to know what *he* went thrrrough. Forrr *us*."

Florence bowed her head for a moment, thinking. "Maybe it's best someone else tells it, then. He'll be far too modest." She glanced around when she heard a flurry of activity in the sick bay. Sean and Carina were both awake now and sitting up, and Meghan was describing what had happened to them as they lamented their uselessness in this mission.

"Plus, Lani needs to know about her mother," Florence

whispered. "And we can't wait for Gunnar to break the news—they'll certainly hear something from everyone who will be glad to see them when we arrive home again." She ducked as they passed through a cloud of evening bugs, and spit a few out of her mouth before continuing. "I spoke with Henry about it, and he doesn't want to tell her. You should have seen the poor boy's face when I asked him. He's in agony."

Simber's muzzle twitched. "We should wait until she's in less pain," he said. "And fewerrr nosy onlookerrrs."

Florence sighed. "I honestly don't see that scenario existing right now. It's going to be messy no matter how it happens."

Simber's determined face didn't falter. "We wait forrr ourrr leaderrr."

LISA McMANN

The Long Night

There was no wind, and the pirate ship was moving so slowly it almost seemed to be floating backward at times. It made for a smooth ride, though, and the moon reflecting on the sea was a perfect picture. The water looked like glass.

Simber kept his eyes forward toward home, while Florence watched the sea behind them to make sure the people of Warbler weren't coming after them. But all was calm.

"All theirrr ships, but no idea what to do with them," Simber growled. "Is everrrywherrre so dysfunctional?"

It was a rhetorical question.

Lani slept. Samheed watched over Alex, growing more anxious the longer his friend's eyes stayed closed. He teased him, daring him to wake up. "Come on, man," he said, his voice strained. "You think you hit that tree hard? Try galloping full speed into a glass wall." Samheed's nervous smile fell away when Alex didn't respond. He swallowed hard and tried again. "You got me good, you know. I owe you one. Hey, remember, uh, remember that time in the lounge where . . . ?" He choked on the words and couldn't finish. Instead he closed his eyes and pressed his fists into his temples, trying to force the watery grit from his eyes.

Samheed shook his head slowly, thinking what a mess he'd turned into over the past weeks. And while the Artiméans moved about the ship busy with chores, or captured a bit of sleep, Samheed couldn't stop the questions that were driving him crazy. He glanced at Lani sleeping, and drew a finger across her forehead to catch a strand of hair that had fallen over her face. And then he got to his feet and wandered about the ship, trying to work out his inner jumble of emotions. He had so many questions, and no one was talking about important things. Was he just supposed to wait until they felt like explaining themselves? He didn't think he should have to ask what took them so long, but nobody seemed to feel the need to apologize for the lengthy delay.

Maybe they just didn't understand how horrible it was on Warbler, Samheed thought. But then he looked at Sky. *No. She knew. Her brother knew. Even Meghan had a clue.* It hurt. And it made him angry.

Samheed ducked his head as he walked past the muttering captain. He'd met the statue before by accident once, thinking he was going into a dressing room. Boy, was that a mistake. He took a punch to the mouth from the crazy peg-legged statue before he knew what hit him, and ended up with a fat lip. At least the weirdo was useful for something.

He found himself at the bow, straining his eyes in the dark, looking for Artimé. There was a faint glow in the distance, and he thought that must be it. He couldn't wait to get home. He reached around his neck, forgetting that the thorns were gone, and he felt the indented scars all the way around. And then he remembered the squirrelicorn. He looked around for Rufus, finding him balancing on the railing nearby with a group of others. Samheed wandered over.

"I'm sorry about the soldier you lost because of me," Samheed said solemnly. "I don't know how it happened, but I know Alex was really upset about it."

Rufus and the other squirrelicorns bowed their horned heads at Samheed. "Thank you," one of them, not Rufus, spoke up. "That was Gremily. She was a terrific soldier and we miss her. But it was not the mage's fault. He would never do anything to hurt us."

Samheed tapped his hand lightly on the railing and nodded, feeling awkward now, unsure what else to say. And thinking it was strange that Rufus called Alex a mage. Even though they all were mages, the Unwanteds tended to reserve that term for Mr. Today as a sign of respect. But maybe creatures thought about the word differently. The squirrelicorns turned back to their conversation, giving Samheed the excuse he needed to walk back to the bow and stare toward home.

After a while, Meghan joined him. She slipped her arm around his waist in a side hug and brought his arm up to hug her shoulders. They didn't need words to transmit what they were feeling. After a while Samheed turned to look at her face. He smiled, and she smiled back, and then he looked more closely at her. "They didn't get your eyes," he said.

"No. Thanks to Lani."

"She never mentioned it."

"Of course not." Meghan gazed over the water, a wry grin on her face. "Wait—how could she have mentioned it?"

"We—" He began to tell her about their secret tapping language in the cave, but then he stopped. "They were teaching us the sign language," he said, not looking at her.

"Ah," Meghan said. "Well, the way it happened was that you were on the table. They'd just put my thorns in, and Lani managed to cause a commotion and scatterclip somebody to the wall so I could run for it."

Samheed swallowed hard. "She's pretty amazing," he said, trying not to betray his feelings. He had to put them away now, he knew.

"I've always thought so," Meghan said. "But you didn't." She leaned into him. "Sounds like you gave her a chance."

Samheed started to protest. "I've always thought—"

"No, you haven't." Meghan's soft laugh rang out over the water.

"Yeah, okay. You're right." Samheed squeezed his fist in his pocket. "But I respect her now. She's the only thing that . . . kept me . . ." He trailed off, reprimanding himself.

Meghan raised an eyebrow at his heartfelt admission. It wasn't like him to speak so openly. He seemed so different now. But people change when circumstances change, she knew that well enough from the aftereffects of the Purge. She didn't say anything.

They stood for a long moment.

"So then you escaped," Samheed said, going back to their conversation.

It took Meghan a second. "Yes. There was a huge group of Warblerans coming, but I ducked out just in time and managed to find my way out the south hole by the lagoon. There weren't many others roaming the tunnels."

"Probably all working," Samheed mused.

Meghan shrugged. "I made a mad dash for the beach, and zigzagged so no darts hit me—I don't think they expected anyone to approach from that direction. It was pretty miraculous, actually, that I got out of there."

"I'll say."

"So I swam back to the white boat, but I was bleeding a lot, and so exhausted. Nobody came after me." She shook her head. "I don't understand why."

"They're not allowed to go into the water," Samheed said. "That's why they didn't follow us to the ship earlier. The queen doesn't want anyone to learn how to swim. She wants them to fear the water so they don't dare to escape." He paused. "That's what I heard, anyway."

A heavy sigh escaped Meghan's lips. "Wow."

"So, ah, then what?" Samheed glanced at her, growing fidgety as his troubled soul began to bubble. "You . . . what? You drove the boat to Artimé and they threw you a month-long party or something?" He cringed and shook his head, cursing himself under his breath. "Aw, cripes. I'm sorry. That was totally—"

"It's okay," Meghan said softly. "Really. I understand how you must have felt."

Her words struck him like a slap to the face. He wanted to laugh. "Um, no. I don't think you do," Samheed said, unable to keep the bitterness from rushing out. He pulled his arm off her shoulders and let it drop to the railing, bouncing his fist on it a few times. And then he turned his head to face her, his lost eyes searching hers. "Is anybody ever going to explain what took so stupid, blasted long?"

Meghan looked at him, her expression unreadable, and pulled her arm from his waist. She put her elbows on the railing, taking care to put space between them. She tapped her lips, eyes narrowed, reminding herself that they knew nothing, and that this was going to be hard. She wanted to yell, but in an even voice, she continued, pretending like he hadn't just been a total jerk. "When I got to the boat, I was too weak to climb in, so I hung on to the ladder."

Samheed shuffled his feet and said nothing.

"I don't know how many hours passed," she continued. "Eight? Ten? I was delirious and freezing and bleeding, and nobody knew we were gone. They were all busy with preparations for Mr. Today to go on holiday." She sniffed, but didn't cry. "Amazingly enough, when they saw the boat was missing, Alex managed to figure out from our comments earlier in the day that we were going on an adventure and we'd taken the boat. He and Simber began searching. Finally they saw it in the Warbler lagoon."

Samheed gazed out over the water, unblinking.

"So Simber dropped Alex into the empty boat and went flying over the island looking for us. It took Alex a while to notice

LISA McMANN

me. I couldn't speak. I managed to make a splash, I guess—I don't remember that part. Alex heard it and found me clinging to the ladder. He hauled me into the boat. When Simber came back without you guys, they didn't know what to do, but I was unconscious, and they finally decided they had to get me home before I died."

Samheed closed his eyes. "Okay, yeah, I'm sorry. I mean, I know it was hard for you, and at least Lani and I didn't have to sit in cold water for half a day. But that doesn't explain why it took a *month* for you guys to come back. I mean"—his still hoarse voice grew louder and cracked, and he held his head as if it were about to explode—"I mean, Lani sent those stupid seek spells day after day after day! And nobody—*nobody*—"

He put his hands over his face, and his voice grew dark and cold, booming over the calm sea. "Meghan, you cannot *possibly* imagine, not in a million years, how helpless and horrible it felt to be blind and alone and to call out for help with that spell and have no response, day after day after day, not one hint that you were getting them—" The tears overflowed his red-rimmed lids and ran down his cheeks. He turned to face her. "And I can take it, okay? I'm tough, I don't need anybody, I don't need you guys," he said, sounding like the old Samheed, not knowing what crazy words were falling out of his mouth, "but how—*how* could you do that to Lani? How? I can't imagine a single reason big enough that would keep you guys from helping us for so long."

He was growing hysterical, and he couldn't stop. "Where *were* you? Where were Lani's parents? Where was Mr. Today?" He ripped his hands through his hair and then held them out, like a plea. "Don't make up some crazy story just to try to get me to calm down, okay? Just admit it. Somebody, will you please just admit it? Say you screwed up and you're sorry, and I'm telling you, Meg, I'll respect that a whole lot more than this junk we're all dancing around now—this ignoring it, or pretending like everything's fine, and I promise you that's all I need to hear and it'll be all good again." He sniffed hard and swiped his arm across his face. "It'll be good again."

Meg closed her eyes and dropped her head.

Samheed's voice softened and he put his hand on her shoulder. "I'm sorry. I'm not mad at you, Meg. I know you couldn't do anything. But what about them?" he turned and waved his hand across the ship, seeing for the first time that

LISA McMANN

Florence, Simber, Sean, Ms. Octavia, and Henry were all standing nearby listening to them, the most somber looks on their faces. Beyond them Lani was sitting up, watching with her fingers at her lips. And Alex—Alex was awake and on his feet, leaning over the railing, Sky and Crow holding him up as he vomited into the sea.

After a moment, Sky shot a sad glance over her shoulder toward Samheed, and then she pulled a small towel from her back pocket and helped Alex wipe his mouth. She and Crow eased him into a chair, where he put his elbows on his knees and his head in his hands.

Samheed paled when he saw Alex, knowing his friend had heard him. He turned away, pressing his fingers into his eyes and fighting an inner war once again.

Meghan's lip quivered but she stood tall, not sure what to say. She glanced at Simber, and then at Sean, and then at Alex, whose long dark ringlets were tangled once again and hung down over his fingers. With effort, he lifted his head, looking at Simber, who nodded back to Alex.

Alex held up a shaky hand, taking a gentle breath and focusing on speaking. "Thanks, Meghan," he said. He paused as a wave of nausea passed over him, and sweat beaded his forehead. When he could speak again, he said, "Sean can take it from there." His voice quavered, but his words were quiet and decisive, like a leader's. "But first . . ." He looked at Samheed and weakly held his arms out to his friend.

When Samheed hesitated, Alex said, "Come on, man." He took another painful-sounding breath and tried again. "I just hurled, and my head is split in half. Help a guy give a proper greeting, will you?"

The Tale Is Told

Samheed lowered his head and shuffled off toward Alex. "I'm an idiot," he said, kneeling down in front of Alex's chair. He reached out and the two friends hugged, Alex wincing only a little when Samheed patted him on the back. "I'm glad you're okay." Sam sat back and looked at his friend. "You look terrible, though," he remarked.

Alex gave him a shaky half grin. "At least I don't smell like you."

"Hey," Samheed said. The others nearby snickered. "I worked hard all day to smell this manly." He let his smile fade, then said earnestly, "I'm sorry for sounding like a jerk."

"Well, under the, um, circumstances," Alex said, "I—" He turned green. "Oh no. Hold on a second." He looked for Sky, who saw his face and rushed over, helping him to the railing just in time.

"It's the medicine," Henry said, nodding importantly. "He might yodel groceries all night long!"

Alex groaned from the railing, letting his arms dangle over it. "Somebody kill me now."

"No!" shouted Florence, Octavia, Simber, Rufus, and all the humans who had lived through the disaster on Artimé. Death of the mage was no joking matter. Their faces reflected the fear that it could happen again.

Lani shot Samheed a quizzical look. "I think maybe we should let them do the talking now."

The light moment of banter faded. Carina got up and offered her seat to Samheed so he could sit next to Lani. Sky helped Alex ease back into his spot on the other side of her. He wiped the sweat from his brow with his shirt and let his head rest on the back of the chair. He closed his eyes. "I drove the boat with Meg," he said, his voice wrecked and full of grit. "Simber flew above us. And slightly to the right," he said, his hand stretching out before him, placing Simber in his mind. "He was guiding us home in the dark. We made plans to come back for you the next day. And then—and then Simber—" He heaved an uneasy breath, and brought his forearm to cover his eyes as the memories flooded back. Alex began to shake uncontrollably.

Lani looked up at Henry in alarm. "Is that the medicine too?"

"No," Henry said softly. At that moment his face wore the experience of an old man. "He's crying."

"Why?" Lani reached a hand out and slipped it in Alex's, her face filled with concern.

Samheed watched, surprised. He'd never seen his friend like this. Sky put her hand to her mouth and looked away, crying too, and Crow slipped his hand in hers.

"Sean," Simber said. The cat growled, watching Alex relive it all again. Florence wiped a tear and flicked it overboard, and Octavia blew her nose loudly into her handkerchief.

Samheed looked around at everyone and his heart slammed in his chest. "What happened?" he whispered.

Sean took a deep breath and let it out slowly, and then he

began. "In one instant, everything changed. Simber froze and fell into the sea. Claire's boat that Alex was driving at full speed stopped running, throwing him and Meghan, who was unconscious, into the water. On land, the mansion disappeared in a poof, turning into the gray shack, and Artimé was gone. Completely wiped out, except for the people. And then a group from Quill attacked."

Lani's mouth hung open. "You're not serious," she breathed. "How could that have happened?" She looked around, bewildered and scared. "Sean?" she prompted. She stared at Henry, but he only looked at the deck.

Samheed's eyes were wild. He stood up and looked all around, as if he might have missed someone. He looked at Alex, shaking in the chair, arm still flung over his face, and he grew pale. "Rufus called Alex . . . No. No way," he mumbled, thinking. And then he gasped and went up to Sean, gripping his shirt, eyes begging the older boy to lie as he whispered, "Where's Mr. Today?"

One Last Tale

When it was over, the ship was wet with tears. Alex had finally had a chance to grieve without having to be the brave one, while Samheed and Lani sat in shock. At Lani's feet Henry fidgeted, his face wearing the strain of one final secret.

They sat like surviving comrades of a lost war, silent, finding comfort in the existence of the others.

One by one the Artiméans realized what hadn't been told, and they slipped away to the lower deck. Even Simber tried to give them time alone by creating a job for himself. With his teeth, he grabbed a rope that was tied to the bow and began pulling, flying out ahead, helping the ship home.

Sky hesitated and then went belowdecks, knowing Samheed could help Alex if he needed it. Even though she'd spent a lot of time with Henry, Sky was a stranger to Lani, and she hadn't earned the right to be in this conversation.

Meghan stole away, finding Sean and Carina standing quietly at the stern.

Soon only Alex, Lani, Samheed, and Henry remained. Alex forced himself to be strong. He gave Henry a long look. Henry returned it with sorrowful eyes and nodded. He scooted over to Alex and rested his chin on Alex's knee, wrapping his arms around Alex's lower leg like it was a security blanket. Alex rested his hand on the boy's head, mussing his hair a little in a comforting way.

"We have one more thing we have to tell you, Lani," Alex said. He breathed shallowly, lungs searing with every breath, his whole skeleton in pain, but he'd turned down a second dose of the medicine because throwing up endlessly was worse.

Lani looked up at him, her face going blank with fear. "What is it?"

Alex leaned forward slowly, pinching the bridge of his nose, thinking. He edged his body up and out of the chair, trying not to gasp in pain, Henry reaching out to help him kneel on the deck next to Lani.

"Al," Samheed said, scrambling to help, but Alex waved him off.

"It's cool. I'm fine," he lied. He rested his elbow on Lani's good leg and took her hand, and then he turned his head to look at Henry, giving him a sad smile and reaching out to bring the boy closer.

Lani couldn't speak.

Alex looked deep into her new orange eyes, feeling the most tremendous sorrow, knowing the next few minutes would change her life drastically, and hating to have to be the one to bear the news. Finally he could delay it no longer. "When Quill attacked us after Artimé disappeared," he said, "the Unwanteds fought hard. They gave everything they had. But they'd lost their magic and were unprepared to fight Quill's way. We had no weapons," he explained. "Because of that, we lost some of Artimé's bravest, who fought to the death for the sake of all of us."

Lani's lip quivered and her already red-rimmed eyes filled

again. "No," she said. A tear escaped, and she looked at Henry. "No," she pleaded.

Henry's face broke. Alex put his hand on the boy's shoulder.

Lani turned back to Alex. "No!" she screamed.

Alex's head tipped back and his lids closed halfway, and then he pressed her hand to his heart. "I'm sorry to tell you that your mother—"

"NO!"

Alex breathed. Lani's screams hurt more than his bones. "Your mother," he said, pausing, waiting for her, but she was already quiet, "was one of those brave people, and she died."

Lani stared at Alex, lips flared, face twisted and streaming with tears. Her body shuddered, and then her features softened as she looked at Henry. She reached out a quivering hand and touched his face, wiping a tear from his jaw and catching another that pooled in the shadow below his eye. And then she pulled her fingers free from Alex, buried her face in her hands, and rocked back and forth.

Alex looked over at Samheed, who knelt on the deck on the other side of the chair. His wild eyes were locked on Lani,

LISA McMANN

and he clenched his fists. Finally he reached out his hand and brushed it tenderly over Lani's bowed head.

Alex checked on Henry, who was crying in silence, and put an arm around the boy. Henry stiffened, then shrugged it off, shaking his head, and Alex nodded. "Sorry," he whispered to the boy.

When Lani finally lifted her head, Alex was there. But she turned to Samheed, raising her arms like a child. He leaped to his feet and lifted her up to him, careful not to hurt her injured leg. She wrapped her arms around his neck and sobbed into his shoulder. Samheed held her close, eyes closed, saying things only she could hear.

"Take me home," she sobbed. "Take me home."

Samheed whispered to her, holding her tightly. Slowly he moved away from the others, giving her privacy to grieve.

Alex watched them for a long moment as the world wavered around him in a haze of pain, and then he dropped his gaze, resting his head in his hand. Beyond the pain, he felt almost like he'd lost something, or been defeated, but that wasn't the right word or the right feeling to be having at a time like this. There was something in that one impulse—Lani turning to

Samheed for comfort instead of him—that said more than anything else could have. That never would have happened before. Those two had always clashed, but there was something there now. Something strong. And even though Alex's feelings for Lani had changed, he couldn't help but curl inward a bit to protect the new emptiness he felt inside.

When he looked up again, he saw that Henry had silently followed his sister, certainly wanting to be near her. She pulled him in, needing him as much as he needed her.

After a minute, Alex took a few shallow breaths and leaned forward to use his hands, pushing his aching body to his feet. Hunched over, he took another searing breath and then straightened, his legs shaking. He reached for the back of the chair to steady himself, missing it on the first try but catching it with his fingertips on the second. He kept his head down, concentrating as a wave of black crossed in front of his eyes. He held himself there, willing his eyes to clear, and then he broke out in a cold sweat. His stomach twisted and he staggered to the railing once more.

Simber looked over his shoulder at his boy. His eyes flashed and he growled low and long, a mourning song in his throat.

A Sleepless Night for the High Priest

Aaron paced the stony, lifeless halls of the palace. He'd tried to sleep but tossed and turned even on the comfortable palace bed. He had a lot to worry about. Artimé was back, or so he assumed based on Haluki's escape and Alex's subsequent rescue of that woman from the Haluki house through that weird glass tube, which had reappeared in the closet. Aaron had fired Bethesda and Liam on the spot, sending them to the Ancients Sector.

But he was surprised that he didn't get much joy from that. His father had ruined it for him, he supposed. Aaron snarled when he thought about his parents. At least he'd have their loyalty. That was something, he supposed, when he seemed to be losing Restorers faster than he was gaining slaves—er, Unwanteds, that is.

His mind turned to Gondoleery Rattrapp, and he willingly admitted that she was his biggest worry right now, for the sheer reason that he did not know what she was up to, and she wouldn't talk to him. Add to that the strange things Secretary had seen her doing through her window, and it was all a bit frightening. He didn't need another magical world to fight against. One was enough; that was sure.

Aaron pulled open the giant door to the driveway, startling the two sleeping guards posted there. "At least pretend like you're protecting me," Aaron said. He waved them off and strode to his new doorway to the sea. There was no breeze tonight, which was rather unsettling now that he'd gotten used to it.

He stared out over the water as the moon went behind a stray cloud, leaving the night as dark as it had ever been, excluding the lights of the palace behind him, of course. Just as he turned to go back inside, something caught his eye. It was light, moving across the water not far offshore. His eyes

LISA McMANN

widened and he hastened back behind the wall, peering out. "What in Quill?" he whispered.

As he stared, he began to make out an outline made up of dots of light, and he could hear people talking, though the sounds were too muffled to understand what they were saying. It was a—a palace on the water, with strange flags pointing to the sky. It was nothing like that white boat that had belonged to the old mage. This thing was enormous. He stared as it passed, wondering if it used some sort of jalopy oil and tires that reached to the bottom of the sea to make it move.

He had never seen anything like it. As it passed out of his vision, he crept out through the doorway once more to watch it, fascinated. "Where did it come from?" he wondered. "And where is it going?"

And then his heart was stricken with fear. Could it be an enemy? One of the enemies Justine had warned about? He clutched the placket of his shirt. How could he have doubted her? There must be other lands, for that vessel obviously didn't come from Quill, and he'd never seen it or heard about it in Artimé. He ran out farther, down the hill toward the water, watching it start to turn toward the island.

Blood pounded in his ears. His brain told him to run, to alert the Quillitary, but his arms and legs wouldn't obey. He could only watch in horror as it moved closer to the shore somewhere beyond the Quillitary yard on the desolate side of the island. "What if they land?" he whispered.

And then he remembered the walls, and he nearly laughed at himself, though he would never actually do that. He breathed easier, but still—what if they could break down the walls? Or worse—what if they landed on Artimé and Alex let them in?

Aaron felt the blood drain from his face. His brother wasn't strong like Aaron was. But the last time Aaron saw Alex, Alex had changed. He would never forgive Aaron for killing the old mage. And maybe he would even seek revenge.

It was something Aaron would have laughed off in the past. But now there was more than just a niggling of fear in his heart. Maybe he was paranoid, maybe not. All he knew was that Alex had more strength and intelligence in him than Aaron had ever expected.

He stood on his tiptoes, straining to see the ship as it disappeared around the curve of the island. He looked back at the block opening he'd made, grateful the secret vessel of the night

LISA McMANN

hadn't seen it. It was the weakest part of the island, he realized. He would have to have the blocks put back up immediately.

But now he had to decide—should he alert the Quillitary even though they weren't wholly in the Restorers' camp? Should he alert the Restorers even though his numbers were dwindling and their loyalty and competence were questionable? Either one would make him look weak if nothing happened. And he wasn't quite sure just who would be best to share the news of other lands with. Realizing his current state of instability made him nauseous.

Clutching his stomach, he walked back to the palace pondering everything.

Meanwhile, in his office, Matilda the gargoyle had climbed out of her box in the closet and crawled up the wall to the window. She straightened the pink ribbon that wrapped around one of her horns. When she saw the lighted ship pass by the opening Aaron had made, she lifted a hand to wave. And then she smiled, knowing immediately that Charlie had seen her and had waved too.

Land Ho!

Captain Ahab, who was considerably more calm when the volcanic island was out of sight behind him than he was when its belching flames were in plain view, shouted out their arrival to the shore of Artimé. The moon had left them and it was as dark as dark could be. Soon the captain called for the sails to be lowered. He dropped the anchor.

Meghan found Alex slumped over the railing. "Oh dear," she said, rushing over to him. "Are you okay?"

"Just a little pain," Alex whispered.

Meghan bent down, slipped his arm over her shoulder,

and supported him. "Come on," she said. "Are you done throwing up?"

"I think so," he said. "Don't shake me."

"I'll try not to," Meghan said. She helped him walk a step at a time, pausing in between, as others, oblivious, sleepy, and eager to get to their comfortable beds, flooded to the gangway.

Simber circled around and dropped the rope into the ship, then hovered near Alex. "Let me take you," Simber said.

"I'm okay," Alex replied, tilting his head up. "You should take them in first." He lifted a heavy arm and pointed to Samheed and Lani, who sat together in a corner.

Meghan lifted a brow and glanced at Alex. He dropped his gaze. Simber sighed and circled around again, unable to simply fly in reverse.

"I'm herrre to escorrrt you," Simber said to Lani. "I'm surrre yourrr fatherrr will be rrrelieved to see you." He dropped his back paws on the deck but kept his wings flapping to keep from capsizing the ship, and then he arched his back and opened his enormous mouth.

Samheed placed Lani into Simber's jaws and climbed up on the great cat's back. Simber lifted off and Meghan looked around, anxious to get off the ship. She spied Henry and Crow heading down the stairs and Sky hanging back.

Meghan smiled. "Hey," she said.

Sky gave a nervous wave. "Hi, um, I just was making sure he was okay. Do you need any help?"

Alex lifted his head at the sound of Sky's voice. He tried to smile. "I might need an extra hand up the stairs in the mansion in a bit."

Meghan rolled her eyes. "Don't be silly, Alex. You're going to the sick ward."

"No way," he said.

"Well, if you're stubborn, you can take the tube directly."

"That's so . . . clinical."

Meghan laughed, and Alex forced himself not to. "Ow," he breathed.

Sky hesitated and tapped her shoe against the staircase, her face flushing. "Okay, well, Simber's back for me, so I'll be in my room if anybody needs me later," she said, and then she disappeared down the stairs to the gangway, where Simber waited to shuttle her ashore.

Meghan turned her head to look at Alex, who was gazing at

LISA McMANN

the spot where Sky had been. He closed his eyes and breathed in as evenly as he could.

A moment later Simber was back from bringing Sky ashore.

"Is everybody else off the ship?" Alex asked. He didn't bother opening his eyes.

"Florrrence is counting. You'rrre the last two, plus the captain, who is waiting for you to go firrrst."

"Nice guy," Alex whispered. He swiveled with Meghan's help and eased back into Simber's mouth, while Meghan climbed onto Simber's back, and then they were off to the mansion.

Inside their beloved home, the fox and the kitten hopped into the tube, heading for who knows where, as Alex, Meghan, and Simber walked in. It was quiet inside; the only movement came from the last straggling passengers, who headed straight to their rooms. Florence came in with the captain, who clomped past the others to the tubes, muttering, "Blast my skull!" as he disappeared, no doubt heading for the theater.

"To the sick bay with you, Alex," Florence said.

Alex glanced into the hospital ward, where Lani lay in a

new bed next to her father's, across from Claire Morning. Samheed stood by Lani's side, holding her hand. Alex's lips parted, and then he shook his head. "No way. No one else needs to witness my spew." He tried to smile, but he could feel the heat coming to his skin and the uneasiness in his gut returning.

"You look flushed," Meghan said. "Do you have a fever?"

"Just tired. Promise." Alex turned to Simber and put a hand on the cat's neck. "Thank you," he said. He looked at Florence. "Thank you," he said to her. And then he looked at Meghan. "And thank you. I am going to bed. Simber, if you need me . . . you know how to reach me." He shuffled blindly to the tube as sweat dripped into his eyes.

"Good night, Alex," they said, each of them exchanging glances with the others, more than a little concerned.

He stepped into the tube, looking longingly at the steps he preferred to take, and with careful deliberation pressed the combination that would take him to his room. He leaned against the cool glass, the pain causing nausea, which prompted sweat to pour down his back. When he opened his eyes, he had reached his room.

Finally Alex could stop pretending to be the brave, strong leader of Artimé. His skin felt like it was on fire. He pushed himself upright, ripped his drenched shirt off, and staggered out of the tube as his room began to swirl around him. He dropped to his knees, clutching at the edge of the coffee table, heaving as the pain tore through his body and head. He gasped and groaned, his sweating hands slipping off the table and his arms slamming to the floor, jolting him. Every gasp for air felt like a knife to the back. He gave up trying to make it to the nearby couch, much less the bed, and melted to the floor as the world went black.

Clive stared, eyes wide, lips parted in shock. "Alex?" he said. He waited, and then he pounded his face against the blackboard, straining and pushing as hard as he could. "Alex," he yelled, "I'm sorry! Please don't die! Don't die!"

But Alex didn't move.

The Fourth Rescue

As Simber napped on his pedestal for the first time in days, he had a terrible dream about crashing into the sea and Alex calling out to him for help.

"Simber!"

The cat startled awake, immediately alert. He looked at Florence. She stood on her pedestal as usual, but her eyes were closed and she was asleep. Perhaps he was imagining things. He sampled the air and leaped down to see if there was anything amiss.

"Simber!" he heard again, and he ran toward the voice, skidding over the marble floor to the dining room, where Oscar the blackboard called out to him.

LISA McMANN

"What is it?" Simber asked.

"It's Alex. His blackboard, Clive, says Alex is dead on the floor."

Simber froze. And then he turned on a dime and raced to the stairs, thundering up them in three strides and waking Florence in the process. She chased after him, having no idea what was happening.

Simber skidded to a stop on the balcony. "Can you see this hallway?" he asked, pointing to the boys' hall.

"No," she said.

"Get Samheed from the hospital warrrd and send him up here." He turned and ran down the boys' hallway, stopping at Alex's room.

"Alex," Simber growled. He listened. "Clive, can you open this doorrr?"

"No, I'm sorry!" Clive called.

Simber growled. He looked all around, and then he backed up. "Look out," he called. He took a running start and slammed into the door, his shoulders and wings crashing through the walls on either side. Wood framing, the door, and chunks of the wall splintered across the room.

"Helllp!" Clive yelled. "Intruder!"

"I *am* the help, you dolt," Simber said. He found Alex sprawled out on his side and nudged him, then pushed him over onto his back as pounding footsteps approached from the hallway and then came to an abrupt stop.

"Ho-lee cats," whispered Samheed, looking at the mass destruction. "It looks like a hurricane hit." He rushed over to Simber. "What happened? Is he okay?" He could hear doors opening up and down the hallway as sleepy students peered out to see what had caused the crash.

"He's alive. I need you to tell everrrybody to get back inside theirrr rooms. Clive, tell theirrr blackboarrrds to call them in too. Say it's forrr safety. Make something up."

Clive nodded and disappeared.

"Are you bringing him downstairs? We'll need another bed."

"No," Simber said decisively. "The head mage doesn't ask forrr anything, but he cerrrtainly doesn't need to be on display. I say he gets a prrrivate rrroom when he's sick." He growled to prove his point.

"I totally agree," Samheed said, a little nervous.

"Help Clive clearrr the hall, and then you and Florrrence

go sprrruce up Marrrcus's aparrrtment. It's time Alex lives wherrre he belongs."

Samheed paled. The news of Mr. Today's death was still so fresh.

Simber noticed his hesitation. "Errr, scrrratch that. Ask Florrrence to do that, then you monitorrr the halls. The boy needs some dignity and prrrivacy. Nobody needs to see him . . . like this."

Samheed nodded, and in a flash he was gone.

Simber sat on his haunches and used a front paw to cradle Alex's head and shoulders as he scooped the boy into his mouth. He waited a few minutes until Samheed returned at a full sprint.

"All clear," he said, huffing.

Simber nodded, unable to speak, and with the utmost gentleness, he carried Alex to the head mage's living quarters. Samheed followed him into the mostly secret hallway and stood outside the door, waiting to see if he was needed.

Florence, who had to stoop a little bit inside the apartment, looked up from smoothing the comforter. "Fresh linens, good as new." She leaned toward Simber, picked up Alex from his mouth, and laid him down in the bed. "Carina's back," she said. "Isn't she a nurse?"

"She helped out Marrrcus when he had a bad case of the flu thrrree yearrrs back," Simber said. "She can access the hallway. You trrrack herrr down. I'll get Octavia."

Samheed cleared his throat.

Florence looked up. "Oh, sorry. You can go to bed, you poor thing. Thanks for helping."

"Well, actually, what I was going to say was that with all of Alex's yakking and stuff—"

Simber cringed. He'd heard enough hairball terminology for one day.

"I mean, the vomiting and all the sweating, he's probably dehydrated. He hadn't drunk anything since I've been with him. I'd start there."

"Hmm." Florence nodded. "I never thought of that."

Simber shrugged. "Me neitherrr."

Samheed shook his head. "Statues," he muttered. "I'll get some water."

Florence nodded. "I'll get Carina and Octavia."

Simber stayed by Alex's side, vowing not to leave until the young mage woke up.

While Alex Slept

Simber remained by Alex's side, waiting for him to wake up. Alex moaned and muttered, shouted and cried in his unconscious state. He fought battles with Quill and Warbler over and over, and he fought imaginary battles that had never happened, or perhaps that were still to come. Day after day he lost Simber to the sea, Mr. Today to the spell, Lani and Sam to the silence, and Sky to his stupidity.

In the days while Alex slept, Gunnar Haluki and Claire Morning felt well enough to leave the hospital ward. They began to get some fresh air and exercise, and Claire even took Gunnar for a ride in her boat.

Claire also began teaching again, and in the evenings she and Gunnar spent hours and hours in the Museum of Large, combing through Mr. Today's books on healing. Whatever she could find she brought to Carina and Henry, and they shared them with the other nurses, and all of them spent many long evenings with books sprawled out over a table in the dining room. One day Ms. Morning appeared via blackboard, inviting residents with science skills who were interested in being on the healing team to join her. "It's about time we improved our skills in this area," she said, her face glowing again and her honey-blond hair shining on blackboards everywhere. "We never needed extensive knowledge and medical spells before. But ever since the battle with Quill, it has become obvious that Artimé is sorely lacking in this department. If you feel especially gifted in this area, please find me in the dining room most evenings from seven to nine."

It was good for her to keep her mind busy after all she'd been through. But every now and then she thought about Liam and what life might be like if he'd chosen her over his blind allegiance to a broken government. He was on the verge of coming around; she could feel it those last days in Gunnar's house. Maybe Liam had a heart in there somewhere. But that he'd been willing to tie her up and keep her in a closet—that was something she'd never be able to forgive. People who care about each other don't hurt each other or make each other feel small. Period. End of sentence. It was obvious that Liam's problem was much bigger than just feeling like he had to obey a high priest who was doing terrible things. He wasn't the man she'd always hoped he'd be. And that was sad.

She sighed and dove into her work, trying desperately, among other things, to find something that would help poor Alex.

Henry's magical stitches were an extraordinary creation. Lani was soon able to hobble around and her slashed thigh was healing quickly. She moved back to her room upstairs too, leaving the hospital wing empty again, but no one knew how to make it disappear again except Alex, so it remained.

One day Ms. Octavia removed the hospital wing's wooden doors and created new ones made of stained glass, designing a beautiful portrait of Mr. Today on the lawn in all his brightly colored glory. Below she etched a tribute: *In loving memory of the heart and soul of Artimé, Marcus Today*. By the end of the first day, more than a hundred tokens of love had been placed in front of the portrait from all imaginable sorts of residents. Piles of acorns, potted flowers, seashells, as well as dozens of poems, stories, drawings, songs, scripts, and crafts.

Meghan stood for a long while staring at the new picture. And then she pulled from her pocket a tiny music box and set it on the floor at the mage's feet.

In the days while Alex slept, Meghan spent extra time in the music room retraining her voice. One day she invited Sky to join her, thinking Sky had the most beautiful, husky, soulful voice she'd ever heard in someone near her own age. But while Sky appreciated the offer and agreed to sit in the room and listen to Meghan, Sky didn't want to sing. "I'm not creative like you," she said, her face growing warm.

Meghan turned away from her music stand to look at the girl. "Of course you are!"

"I don't sing or draw or act or play an instrument. I can't make things."

Meghan tilted her head. "That's not what 'creative' means, you know," she said kindly. "Creativity is in everything. Even the people of Quill are creative, but they'd be horrified to be called that."

LISA McMANN

"They are? But I thought they got rid of you guys because of that."

Meghan tapped her lips with her forefinger. "You know, I've been thinking a lot about that. Mr. Today once said that Justine was afraid of people who might not follow directions blindly. And someone, somewhere along the way—Justine, probably—decided that the kind of people who *got caught* being creative were bad. The ones who hid it didn't get sent to their deaths. And it's so *sophomoric*," she mused, trying out a new word she'd learned as her thoughts came together. "Because she valued the people who could write, but she didn't want very many of them because they would be a threat to her. And when you think about the Quillitary—those people make armor and work on their vehicles and plan attacks, and that's all creative, but it's the kind of creative that furthers the goals of Quill." She ended on a triumphant note, excited to have made this connection. "Like Aaron—he's very creative. He figured out that whole Favored Farm thing—remember where we stole food from when Artimé was gone?"

Sky nodded.

"He designed that. But see, his creativity helps advance the goals of Quill. And ours doesn't. That's the difference."

"So Alex's brother doesn't think he's creative?"

"He doesn't *want* to be, because Quill turned 'creative' into a bad word. And it's not a bad word." Meghan shook her head. "What a way to mess with our minds. It's amazing we don't all need a psychiatrist."

"What's that?"

Meghan laughed. "Oh, I don't know. There was a psychiatrist in one of Mr. Appleblossom's plays, but we don't have them here. He said it's a brain doctor who asks weird questions about your mother or something."

Sky sucked in a breath.

Meghan clapped a hand to her mouth. "Oh, Sky, your mother," she said. "I'm sorry." She didn't know what else to say. She remembered Alex's promise to rescue the woman, but now, with him so ill, she wasn't sure what would happen.

"It's okay," Sky whispered. "But, um, I need to go. I think I have . . . something . . ." She hurried out of the room, Meghan following after her for a moment, then stopping and pounding a fist against her forehead.

Sky ran to the shore, where she could be alone. She sat

LISA McMANN

401 « Island of Fire

down near the water's edge and stretched out her legs so the surf could rush up under her heels and help them sink into the sand, anchoring her there.

She looked to the west, where Warbler stood, and then beyond it, straining her eyes for Pirate Island and finding it in the distance, marked by the spray that crashed against the side of what they now knew was a volcano. Her mother's face danced before her and she felt a numbness creep over her body as she tried to forget about her mother being pulled away by that pirate, like he was threatening her, hurting her.

And even though her mother had insisted that there was no way to rescue her, Sky couldn't help but think there had to be something she could do. It was more than a wish. It was her duty. And time—too much time—was slipping by without any word from Alex about going back there. Soon, Sky knew, she'd have to do something. But something kept her waiting for Alex . . . wherever he was.

In the water in front of her the pirate ship floated, and she wondered what would happen if an entire ship full of people got sucked into the volcanic drain. Would they drown? Would the ship stay afloat and come back out again once the volcano had been filled? Or would the ship get pulled into a different place, where the pirates could collect the goods and people from it? She remembered how elaborate the reverse aquarium had been. A full garden meant they had to get seeds and dirt from somewhere. And the play area for the children—how could they have built that without supplies? There must be a way in and out. After all, her mother ended up in there somehow, and so did all the other pirates and people.

Sky lifted her face to the sun and wondered if Alex really meant it that he'd help her go back to save her mother. He'd obviously been avoiding her ever since they'd returned—and maybe that was why. She hadn't seen him anywhere. Granted, she'd heard he was pretty bruised still, but it had been days and days since they returned. And he wasn't in the hospital ward, so he must not be too badly hurt.

She drew a heart in the sand with her finger, and then quickly wiped it away. Alex had made it clear he wasn't interested in her like *that*. Even though she was certain he'd enjoyed the kiss. . . .

But it wasn't meant to be. After a moment, she got to her

feet and looked around the beautiful grounds, her eyes stopping at the jungle with its trees and vines everywhere. With grim smile, she set out for it.

In Quill, while Alex slept, Aaron demanded the wall be put back up again. But when it was back up, all Aaron could do was think about how he couldn't see anything, and what if someone were sneaking up on them right now?

He lasted a day with the wall in place again before he demanded it be taken down once more, this time making it a window up off the ground, rather than a door, so that anyone coming up the hill from the outside would have trouble trying to get in through it without help.

Aaron assigned two guards to stand in front of it at all times, peering out, and then he fired them, not trusting anyone to watch for things as competently as Aaron could do himself.

And so it was that Aaron became quite decidedly obsessed with being attacked by outsiders, so much so that he spent many sleepless nights crawling up into the window and watching for enemies.

The Eighth Day

I n the dark of the night on the sixth day after their return to Artimé, Alex opened his eyes for a little less than a minute. He stared at the ceiling, unable to focus. And then he closed his eyes again.

Over the course of the seventh day, he opened his eyes a few more times, but it was too hard to keep them open.

When light beckoned from the other side of his lids on the eighth day, Alex's body finally decided it was ready to emerge from its cocoon. His eyelids fluttered and then opened. He squinted, having no idea where he was or why there was so

LISA McMANN

much sunlight in his room when he didn't remember having a window. Slowly he turned his head to look around.

It seemed like his room, anyway—all his things were there. But it was so much bigger than his room, which was extremely puzzling. "Where am I?" he croaked. His throat was dry.

There was a noise beside him, and soon Simber's body and face rose before him. "Hey, Sim," he said. And then he frowned. "How'd you get in here?"

"Alex," Simber said. The cat peered at him. His nostrils flared, and then he smiled. "Welcome back. You'rrre in your new rrroom now."

Alex blinked. "What?" He took a breath, feeling muted pain, and everything flooded back to him. "What time is it? I didn't mean to sleep so late—I have a ton of stuff to do." He tried to ease up to a sitting position but gave up after a few seconds, totally spent.

Simber told him everything that had happened, how Clive had called for help, how Simber had slammed through the door and walls and destroyed Alex's room, how he'd found Alex collapsed on the floor. And how they'd brought Alex here, to the mage's living quarters, and made it his own.

"From what Clairrre can tell, you brrruised severrral rrribs and prrrobably frrractured some too. How does it feel to brrreathe?"

"It hurts if I take a deep breath, but not as bad as it did. How long have I been here? Did I sleep a whole day and another night?" he asked, incredulous. "I've never slept that long in my life."

"Today is the eighth day since we came back frrrom Warrrblerrr," Simber said.

Alex's eyes opened wide. "Whoa," he said. And then a cloud passed over his face and he tried once more to sit up. "Oh no," he said. "I have so much—"

"Rrrelax, Alex," Simber said. He pressed a cold paw gently on Alex's chest. "You have to get well firrrst. Everrrything is fine herrre. We'rrre all pitching in. Clairrre and Gunnarrr arrre back to normal, Lani is too. Arrrtimé is once again a well-oiled machine."

Alex sank back into his pillows. "So Lani—"

"Fine."

"Meghan?"

"Fine."

"Carina?"

"Fine. They'rrre all fine."

"Even—" He blushed. "Never mind."

"She's fine too."

Alex put his hands over his eyes and tried to hide his dumb grin. "Ack," he said. "The cat knows all. The cat knows all. When are you going to get that through your thick skull, Stowe?" He shook his head slowly, furious with himself for being so obvious. "Stop looking at me."

Simber snorted.

Alex peeked out around the side of his hand. Simber was looking pointedly at the wall where Clive hung, though the blackboard's face had yet to make an appearance. Simber chuckled to himself.

Alex's blush faded and he hastily changed the subject. "Where are all of Mr. Today's things?"

"Packed in a giant chest in the Museum of Larrrge. It's all therrre for you wheneverrr you want to go thrrrough it. Oh— except forrr this." He turned his head suddenly and padded to the side of the enormous room. "We found it on the drrressing table. It has yourrr name on it."

Simber brought him a book, setting it on the bed. "It looks

LISA McMANN

like he meant to give it to you beforrre he planned to leave on his holiday."

Alex picked it up. The corners of his mouth rose a fraction as he read his name in Mr. Today's handwriting. He removed the note and looked at the book, reading the title: *The Triad: Live, Hide, Restore.* His mouth dropped open. He paged to the third section and read a few sentences.

"You've got to be kidding me," he said. He looked up. "Is this a joke?"

Simber shook his head. "Why?"

"The restore spell. It's right here." He quoted, "*Wearing a robe, stand on the back stoop of the gray shack (near the gate). Say the words 'Imagine, Believe . . .'*" Alex snapped the book shut and let his head fall back on the pillow, not even sure how he was feeling. "Seriously," he muttered, staring dumbfounded at the ceiling. "Seriously, Mr. Today? You couldn't have handed this to me an hour earlier?"

Simber ducked his head.

"It's not funny," Alex warned. "There is nothing funny about this."

Simber lowered his head farther, his neck shaking.

"Don't even," Alex said, disgusted. He threw the book at the wall, which didn't quite have the velocity to hit it, seeing as how Alex was so pathetically weak. It flopped to the floor. Alex stared at it, shaking his head. And then he pressed his lips together to keep them from twitching. "You are a bad," he said with a little hiccup, "bad cat." He tried to breathe slowly, but soon he was trembling. "Ow," he said between laughs. "Ow. Seriously. You're killing me, man." He snickered and winced.

Simber was laughing so hard the bed shook.

When at last the shaking stopped, Alex was sore and exhausted. But there was also something huge missing from his life.

"So," he said, "you got any food in this fancy place?"

Within a few days Alex was walking around his room with a cane that Henry and Crow had carved for him and sent along with Simber. Those who could access the secret hallway to visit did so, updating him on everything that was going on and bringing him more and more flowers and gifts as the days passed and word got out that he'd been badly injured and had been recovering all this time. But he never heard from Sky.

He began to puzzle over Sky and Crow's mother's rescue, knowing that it would be very difficult. Late in the evenings he would scratch out notes and sketches, ideas of how to do it, but he found flaw after flaw in all of them. But each scrapped plan made him more determined to find the perfect way to succeed. On one visit by Ms. Octavia, he questioned her quite thoroughly about everything he could think of regarding the sea, and came away with even more thoughts that churned inside his head, trying to turn into real ideas. The only thing he needed was time for his subconscious to sort them all out.

When he was able, Alex began to walk and move around as much as he could in the secret hallway, gaining his strength back, calling on his muscles to work and grow again.

Samheed came by every now and then. He wore a pained expression whenever Alex asked about Lani, but Samheed never admitted they were always together, and Alex pretended not to know, though from the big picture window he'd seen them wandering the grounds holding hands. As boring as things were hanging around his room all day, it gave Alex a bit of perverse pleasure to see Samheed feeling uncomfortable about it.

Alex had accepted it by now, and he wasn't sad. He and

LISA McMANN

Lani had always felt more like friends anyway, and he thought it would be pretty easy to just be that again.

Whenever he thought about Sky, though, his chest ached. It was like her heart was inside him, pressing against his cracked ribs. It was probably good that he hadn't seen her in a while, though he longed to. Better to get her out of his head. But when he closed his eyes at night, he could feel her cool, spongy lips pressing against his, and his stomach flopped inside him.

"You have to stop," he said one day, covering his face with his hands. There was no place for romance when one was the head mage. Was there?

"You know," Simber remarked on one occasion as they played a hand of cards, "Marrrcus was alone because he was still marrried to his wife—Clairrre's mother. He always hoped she'd come live herrre. He trrried to convince her many times, but she rrrefused. Still, he waited, just in case, because he loved her."

Alex flushed. He didn't know what to say. But the words slipped in, creating a sliver of hope. "She never came?"

"No."

"Is she still living in Quill?" Alex sat up, curious.

"No. She was sent to the Ancients Sector a few years ago."

It seemed there was a lot about Mr. Today that Alex didn't know. But he'd learned something new. And maybe, one day, there was hope.

Sadly, he'd ruined things with Sky by now. He hadn't even sent her a message or anything all this time, even though he knew she was dealing with her mother's situation. He hadn't even asked how she was doing. And it was too late now—it would look like an afterthought. Better to talk to her in person once he was back to normal.

But still, every day, he walked to the window at the end of the not very secret hallway and looked out, wondering if he'd see her.

One day, finally, he did. She was coming from the jungle, walking toward the shore, doing her very best to balance a freshly made raft on her back.

Alex's cane clattered to the ground.

A Fight

Alex moved toward the balcony as fast as his feet would carry him, which wasn't very fast at all. He grabbed the railing and leaned on it as he maneuvered down the steps, trying not to jolt his body any more than he had to. But he had to reach her in time.

Simber and Florence looked on in surprise at the sight of him dodging other students and residents like a decrepit grandfather on ice skates. They peppered him with questions as he reached the bottom and sped for the door, but Alex ignored them, whipping the door open and stepping outside for the first time in weeks.

He shielded his eyes from the sun and scanned the shore, spotting her.

"Sky!" he cried. He hastened toward her as she dropped the raft in the water, pushing it deeper. She placed a small satchel on top of the raft and climbed on.

"Sky!" he yelled again, and this time she turned her head. Her eyes widened in alarm.

Alex stopped at the edge of the water and stared at her. She held his gaze as the raft drifted in front of him, heading west. Where was she going? Alex didn't know what to say, what to do. Everything inside him crumbled.

She was leaving Artimé.

She was leaving him.

And what was he supposed to do? Watch her go?

The only part of her that moved was her head, turning slowly to hold his gaze as she drifted farther away. The water reflected sunlight that shimmered on her skin, her face, in all its stillness. She was a statue of a girl on a raft, breaking a boy's heart after he broke hers.

Waves of emotion surged through Alex. She *had* to come back! He saw her, she saw him, and now she should come back.

But she didn't. Her raft rolled and dipped over a wave and she drifted farther out to sea. Finally she made a fist, tapped her chest, and held her hand out to Alex. And then she turned around, lying on her stomach at the corner of the raft and using her arms to paddle.

"Stop!" Alex yelled. "Don't leave!" He couldn't see her expression anymore. "Please!" he shouted. But she didn't react.

Alex couldn't stand it. She was going away. She didn't even say good-bye. And she wouldn't be coming back—she'd never make it. He couldn't hesitate any longer. "Sky!" he yelled one last time. And then, despite his pain, despite his weakness, he kicked off his shoes and started running recklessly into the waves. When the water reached his chest he dove in, swimming like his life depended on it.

Onshore, he didn't know a crowd had gathered until they began cheering. Simber and Florence had followed him outside, and now Simber growled and stood up, ready to chase after Alex and pull him from the water.

Florence held him back. "Don't," she said. "Not just yet."

"He'll drrrown. We can't rrrisk it again."

"He won't drown." Florence didn't take her eyes off the boy. "Watch. She's looking back."

More and more people gathered to see what was happening, and when they found out, they began cheering Alex on too. After a minute, a chant started. "Sky, come back! Sky, come back!"

Sky stopped paddling and sat up. She stared at the crowd, and then she stared at Alex and started yelling at him. "What in the world are you *doing*? Are you insane? Go back!"

Alex couldn't answer. It was all he could do to breathe and focus on not drowning. He plowed forward, telling himself to let the pain roll off him.

She stared, dumbfounded. "Alex, I mean it. Go home! I have to leave. I have to save my mother. I'm sorry, but I can't just let her stay there."

Alex was gaining on the raft, and now he heard the cheering behind him, but he couldn't afford to look back. "What—about—Crow?" he sputtered through each knife-stabbing breath, barely getting the words out. "You said—you'd never—leave him."

"He'll be safe with you. I know that. I can't take him with

LISA McMANN

me. I can't risk his life again, now that he's finally happy!"

Alex had to slow down to catch his breath. He flipped over onto his back and began kicking, his chest heaving, his breath coming out in gasps of air and pain. When he could speak, he said, "I can't let you risk yours."

"You big jerk!" she cried. "Why are you doing this to me?"

With an enormous effort, Alex flipped back onto his stomach and pushed himself forward with all he had left. "Why—are you—letting me—" He took one more gasp of air. "Drown?" he said. He fell underwater and was forced to flip to his back again. He managed a cheeky smile as he lunged through the water and reached for the corner of the raft.

The crowd on the shore cheered.

"Get off!"

Alex obeyed. He sank under the water.

The crowd gasped.

"Very funny," she said. But her voice didn't sound as confident as before.

Alex swam under the raft and popped up on the other side, and when Sky leaned over to see where he'd gone, he pushed up and yelled. "Bah!"

She screamed in terror and grabbed on to the edge, but the momentum was there and she fell into the water. The bag she carried plopped in after her.

That's about when Alex remembered that people from Warbler don't know how to swim.

· A Promise

She came back above the water sputtering and coughing. "Help!" she yelled, real fear in her voice as the raft drifted out of her reach. She was flailing so much she was dousing herself.

Alex dove back under the raft in an instant and grabbed her around the waist, pushing her up above the surface and holding her there even as she grabbed two fistfuls of his hair and yanked.

The crowd cheered.

"I hate you," she sputtered.

"I hate you too," he said. He watched her chest heave with

panic, felt her stomach muscles clench against his chest. He directed their bodies sideways, reaching out a long arm to catch the raft again. "Here, grab on. I'm sorry. I forgot you can't swim."

"You're awful."

"I know."

She gripped his hair and looked him in the eye, her lips a white line. "I need to get her out of there," she said.

Alex looked up at her face, treading water and slowly, almost unnoticeably, pulling the raft toward home. "Don't you think you should learn how to swim first?"

She glared at him.

"I could find someone to teach you," he offered. "I am the leader of Artimé, you know."

"You are insufferable."

"Only around you."

"How would you know?" she spat back at him. "You never are." She clenched her legs around his back and squeezed.

He grimaced and his hand slipped from the raft. Her weight on him forced him underwater, where he screamed out in pain. He pushed his hands upward and lunged for the raft once

LISA McMANN

again, grabbing it with the tips of his fingers. He blew out a wet, staggered breath and readjusted his grip on her. His lungs burned.

She looked away. "I'm—I'm sorry," she said. "I didn't know you were still hurt. All this time I thought you were a jerk instead of merely inconsiderate." She let go of his hair and reached out for the raft, just barely grasping it, and pulled it closer, pushing herself up on her elbow to help. "I'll climb back on here—"

"No," he said. "Stay here in the water. Please. I'm sorry— you're right. I was a jerk."

She looked into his eyes, so brown and earnest. "You're just being like this to get me to come back with you," she said, setting her jaw.

Alex tilted his head, about to protest, but then he changed his mind. "You know what?" he asked. "So what if I am? I'm not afraid to say that I care about you and I don't want you to die, and yes, I want you to come back to Artimé with me. So I'm not just 'being like' anything but me. But the truth right here, just you and me and no hiding on top of roofs or in pirate ship stairwells, and no giant cat hovering overhead—the truth,

LISA McMANN

Sky, is that I think about you all the time. And when I'm not with you I miss you, and I feel like we have this, I don't know, connection or whatever, and maybe that's because of all we went through restoring Artimé. But I don't know, you know? You're the one I broke down in front of that first night on the roof, and I hardly even knew you. You're the one I went to when I needed somebody smart to help me solve things."

He was out of breath. He winced and pulled himself up, lurching to get a new grip on the raft. "The problem is, I just don't know what to do. Because there will be a lot of times where I'm plastered with all the messes this magical world makes. And I guess that's a lot—I don't know. All I have is what I've experienced so far, and this job about killed me. So I don't know . . . exactly what, or how much, I'd have left . . . over . . . for someone."

He swallowed hard, and his foot brushed the sandy bottom. "But the one thing I do know, and I'm not just saying this to get you to come home, is that I told you on the ship that I would help you get your mother out of there. And I meant it. I meant it then, and I mean it now. And I'm sorry it has taken me so long to get healthy, and I'm fifty times sorrier I didn't let you know I was thinking about it . . . and you. But if we do this Pirate Island rescue, we need to do it right. And there's no way I'm going to break into an underwater pirate island with a team of people who can't swim, because that would be stupid, and we are not stupid."

Sky was quiet. And then she gently draped her arms around his neck and hugged him.

He closed his eyes, digging his foot into the sandy floor of the sea.

When he turned to see just how many witnesses he'd had to his latest spectacle, the beach was strangely empty.

"You can touch the bottom here," Alex said, loosening his grip so she could slide down to her feet. "Come home with me?"

Sky nodded.

"Stay until we're ready to crush the pirates *and* live to tell about it?"

"Okay," she said.

He cast a sidelong glance at her as they slugged through the shallow waves in their wet clothes. "Promise?"

She grabbed his forearm and almost tripped over her own feet. "Promise," she said, laughing.

Alex caught her and laughed. "Ow. You're seriously killing me now."

Back to Normal

Alex's ribs slowly knit back together over the next months, and Artimé resumed its normal routine. Alex began wearing one of Mr. Today's robes all the time, knowing that if the world disappeared and he didn't have one, they'd be in another mess. After tripping a few times on the long hem, Sky took the robes and tailored them to fit him.

All the various classes, Beginning and Advanced Magical Warrior Training, and picnics on the lawn began again.

And so did Alex's plan for Pirate Island. With Artimé situated on the sea, most Unwanteds learned how to swim whenever they felt like going into the water—there was always somebody older willing to teach a new Unwanted how to hold his breath underwater and how to move through it safely using arm strokes and leg kicks. But now Alex asked Ms. Octavia, in addition to her art classes, to begin teaching an extensive swimming course for those who wanted to volunteer to help rescue Sky and Crow's mother. Dozens of people signed up. After the initial lessons, when some naturally dropped out upon realizing they were not suited for this quest, and only the strongest swimmers plus Sky and Crow remained, Ms. Octavia began to share the secrets of sea breathing with the determined ones who remained.

She began to teach them little tricks and helps that would allow them to eventually hold their breath for an extraordinarily long time by utilizing the oxygen that was stored in their blood, not just in their lungs.

It was the most strenuous, exhausting exercise Alex and the others had ever tried, and the progress was slow. But it was necessary if they were going to succeed.

In the evenings, when Alex wasn't spending time in the lounge with Lani, Sam, Meghan, and Sky; strategizing about Pirate Island; or training his lungs and muscles for the rescue, he went to the

Museum of Large to clean up the mess of whale bones in there. Claire, Gunnar, and Octavia all offered to help, but he declined. It was something very soothing for Alex—an enjoyable, creative task he could do alone. It gave him the opportunity to decompress from his day and think up new ideas for Artimé. Now he understood exactly why Mr. Today had spent so much time fixing up the pirate ship. It was a relief to realize that not every day as mage of Artimé would require him to work at a breakneck pace.

Alex placed each whale bone carefully into its socket, sometimes looking for hours to find the exact piece he needed next. It was a glorious puzzle with hundreds of pieces, and it took him months to finish it.

And when he finally did, he was sad to leave the whale, so he began to sculpt muscles and tendons and tissues over the bones out of materials he found in the sea during their sea breathing lessons. It was his own secret project, and it was amazing to watch the whale take shape as he layered it. One day maybe he'd try to give it a mosaic exterior like Jim's.

Claire Morning, Henry Haluki, and Carina Holiday became the lead researchers and chemists, experimenting with all kinds of serums made from plants they found in the jungle. Henry practiced his magical stitches on various fruits and vegetables that he found in the giant kitchen pantry, and Carina began to work hard on a concoction that would ease pain—and *not* cause a person to vomit incessantly. Sean became a willing volunteer for Carina, who administered the medicine whenever she thought she'd improved on it. They had varied results, including one rather explosive multicolored vomit rainbow that the team oohed and aahed over, and even Sean was impressed once it stopped. He decided to keep a vial of that version in case he ever needed it for a practical joke.

The interest in spell making began to bloom after Artiméans saw the success of the spells Alex, Meghan, Samheed, and Lani had created. After a while, Florence had to limit the number of presentations to one per week, per student. And then, after numerous crazy spells were presented that seemed unlikely to assist Artimé in battle, Florence had to establish a committee of students who would decide if a spell was useful, like the jabbing violin bow spell, or unnecessarily dangerous like the guillotine spell, or merely frivolous and fun, like the pink hair spell. There were definitely a few students who were gifted in this area of spell creation, while most of the others found it to be a passing craze and soon went on to find something different that they could be fabulous at.

Quill's national holiday, the day of the Purge, came again. A new crop of Unwanted thirteen-year-olds arrived at Artimé's gates. Alex, the girrinos, and all the other Unwanteds welcomed them. And for the first time, but certainly not the last, Alex declared that Artimé would hold a masquerade ball the following week to celebrate.

All the seasoned Unwanteds spent the day of the masquerade in preparation, some opting to create magical masks that would change color and shape depending on the mood of the owner, and others choosing to fashion more elaborate, less flashy masks to be worn in a traditional manner. Mr. Appleblossom, of course, was the coordinator and producer of the event, and he was having a most delightful time planning the gala, which would be complete with musical numbers by his students—and of course, the lounge band.

The mood and timbre of Artimé was as high and rich as it had ever been, and the Unwanteds looked forward to a most amazing evening indeed.

Masquerade

Alex opted for a simple pirate eye patch as his mask, which wouldn't clash with his brightly colored robe. He sat at his dressing table combing his hair and trimming the ends of it with a magical finger scissors he created on the spot for such an occasion. He wanted his hair to look nice and fresh, as it had grown into long waves by now.

He shaved the soft dark fuzz above his upper lip because he thought it made his skin look like it was smudged with dirt, and then he checked his chin and found a few stiffer black hairs there to shave as well, which seemed like quite an accomplishment. "I wonder if I should keep these whiskers and give them to Simber in case he ever learns how to use a seek spell," he mused, straightening his tie and jacket underneath the robe. "It seems I grew them my very own self. Very creative of you, Stowe." He grinned to himself in the mirror and patted his pocket, where Simber's stone dewclaw remained. He was in a chipper mood tonight.

He had the benefit of spying on his side. He could look out the giant window at the end of the hall to watch the decorations go up, and when the time came to meet Sky on the balcony, he had the good fortune to be able to see her standing there without her seeing him until he emerged.

She stood in front of the secret hallway, one hand resting on the banister. She wore a burnt-orange gown covered in multicolored sequins. Attached to a stick in her other hand was her mask—a butterfly shape with plumes of orange and purple feathers. She looked in the direction of the staircase, not smiling or frowning, just gazing at the flurry of students as she waited for Alex. Her hair looked glossy and smoother than usual, somehow enhancing both the dark under layer of her hair and the bright natural highlights that had grown even more distinct after so much swimming and training. It jetted down to rest below her collarbone.

Alex liked that Sky didn't try to cover up her scars around

her neck, and he admired her profile for a moment in secret. He watched her face light up as Samheed and Lani joined her at the railing.

"You look stunning," Lani said. "What a great idea to match your eyes to your dress. I wish I'd thought of that."

Samheed rested his hand on Lani's shoulder and glanced down the secret hallway, startling only slightly when he saw Alex standing there. Sam grinned and Alex grinned back. "Busted," he mouthed. Samheed nodded and turned his attention back to the girls as Alex came bustling out of the hallway, pretending to straighten his robe, as if he hadn't been there all the time.

"Fabulous. Gorgeous. Divine," Alex said, mimicking a voice that Mr. Appleblossom often used when playing the part of a wealthy nobleman. His eyes lingered on Sky. "You look amazing," he said.

She grinned. "You look . . . like . . . some weird, psychedelic pirate. A cute one," she added.

"Then my costume is a success," Alex said grandly.

They fell into step together, picking up Meghan as she exited the girls' hallway. Alex linked his other arm with hers, and the five descended the steps in elegant fashion. By the door, Florence wore a cheetah mask and Simber wore a simple black warrior-looking mask.

"Who do you suppose they are?" Meghan asked.

"Wow, I just can't tell," said Lani.

Florence opened the door for them and they swept out onto the lawn, which was glowing with light and color. Ms. Morning played in the band with the fox (and the kitten, who played a tiny triangle), and there was an enormous spread of food and drinks.

The five mingled together and apart, laughing and chatting with people they hadn't had a chance to chat with in a while, and everyone made a point to be kind to the newest batch of Unwanteds, who wore looks ranging from shock to pure fright on their faces.

Alex said a few words of welcome to everyone but kept it short, which is what Meghan told him to do. After that the party continued late into the evening with dancing, everyone changing partners and having a blast.

And so it happened that when an enormous boom echoed in the sky, only those on the outskirts of the party and the very best music students could distinguish the fracturing noise from the kettledrum in the song the band was playing. But

LISA McMANN

when flashes of fire lit up the air, it was hard to miss.

The music stopped immediately as a gasp rose up from the crowd.

"What was that?" Meghan asked. She grabbed Alex and Sky and they ran to the shore, straining their eyes to see in the darkness. There, amid a cloud of smoke, they saw a large piece of something falling from the sky. It whistled as it fell, and hit the water with a smack that rang out. Soon there was the raining sound of the splash coming back down before all was quiet again.

Half the Unwanteds ran into the mansion in fear, and the other half lined the shore as Alex ran to Simber to see if he could see or smell anything.

"Whateverrr it is, it's floating on the waterrr," Simber said, eyes narrowed. "It's big. And I smell . . . something."

"What do you smell?" Alex said, craning his neck uselessly, for it was too dark to see anything.

"It's . . ." The cheetah sampled the air once more as if he wanted to be sure. "It's death." He rose up on his haunches.

Alex glanced at Sky. "I need to take a look," he said, an apology in his eyes.

Simber glanced at them. "May as well have two of you."

Alex looked at Sky, and then at himself. "We might have to go in," he said. "Sim, we're going to do a quick change of clothes and grab some lights, and we'll be back in a flash. Less than a minute. Right, Sky?"

Sky nodded, excited, and the two of them raced into the mansion, Sky pulling her dress up a little so she could take the steps two at a time. "Unzip me!" she cried.

Alex fumbled with her zipper and yanked it down her back while running. "Meet back on the balcony!" he shouted, and they split at the top of the stairs and went down their respective hallways, stripping the formal clothes off as they flew into their rooms. Alex tossed his robe, jacket, tie, and mask on the bed, kicked his shoes at the wall, and slid into his normal day clothing. He fumbled with his sandals for several agonizing seconds, and then decided just to go barefoot. He whirled the robe over his shoulders once again, patting the inner pockets to make sure they were full, shuffled around trying find a component that would shed light, and then raced to his door and flung it open.

What he saw on the other side of the door stopped him cold.

LISA McMANN

A Visitor

What—how the—" Alex exploded. "How did you get in here?"

Without a second thought, the High Priest Aaron Stowe threw a punch, hitting his brother square in the jaw. Alex reeled back into his room and caught himself on the bed, then scrambled back and charged at Aaron, slamming into him and knocking him flat in the hallway.

The two scrabbled on the floor until Alex gained the upper hand, thanks to his recent strenuous workouts, and pinned Aaron to the floor.

"What the world is wrong with you?" Alex shouted, breathing hard.

Aaron, who looked like he was in a state of shock, whimpered, "Don't hit me."

Alex stared at his brother through narrowed eyes. "Why not? I should kill you."

"I didn't mean to punch you," Aaron said, regaining his composure. "It was a reaction. You practically exploded out of there. I wasn't expecting it."

Alex's mouth hung open. "Why don't you tell me just what you were expecting?"

Aaron struggled. "Will you let me up?"

"No!"

"All right," Aaron said, his voice straining to remain calm.

"How did you get in here? Don't make me ask you again," Alex warned. "I could kill you approximately a hundred and fifty times with a flick of my finger if I wanted to." It was a lie, but it was a good one.

Aaron tried to melt into the floor. His breathing grew ragged. "I came through that glass thing. From Haluki's house."

Alex's expression didn't change, but inside he was kicking

LISA McMANN

himself. He'd meant to do something about that after he rescued Ms. Morning, knowing that the guards had probably figured out what the tube did. But there had been so much happening back then that it had slipped to the bottom of his list of things to do. And after his injury, the entire list had all but disappeared.

"Well, what do you want? Last time I tried to get you to come in here, you didn't want to have anything to do with it. So get out. Here, I'll help you." He let Aaron up, not letting go of his brother's shirt, and shoved him toward the kitchenette's tube.

Aaron stumbled, throwing his arms out to catch himself. "Alex, I came here because I saw something, and this was the quickest way. There was an explosion in the sky over in this direction, and I . . . I just know it's got to be one of the enemies attacking us." His face was rather pale.

Alex was starting to believe Aaron really *was* scared, and he wasn't sure what to make of it. He glanced down the hallway to the balcony, where Sky paced anxiously. "How could you see anything at all from Quill? Oh, wait," Alex said, remembering something he'd seen when he was slung over the pirate ship railing on the way home from Warbler. "You made a hole in your wall, didn't you?"

Aaron's eyes widened. "Yes. How did you know?"

Alex nodded secretively. "I have my ways." It felt good to have the upper hand for once. He glanced at Sky again. He hesitated, debating about what he should do with Aaron. If he forced him back into the tube, Aaron could just come again later, and he could wreak a lot of havoc in Alex's new office, which didn't have a lock on the door. Plus there were the monitors. . . . He let a frustrated sigh escape, and then in a flash he shackled Aaron's wrists with a spell and grabbed his arm. "Fine," he said. "Sit here in the hallway until I come back. I'll destroy that tube later." He reached for the door to his private quarters and pulled it closed, putting its magical lock in place, and then he went down to the office door, closed it, and pretended to lock it so Aaron wouldn't even try to get in.

Aaron, who had followed Alex's gaze the second time he'd looked down the hallway, barely resisted the shackles and couldn't turn his head away. He frowned. "Who is that?" he said in a quiet voice.

Alex glanced at Aaron and turned to see what he was staring at. All he could see was Sky, and he wondered if there was some picture or artwork on this side of the opening like there was a mirror on the other side, though he didn't know why there should be. He narrowed his eyes. "What do you mean?"

Aaron's Adam's apple bobbed. "That girl," he said. "On the balcony."

Alex's heart jumped to his throat. "You can see her?"

Lights

O f course I can see her," Aaron said, snapping out of whatever trance he'd been in. "She's standing right there." And she was the most beautiful girl he'd ever seen. Not that he spent a lot of time thinking about girls, what with all the takeovers and falls from grace and rises to power. But he'd turned his head a time or two, just like anyone might expect.

Then he looked down at his hands and realized what Alex had done. "You shackled me? How dare you? Did you forget who I am?"

Alex just stared at him with a look of horror on his face. *Impossible*, he thought.

LISA McMANN

"What?" Aaron said.

"Describe her."

"Honestly, Alex, don't you think we should figure out this explosion thing? If the island is being attacked, maybe we ought to, you know . . . consider . . ." His mouth went dry, hardly believing that he'd almost proposed working together. But right now Aaron wasn't sure what kind of support he had, and he'd do anything to keep his place in the palace. Absolutely anything. Still . . . He jiggled his arms impatiently. "Take these things off my wrists." It was annoying.

"No. I changed my mind. You're coming with me."

"This is ridiculous. I let you walk unshackled in Quill," Aaron said.

"That's because I'm not a stupid tyrant, you jerk. If I take the shackles off, I'm guessing there are at least a hundred people out there who would kill you as soon as look at you. With the shackles, and with me, you might live. Did you forget who I am?"

But Aaron wasn't listening. He was looking at the girl again. "She looks . . . emotional." He said the word with disdain, but it didn't change the way his stomach flipped.

"Come on," Alex said, tugging on his arm. "She's anxious because I was supposed to meet her five minutes ago to see what the explosion was."

"Ah, so you heard it? Did you see the fire?" Aaron's eyes shifted nervously as Alex dragged him down the hallway.

They reached the balcony, and the girl's face changed from anxious to relieved to surprised when she saw the nearly identical image next to Alex. Her eyes flew to Alex's with a question, but all Aaron saw was the amazing color of her irises—he'd only seen color like that for the first time just recently, having watched—with a bit of fear—the sun disappear at night.

He frowned, remembering the explosion again, which wasn't quite as frightening now as it was when he'd watched it all alone at the edge of the sea.

"Sky, I'm sorry," Alex said, and he picked up his pace to a jog down the stairs to keep up with the girl. "I had an unexpected visitor."

"You say that with such pleasure," Aaron said.

"Ooh, sarcasm. You've allowed yourself to emote. What progress," Alex replied.

Aaron watched the girl. "I'm the High Priest Aaron. Stowe,"

LISA McMANN

he added, and then felt heat rising from his shirt collar.

"I know who you are," the perfectly named girl replied, not looking at him.

"Usually people bow," Aaron explained, sure she would be impressed.

"Don't get your hopes up, Jerkface," Sky said. She ran ahead.

"Get Sean, will you?" Alex called after her.

"I'm already on it."

Alex grinned.

Aaron looked at Alex as they reached the bottom of the steps. "What? What is that? Jerkface? Is that good?"

Alex snorted. "Yeah, Aaron. It's really good. I think it means she likes you." Seconds later they pushed through the door to the lawn, where a bevy of Unwanteds were gathering with spell components drawn and fury in their eyes.

"Look who I found," Alex said. He spied Sean and shoved Aaron in his direction, knowing the rest of Artimé would pounce if Aaron tried to do anything.

He ran after Sky and they mounted Simber's back. Simber took a few steps and leaped out over the water, reaching top speed so fast that Alex and Sky could barely hang on.

"Sorry about the delay," he called out to Simber. "Aaron saw the explosion and got in through the tube." He rubbed his jaw where Aaron had punched him.

"That's trrroubling."

"I meant to do something about that tube."

Sky's face was concerned. "But how did you get him through the wall? Did you find a spell for that after all?"

"No," Alex said. "That's even more troubling. He can see it. The opening, I mean."

Simber turned his head sharply. "He can?"

"Yes. I almost fell over. It's not good."

Sky looked at Alex. "What does it mean?"

Alex considered all the dreadful possibilities. "It means he's a lot more powerful magically than we ever imagined." A swirl of fear dove through him. "If he ever finds out . . ." He shook his head and didn't finish.

They reached the wreckage of whatever had exploded. Simber hovered above it. Alex lit a spotlight spell component and pointed it at the water.

The light reflected on a clear panel, like a window, which was held in place by a massive rounded white structure. It was a vessel—sort of. But it was obviously not seaworthy, at least not anymore. It had already begun to sink.

"What is it?" Alex asked. "Do you see anyone in there? How do we get inside it?"

Simber stared down at the vessel, only the point of it showing above the water now. "Two, maybe thrrree humans, he said after a minute. "I can't see verrry farrr with the sea bottom all stirrred up. But they'rrre all dead."

Sky and Alex looked at each other in alarm.

Simber sampled the air, his eyes closing halfway as he concentrated. "Definitely thrrree of them." He rose in height. "I don't think this is a good time to go down therrre. Therrre's nothing we can do. Let's wait until daylight." The statue looked back at Alex. "But it's yourrr call."

Alex hesitated, thinking about going down into the dark water to see dead bodies. "No, you're right. We'll send a team out in the morning."

Simber marked the location mentally, then turned back toward Artimé, and all three were silent until they landed.

The people of Artimé gathered around. Sean and another man whom Alex didn't know were standing on either side of

Aaron, gripping his upper arms tightly. "What is it?" Sean asked, followed by echoes from the crowd.

"We don't know, exactly," Alex said. "It's some kind of vessel with humans inside. It's sinking. And they're dead."

Some of the Unwanteds gasped. Aaron looked relieved.

"But it came from the sky," Meghan said.

Alex shrugged. "Maybe it's an air vessel, not a water vessel," he said, musing. "Don't we have a book about such things in the library?" He looked at Lani and Mr. Appleblossom.

"I don't know." Lani's voice was a mystery.

Mr. Appleblossom looked troubled, and not just because his party had been ruined. "This thing has surely happened once before," he said. "The craft had fans that kept it in the air. But by the time it washed upon the shore, no humans lived to tell about their scare."

Ms. Morning nodded. "I remember that. Father kept the pieces he found, Alex. They're up in the museum."

Alex remembered seeing something up there with a fan attached. "But where did it come from?"

"We don't know," Simber said. He bared his teeth at Aaron.

Aaron narrowed his eyes and shifted uncomfortably. "Well, then. Now that the intruders are dead and everything is fine and I find no reason to, ah, attack you, I'll just be going now," he said. "Can someone uncuff my wrists? I'll show myself out." He flashed a patronizing smile as if he expected the Unwanteds to do what he asked.

Everyone ignored him.

The speculation began about the thing that had exploded in the air. Did it come from the stars? The moon?

"Please understand that things don't work that way," Mr. Appleblossom began, waving his hands and trying to raise his voice above the crowd. "It flies from side to side, not up to down." He drew a finger across the sky. "It uses wings—like Simber, but no flap—and isn't meant to crash to sea or ground." He cringed at the imperfect rhyme.

Samheed patted the man's shoulder sympathetically.

Alex, Sky, Samheed, Meghan, and Lani gathered in a group to try to figure out where the thing could have come from. And then Lani blurted out, "Sometimes don't you just wonder how *we* all got here? I mean our ancestors, before Mr. Today and Justine started Quill."

That left them all silent and thoughtful. Aaron stared at Lani. "What do you mean, before them?"

Lani startled. Most of them had forgotten that he was still standing nearby, waiting to be let free. But Lani didn't have time to answer him, not that she would have anyway, because Simber rose quickly and stared out over the sea to the west. Alex followed his gaze, and then he sucked in a breath.

"Oh, crud," he said. He raced to Simber, made sure he wasn't imagining things, and said quietly, "Is that—?"

Simber growled long and low. "It is."

Alex tried not to panic. He stood by Simber's side collecting his wits and gathering courage through a few mostly pain-less deep breaths. Florence moved over to them as well. Alex turned to face the partygoers, his face stricken, as hundreds of tiny lights appeared, dotting the surface of the sea between Warbler and Artimé.

The time for merriment and discussion about flying objects was over.

"Everybody," Alex said in as calm a voice as he could muster. "It appears we are under attack. I need you to go inside and get dressed for battle."

LISA McMANN

The hundred or so Unwanteds that remained stood stunned, and then several of them gasped and jumped up, trying to see what was happening. The lights slowly grew stronger.

Alex called for attention once again, but the panic was palpable. "Warriors, you'll find instructions on your blackboards in a few minutes. As soon as you have them, return to the lawn. Go quickly now!" There was a split second's hesitation before the alarmed Artiméans stampeded to the mansion door.

Alex looked around, anxious, scanning the crowd for his closest friends, and he saw Sky at a run, dragging Crow by the hand and rushing up to Sam and Lani.

"They're coming for *us*!" Sky screamed. "Lani, Sam, Crow— we have to go back with them or they'll attack Artimé!"

"No!" Alex shouted. "No one is going back there. Artimé fights to protect its people."

Sky's eyes blazed. "I won't be responsible for anyone's death!" she yelled back at him, her voice ragged.

Crow started crying as people pushed past him.

"Sky—" Alex said, but Lani caught Alex's eye. She grabbed Sky's arm and pulled her and Crow inside.

Alex turned to Florence. Outwardly he was calm and

collected, but inwardly he felt like he was bordering on hysterical. He pulled his little notebook from his pocket to sketch out their plan of defense, knowing that Artimé was the most prepared it had ever been yet feeling like they were about to be overwhelmed.

He focused, turning away from the flurry and chaos at the mansion door, while the High Priest Aaron Stowe, more afraid than all the rest, wrenched his arms free from his guards and lost himself in the crowd, still shackled. He tripped up the stairs, and before anyone cared enough to stop him, he careened down the secret hallway and into the kitchenette, and stumbled into the tube.

Faced with an array of buttons this time, Aaron panicked. "Which one?" he whispered like a man possessed. "Which one!" He hesitated, and then he slammed his shackled fists into all of them.

No more than an instant later, the high priest of Quill faded away.

Mr. Today's Clue:

FOLLOW THE DOTS AS THE TRAVELING SUN,

MAGNIFY, FOCUS, EVERY ONE.

STAND ENROBED WHERE YOU FIRST SAW ME,

UTTER IN ORDER; REPEAT TIMES THREE.

SAM & LANI'S TAP SYSTEM:

A=1 TAP

B=2 TAPS

C=3 TAPS

D=4 TAPS

E=5 TAPS OR 1 SLAP

F=6 TAPS OR 1 SLAP 1 TAP

G=7 OR 1 SLAP 2 TAPS

H=8 OR 1 SLAP 3 TAPS

I=9 OR 1 SLAP 4 TAPS

J=10 OR 2 SLAPS

K=11 OR 2 SLAPS 1 TAP

L=12 OR 2 SLAPS 2 TAPS

M=13 OR 2 SLAPS 3 TAPS

N=14 OR 2 SLAPS 4 TAPS

O=15 OR 3 SLAPS

P=16 OR 3 SLAPS 1 TAP

Q=17 OR 3 SLAPS 2 TAPS

R=18 OR 3 SLAPS 3 TAPS

S=19 OR 3 SLAPS 4 TAPS

T=20 OR 4 SLAPS

U=21 OR 4 SLAPS 1 TAP

V=22 OR 4 SLAPS 2 TAPS

W=23 OR 4 SLAPS 3 TAPS

X=24 OR 4 SLAPS 4 TAPS

Y=25 OR 5 SLAPS

Z=26 OR 5 SLAPS 1 TAP